DREAMS
AND
SECRETS

By

Judy Goodman Howard

Published by Take Me Away Books, a division of Winged Publications

ISBN-13: 978-1-946939-31-9
ISBN-10: 1-946939-31-5

As storm clouds from the sky.
Spread azure wings and drift away,
And teach me how to fly.

Smooth out the rocky road I've trod.
Make way for better things,
And lead me to the hand of God
On gentle bluebirds' wings.

"Are not two sparrows sold for a penny? Yet not one of them will fall to the ground apart from the will of your Father... So don't be afraid; you are worth more than many sparrows."

Matthew 10:29, 31 (NIV)

Chapter 1

Missouri, August 1937

"Hey, are you dead?"

"Dead?"

"Naw, he ain't dead. Look at 'im. He's a-breathin'."

Zeb opened one eye to a slit, reluctant to face the reality of wakefulness on the front porch of Hollisters' store—a place that, for the moment, resembled an oven more than a porch. Wade County, Missouri. Might as well be in the Sahara Desert. Couldn't be much hotter. Sweat ran down the back of his neck, saturating his shirt.

Four-year-old Duke Banks stood to his right, his face an inch away from Zeb's. Duke's twin brother,

Luke, stood at the other side.

Leaning forward, Luke dropped a rope, looped several times, over Zeb's head.

Duke patted his brother on the back and grinned at Zeb. "You're lassoed."

Luke nodded, "Lassoed."

Zeb gave a slight tug at the rope, but made no attempt to remove it. "Guess you got me."

A door slammed, and a smaller child appeared. "Pway?"

Grinning, Zeb hoisted the tiny boy onto his lap. "Davey, get that harmonica out of my face. It's too hot to play."

Davey solemnly examined the instrument, then focused a wrinkled-brow look on Zeb. "Not hot."

"No, the day is hot, not the harmonica." He rolled his eyes. "Alright, one song."

"Mazin' Gwace?"

Zeb's heart went out to the kid. What a life, and only two years old. "Sure. Why not?"

As the song ended, a short balding man, tugging on a rope attached to a calf, stopped in front of Zeb, who slipped the harmonica into his shirt pocket as Davey hopped down and took off with the twins.

Zeb eyed the little man. He'd known Fred and Hazel Hollister, owners and operators of Hollisters' store, since his preschool days. "Whatcha need, Fred?"

The older man sighed. "Well, this here little calf is without a mama, and I need you to do something for her to keep her alive. I'm worried about her."

Who you need to be worrying about is Davey.

Zeb eyed the animal. "This calf is three months old and probably weighs two hundred pounds. There's nothing wrong with her."

"Couldja look at her anyways?"

Bending over the healthy calf, Zeb heard a loud "ROH" and turned in time to see Davey's small terrier take a playful nip at the calf's hind leg. The young bovine jumped with a start, jerking the rope from Fred's grasp. Trailing it behind her, she tore across highway 34 toward the woods.

"Catch 'er!" Fred yelped.

Zeb, with Luke's rope still dangling from his neck, loped across the highway and into the woods, the calf already out of sight. His feet beat out a rhythm on the worn path, the hot, dry air making his breath come in short gasps. The desire to find a place to lie down slowly but surely demanded control of Zeb's mind as the August heat took its toll. Soaked in sweat, heart pounding, he sank spread-eagle onto the cool forest floor.

Sometimes he wondered if the struggle to become a veterinarian was worth it. His teacher salary barely kept the family afloat, and attempting to save for vet school was slow and discouraging.

A movement caught his eye. He bolted to a seated position as a scuffed brogan shoe beneath a faded pant leg dangled above him.

Springing to his feet, he slapped the shoe with the palm of his hand. "Hey, Mac. What're you doin' up a tree?"

No response.

Grabbing the shoe, he shook it back and forth. "Mac."

A sharp cracking noise made Zeb start, as the entire branch gave way. Staggering backward, he lost his balance and landed with a thud. A shower of small, pungent objects bombarded him on the head and face, as a second thud sounded beside him.

Shielding his face from the spray, he turned to see a figure sprawled on the ground a couple feet from him. "Hey, buddy, are you hurt? You took quite a tumble."

Huge blue eyes peered at him from an oval face framed with wavy, shoulder-length blond hair.

He did a double-take. "You're not a Mac. You're a girl."

The girl stood, brushing dirt and debris from blue overalls over a thin green shirt that hung loosely on her slender frame. She couldn't be more than nineteen. Her face showed concern. "Oh, my goodness. Are *you* hurt? Did anything hit you?"

Picking up one of the smelly tidbits, he held it before her. "This."

She reached out and took it. "Oh, I'm sorry. My pig snout spilled all over you."

Gathering up the morsels and stuffing them into her bib pocket, she popped one into her mouth straight from the ground.

Zeb's stomach lurched. He took a deep breath and swallowed before speaking. "Your pig snout?"

"Sure. It's delicious. Try a bite." She held up a piece and pushed it toward his face.

"No, thanks. I already know how it tastes." He scooted to a sitting position against the tree trunk.

The girl lowered herself onto the fallen branch and brushed the hair out of her eyes, never taking her gaze off him. Leaning forward, she extended a hand. "Hi. I'm Katie Gallagher."

He accepted the greeting. "I'm Zeb Harlow. And if I may be so bold as to ask," he glanced overhead, "what were you doing up there?"

Katie tucked her hair behind her ears, lazily eying the place where the branch used to be. "Oh, you know. Having a snack. Talking with the Lord."

This was one relaxed female. Not sure how to respond, Zeb hesitated for a moment. "Sorry about your pig snout." Heat rushed up his neck and engulfed his face.

For crying out loud. That was a dumb thing to say.

~

Katie grinned at the guy's obvious embarrassment. "Oh, it's okay. I can get more. Hazel fixes it for my little cousins all the time. They're twins—just four years old—but they know what's good."

She reached out and gave him a friendly punch on the arm. He leaned away from it, making her smile again.

She stood. "I'll be heading over to Hollisters' store pretty soon to pick them up. They're over there playing with Davey. He's only two-and-a-half, but they're good friends. A nice way for the three of them to spend a Saturday."

Zeb nodded. "I'm their school teacher. We let them start this term since they'll turn five in September. They're good boys. Well behaved. Both quiet, especially Luke."

Katie pictured the boys' antics at home and chuckled. "Says the schoolmaster. I suppose you've noticed Luke echoes the end of all Duke's sentences."

Zeb nodded again. "I've noticed."

"Well, don't kid yourself. He's his own guy when he thinks they're alone."

Zeb grabbed a still-attached, low-hanging branch and pulled himself to his feet. "I'd better go. I've got an ornery calf to locate somewhere out there in Frog Hollow, and a feisty dog to reprimand when I get back to the store. Nice to have met you."

Katie shook her head. "Don't bother to reprimand the dog. Whatever he did, it's been too long now, and he won't even know why he's in trouble." She gave Zeb another punch on the arm, and he drew back. For some reason, she found this mildly amusing.

Then she slapped her leg as a thought surfaced in her brain. "Frog Hollow? My uncles live there. I *know* Frog Hollow, and I'm no stranger to critters. Let me help you find that wayward calf."

Zeb shrugged, did an about-face, and headed deeper into the woods. Katie followed. The tall, slender man in a faded blue cotton shirt tucked into equally faded jeans reminded her of a regular farm boy. He looked to be barely older than she, early twenties at most, with maybe a hint of school teacher—if you used your imagination. His huge cowboy boots—at least a size eleven, if she were guessing—covered a great deal of territory with each step, and she trotted to keep pace.

Not bad. Not bad at all. But way too young. Add twenty-five years to this dude, and he'd be just what the doctor ordered for Mama. But then Mama had made it clear she didn't want another man.

Zeb halted so abruptly that Katie almost ran into him. He turned toward her, dark eyes sparkling, a finger across his lips. "Shhh. I see her. Behind that blackberry bush. Her rope's caught in the tangle." He inched forward, then whispered over his shoulder. "I'll work it loose and we'll take her home."

Katie watched in silence as Zeb inched toward the struggling calf from behind. Speaking softly, he grabbed the rope, pulled taut by the still straining animal, and began to work it loose from the tangled mess.

Katie's nerve endings tingled, anticipating what would happen the moment that heifer realized the rope had gone slack, but she remained a silent observer.

Finally Zeb tilted his head in her direction and mouthed the words, "Got it," as he pulled the rope free of the bush and stepped out, waving the frazzled threads in the air.

Free again, the wild-eyed critter bolted. Zeb clung to the rope and was thrown to the ground, dragged on his stomach by the fleeing calf.

Katie could contain herself no longer. "Let it go!" She sprang into action. In one flying leap, she landed astride the animal's back, arms around its neck, and wrestled it to the ground. Flipping the calf onto its side, she called to Zeb. "Give me your rope."

He pulled it over his head and held it out to her. She snatched it and twirled it around three of the calf's legs, rendering the animal helpless.

Zeb got to his hands and knees, then pushed to a standing position. "Hey, girl, that was some pretty fancy footwork—for a female. You act like a rodeo gal."

The old familiar tightness invaded her throat, and tears threatened. But she forced a grin and playfully jabbed him in the arm. "Not anymore."

"You mean you used to…" He waved a hand in the air, revealing a nasty rope burn across the palm.

Katie changed the subject. "That calf's not going anywhere. What say I go get Uncle Everett and his mule to give her a little lesson in manners and escort her home?"

~

Before Zeb could reply, Katie spun on her heel and bounded through the woods at a fast clip. He watched her go, then turned to the calf. "You heifer. Now look at what you've caused."

The animal stared up at him, all the fight drained from its now still form. Zeb stared back. Poor little calf. Tried to run away. Didn't quite make it. He empathized with the creature. Drained. Can't get up. Or maybe not enough fight left to make the effort worthwhile.

He raked a palm across the side of his face, but jerked it away as perspiration, mingled with afternoon stubble, touched the raw skin left from the recent rope burn. He examined his smarting hand.

That stings. Sometimes life stings.

He leaned against the tree and eyed the calf again. "Yeah, you and me both, girl. But things always get better." *Don't they?*

"There they are, Uncle Everett." The now familiar voice invaded the stillness, and broke Zeb's reverie.

Katie, accompanied by Everett Tillman riding muleback, approached the inert calf. Zeb knew the overall clad, gray-haired man well. Residing with his younger brother, Rance, on the old home place ever since the death of their father, Ben Tillman, he had a reputation as one of the best gardeners, cooks, and cowpokes around.

Nearly as spry as his much younger counterpart, he dismounted and knelt by the animal. In seconds the calf was on its feet, rope secured to the saddle horn, and Everett was back astride the mule.

"We'll be headin' on over to Fred's. He's prob'ly fit to be tied by now." The man raised a hand in a wave, and chuckled.

Katie returned the wave. "Thanks, Uncle Everett."

"All in a day's work. See ya later, kids." Giving the mule a nudge, his took his charge and left.

"That's that." Katie stuck her hands in her pockets, and rocked back and forth on her heels. Then her face changed into an expression Zeb hadn't seen until now. Panic?

"What's wrong?"

In an instant, she rallied and took on a not-quite-believable look of nonchalance. "Nothing. I think I may have lost something." Dropping to all fours, she began riffling through the area of her recent tussle with the calf.

Zeb bent over her. "What is it? I'll help you look."

"Oh, just a little pin. I had it in my pocket."

When the search proved fruitless, Katie stood, chin quivering. "Well, I guess we're not gonna find it. Dumb ol' me." She jabbed his arm and produced a mirthless giggle.

For some reason, this was more than just a pin. It was important to the gal. But why?

"Katie?"

"Yeah?" Her smile didn't reach her eyes.

"Could you have lost it when you fell out of that tree?"

Biting her bottom lip, she gave a half-hearted nod. "Maybe."

"Well, it can't hurt to go look, can it?"

Katie offered no response, but fell into step beside Zeb as they retraced their path to the fallen branch.

When a search near the broken limb rendered nothing, Katie sat cross-legged on the ground, head lowered. Zeb sank onto the fallen limb near her, not knowing what to do. "I'm sorry."

She didn't look up. "You can't help it. I shouldn't have been so careless."

Zeb's heart went out to this girl he hardly knew. "Maybe it can be replaced."

She drew in a long breath, then let it out slowly. "It's not that. The pin was a gift. Grandma gave it to

Mama. Mama gave it to Aunt Ella. Then, when I came here to stay and help her with the twins, Aunt Ella gave it to me. She trusted me with it. It was a bluebird. You know, bluebirds bring happiness."

He nodded as he understood, then focused on a birch in the distance. *Maybe I need to find ME a bluebird.*

Katie raked a stick through the dry leaves in front of her. "Aunt Ella'll be *so* upset. She doesn't need this stress with the baby due next month and all."

Zeb scuffed the toe of his boot in the dust before him. Something glinted in the afternoon sunlight. "Katie."

She jerked her head around, and her eyes widened. Scrambling in the direction he pointed, she grabbed the object and cradled it to her. "That's it! You found it."

The pin was indeed a delicately crafted bluebird, its wings spread in flight. It reminded him of his last year as a student in Bluebird Valley School—the year Miss Ella had been his teacher for a time and had worn the pin every day. Those had been happy days for Zeb, some of the happiest he'd known.

He'd been in eighth grade for the umpteenth time, never having attended enough days in one term to graduate, and never really caring.

Then Miss Ella Tillman, wearing that very pin, had waltzed onto the scene, a first-year teacher barely older than Zeb. She'd played the piano and told him his baritone was outstanding, encouraged him to attend school on a regular basis, and taught him to believe in himself again—because *she* believed in him.

He'd graduated eighth grade that year, and Miss Ella had married Marcus Banks.

After attending four years of high school, Zeb had returned as the Bluebird Valley schoolmaster, and now had the honor of teaching Luke and Duke Banks, Miss Ella's twin sons.

His heart warmed at the thought of this lady and the part she played in enriching his life. *Maybe there really IS something to this bluebird thing.*

His thoughts returned to the present as he watched Katie transform back into the carefree gal he'd met less than two hours ago.

"Oh, Zeb, how can I ever repay you? I thank you. Aunt Ella thanks you—even though she doesn't know it's necessary." She paused, a twinkle in her eye. "And we're not going to tell her. Are we?"

Zeb smiled. "She won't hear it from me."

Katie gave him a playful punch on the arm. "Good job, Teach."

He reciprocated, jabbing her lightly on the shoulder. She stepped back, emitting a slight gasp, then raised her eyebrows as a wide grin spread across her face. "It's late. I'd best run and get the boys."

Zeb followed her easy gait to the woods' edge. She stepped from among the trees and hesitated, staring intently across the road. His eyes followed her gaze, and his heart stood still.

Chapter 2

Katie stared in horror as a thin, scruffy man reeled precariously against the store's lone gas pump, Davey under one arm, kicking and wailing at the top of his lungs. Fred stood pointing a rifle at the man, while Hazel approached waving an iron skillet above her head.

Katie sucked in a breath and clamped her lips between her teeth.

Jesus, take charge.

"Let's go." It was more of a command than anything else, but Katie obeyed. They cleared the ditch and sprinted across the road together, Katie taking two steps each time Zeb took one.

Dashing by the man, in one motion Katie snatched Davey from his grasp and headed for the store.

The rifle fired. Katie froze. Hazel screamed. "Good grief, Fred. You could've shot the baby."

Fred glared and waggled a finger at Zeb. "I couldn't have shot nothin'. He grabbed my gun and pointed it toward the sky."

Katie stumbled to the porch and collapsed on a step with Davey in her arms. The child snuggled against her. She rubbed his back. How could anyone terrorize this innocent little boy?

The man at the gas pump staggered in the direction of the porch. "Anybody got 'ny hooch around here?" Grabbing a support post, he slid to the ground and gave Katie a glassy-eyed stare. She turned away in disgust.

"Cryder Zarbone, you get up and get off this property right now. You're already soused." Hazel stomped past Katie and Davey, waving the skillet again.

"But, Mish Hazhel," the man blubbered, "I jusht need a little drink of hoooo—Ouch! Your confounded dog bit me." He grabbed his ankle. "It's a-bleedin'."

Duke came strutting around the side of the building, a huge grin on his face. "That wasn't no dog. That was Luke."

Katie didn't want to scold the child. In fact, she thought a little pain might jerk Mr. Zarbone down a notch or two.

It is Mine to avenge came to mind.

She beckoned the twins to her. "Why, Luke? Why did you bite the man?"

The child eyed her, then tugged his brother aside and whispered in his ear.

Duke put an arm around Luke and declared

matter-of-factly, "'Cause he tried to steal Davey."

Katie hugged the child to her and tried to shake the sense of foreboding generated by Duke's words.

Zeb knelt beside the distraught Mr. Zarbone. "Here, let me have a look at that leg."

The man winced. "No. You ain't no doctor. You're a vet."

Katie came to attention. A teacher, *and* a vet? Jack of all trades, master of none? Or maybe a journeyman unsung. Interesting.

"Get some alcohol and clean rags." Zeb barked the orders.

Mr. Zarbone brightened. "Alcohol?"

"Shut up, Bone. Hazel, do it now."

To Katie's surprise, Hazel disappeared into the store and promptly reappeared bearing the supplies. Zeb held Bone down while Hazel soaked the wound with rubbing alcohol.

Amid Bone's kicking and flailing, accompanied by shouts of, "Ow, stop, it burns, you're a-killin' me," Zeb and Hazel managed to wrap the man's ankle and pull him to his feet.

Zeb grasped the teetering man's shoulders and faced him. "Go on home, Bone. Sleep it off."

Bone pitched forward and locked elbows with Zeb, nearly dragging them both to the ground. Leaning against Zeb, the drunk man stared toward Katie and Davey. Knots formed in her stomach as his eyes blazed. "I'll sleep. Oh, I'll sleep. But when you sleep, beware."

"Okay, that's it. You're gone." Zeb grabbed the man's arm and dragged him across the gravel drive.

15

Bone staggered and swayed onto the highway, then paused and, turning back, shook his fist and spewed in her direction. "You gotta sleep sometimes. And when you do—I'll be your worst nightmare."

Goosebumps started in Katie's toes and made their way over every inch of her body. She hugged Davey tighter, her eyes only faintly focusing on Zeb as he twisted Bone's arm behind his back and escorted him away from the Hollisters' property.

Davey squirmed on Katie's lap, bringing her back to reality. "Bad man?"

"Yes, but he's gone now. It's okay."

The child reached up and placed his hands on her cheeks. Then he leaned back and glanced toward the road. "Bad man."

Zeb, wiping his hands on his pant legs, covered the driveway in purposeful strides. "You can put down that skillet now, Hazel. He's on his way home."

Hazel laid the frying pan on a chair and reached down to take Davey. "That old drunk's just a bunch of hot air. More bark than bite." She shook her head.

Fred pumped the remaining shells from the magazine, and threw the empty rifle to the ground. "I wouldn't be too sure about that."

The older woman settled Davey on her hip and huffed into the store. Fred and the twins followed.

Zeb sank to the porch floor, leaned back against a post, and closed his eyes. He sat for several moments saying nothing, beads of perspiration trailing down his face.

Katie broke the silence. "So. You're a vet, huh?"

"Not officially." He opened his eyes momentarily, then shut them again and massaged them with his fingertips.

She pursued the matter. "A critter doctor who just patched up a human."

Zeb sat upright. His biting tone startled Katie. "Bone is an animal."

"Oh?"

"All he ever does is get plastered and threaten people. He'd as soon steal you blind, and no telling what else, as to look at you."

Katie considered the statement. "Are you afraid of him?"

Zeb pulled his bandana from his jeans pocket and swiped it across his face and neck. Then he turned toward Katie with an unwavering stare, hesitating so long she began to think he wasn't going to answer. Finally, leaning toward her, he cuffed her lightly on the shoulder. "Let's just say he bears watching."

Her mind relived the moment when Bone's blazing eyes met her own, when the threats hung in the air like icicles waiting to break loose, and her body shivered of its own accord. But this was ridiculous. She didn't even know the man. And what could he have against a little boy? He was just drunk and making a spectacle of himself. Of course, that's all it was. And yet.

She drew her knees against her chest and wrapped her arms around them.

~

Zeb watched the young woman retreat into

herself and sit motionless. There was more to this little gal than the happy-go-lucky character she portrayed. Independent, yes. But below the surface a deeper, softer side lingered—a side he'd like to get to know better.

He eased back against the post. "A penny for your thoughts?"

"Thoughts come and go. So do pennies."

Elusive little thing.

Trying to formulate a response, and failing, Zeb glanced toward his house. His younger brother approached, bare feet stirring up miniature clouds of dust with every step.

"The cow's loose and the clothesline's down. Dad said to come a-runnin'."

Zeb sighed. "Okay, Mike. Tell him I'll be right there." Truth was, the man wasn't his dad, or Mike's, and the cow was loose half the time. He got up, brushed off his pants, and started toward the lane. "See ya later, Katie."

The girl bounced to her feet. "Can I help?"

"Don't see how."

But she stayed on his heels.

By the time Zeb and Mike had rounded up the cow, put her where she belonged, and secured the gate, Katie and their mom had righted the clothesline and were sitting together on the front porch.

Mike raced up and hopped on his mother's lap. She hugged him and playfully slapped his leg. "Get up. You're twelve years old. I need to be sitting on *your* lap." He laughed and returned the hug.

There was a red mark across Mom's cheek, and her husband was nowhere to be seen. Not unusual.

Katie stood. "Guess I'd better be getting home now. I enjoyed meeting you, Mrs. Slocum." She averted her eyes from Mom's face and shot a questioning glance at Zeb, but said nothing.

Zeb's brows knit together, and he shook his head. He followed her across the yard to the lane, then stopped when she paused at the gate. "Thanks for helping my mom."

Katie leaned on the gatepost, her eyes glistening. "She's a nice lady. Easy to love."

"*I* think so." Oh, how he'd love to give his stepdad the what-for. Lazy, selfish, arrogant, abusive old goat.

Vengeance is not in your hands invaded his thoughts.

Katie leaned forward and patted his arm. No punches this time. "It'll be okay, Zeb. God's in control. Trust Him." With that, she turned and stepped onto the lane, calling to her charges. "Let's go, boys. It's about suppertime."

Zeb's stomach did a somersault and his eyes went hazy as he watched the three join hands and skip away from him—four bare feet and a pair of brogans. He wished he could add his big old cowboy boots to the three pairs.

Chapter 3

"Zeb, get over here. I've got a job for you." Boomer Slocum's voice cut through the air like a rusty-bladed hunting knife. Zeb's whole body cringed.

"Alright, Boomer." He couldn't bear to call the man Dad, or much of anything else for that matter. He'd be gone in a heartbeat if it weren't for Mom. And Mike.

Ten years. Ten long, long years. Mike had barely even gotten to know their dad. Stupid typhoid fever.

Boomer stood leaning against the side of the house, arms and legs crossed, cocky grin in place. "Dog just now killed a rabbit. It ain't tore up. You need to skin it so's Maw can cook it fer supper."

The dog was gone. Zeb was sure it was Davey's pup who had done the deed, and equally sure Boomer had kicked it again. He pulled out his pocketknife and picked up the rabbit. Poor bunny. Well, at least the little dog had gotten away. Lucky dog.

Zeb performed his *duty*, and held the rabbit out to Boomer. The man hooked his thumbs in his overall pockets and tilted his head. "Mi-i-i-ike."

The boy, carrying a slingshot, dashed around the side of the house and stood before him. "Yeah, Dad?"

One swift slap sent the homemade weapon to the ground. "Get rid of that thing and take that there rabbit in and tell your maw I want me some rabbit and gravy for supper."

Mike took the skinned animal from Zeb and said nothing.

Boomer stood to his full height, a good five inches shorter than Zeb's six feet. "Make it snappy." He flipped the child's ear, then sauntered across the yard whistling.

Zeb bent over, and retrieving the slingshot, took off in the opposite direction. The barn, if one could call it that, was his refuge. He climbed the worn ladder to the loft of the rickety structure, made his way to the far corner, and pulled out the familiar chest bearing the name Zeke Harlow.

The only thing he had left of his dad, it stayed carefully secluded in the one place where Boomer's alleged bad back prevented him from entering.

Removing the tattered Bible, he hugged it to him, and the tears came—silent tears that no one saw, or would ever see.

I see your tears, Son. It'll be alright.

How can it be alright? A grown man, a school teacher, sitting here in a barn loft crying like a baby.

Jesus shed tears streamed unbidden but welcome.

Zeb gently placed the Bible on the hay before him and covered his face with his hands. Soundless, violent sobs wracked his body.

The moon was high in the sky when he returned Dad's chest to its hiding place, slowly descended the ladder, and made his way to the house. He'd missed supper, but Boomer wouldn't care, Mike would be afraid to mention it, and Mom would understand.

Entering the silent house, he dodged creaky floorboards and crept into the room he shared with his brother.

"Zeb?" Mike's voice was a whisper. "I saved you a biscuit."

"Hey, thanks." He devoured the treat, then collapsed onto his mattress.

"You okay?"

Bless the kid's heart. "I'm okay, buddy. I just needed some time alone."

"Did you pray?"

Zeb turned on his side. "I did. People need to pray. It's really important."

A whispered, "I know," followed by steady breathing, drifted from Mike's side of the room.

Zeb closed his eyes. A whirlwind of images raced through his consciousness. Bluebirds flying high above rabbits, chased by little dogs, chased by little boys, chased by a blue-eyed gal in overalls and brogans—suddenly joined hands and paws and wings, and twirled around laughing like they hadn't a care in the world.

Zeb relaxed, willing his mind to become one with them. Then his body tensed. *Wish I had it all together like that Katie girl. Wish I had me a bluebird.*

His head fell back against the pillow as weariness set in, and sleep overtook him.

~

Katie woke Monday morning to the sound of voices in the kitchen. Where had the weekend gone? Zeb hadn't been at church or anywhere else she'd been yesterday. She hoped he was alright.

Duke's voice rose above the others. "Dad, are you sure this is how Mama fixes eggs?"

Marcus ignored the question. "Eat your breakfast, Son. Mama's resting, and you guys need to get ready for school."

Katie hopped out of bed and slipped on fresh overalls and her trusty brogans. "Finish your breakfast and go wait on the porch, you two, and I'll walk with you to school."

Both boys grabbed their lunch pails and headed for the door.

Katie's heart surged. These two little guys had become dear to her during the few weeks she'd spent in their home. And soon there'd be another little guy, or gal, to love. She stuck her head in the bedroom door. "Aunt Ella, I'm headed out with the boys. Anything I can bring you?"

Ella rolled onto her back and stretched out to her full length. "No, but grab a jar of that apple butter from the cupboard and take it to poor Zeb. Maybe it'll brighten his day."

Katie stepped across the room and stood over her aunt. "What do you mean by *poor* Zeb?"

Ella averted her eyes. "It's just that he's always had so many things pushed on him. He never really had a chance to enjoy his teen years, and still gets no time for himself. He needs to have a little fun. Maybe he just needs…"

"Ka-a-atie, are ya comin'?" Duke's voice was loud enough to rattle the rafters.

Katie was loath to end the conversation. "Needs what, Aunt Ella? What does Zeb need?"

Ella reached up and patted her niece's arm. "Go on, girl. Grab the apple butter and get our lads to school on time. We'll talk later."

Katie's thoughts raced. What about Zeb? Why was he *poor* Zeb? What did he need? And why did she care?

Once across the highway, they started down the lane between Zeb's house and Hollisters. Beside the store, Luke stopped and pointed toward the building. Davey stood at a window, waving. "Duke. Wuke."

The boys waved back. "See you after school, Davey." Then Duke took off at a run down the lane in the direction of the school. Luke followed.

Katie glanced back at the small child. His lips puckered, and he held up one hand in another slight wave. "Bye." And he disappeared into the room.

Something wasn't right. Cryder Zarbone's face and drunken threats invaded her mind and took up residence. Was Davey in danger? Was *she*?

Katie quickened her steps.

The schoolyard was filled with laughing, cavorting children of all sizes, her cousins and Mike among them. Zeb stood near the front door. When he saw Katie, his expression brightened, and he hastened toward her. "Well, hello, Miss Katie. What brings you to our humble hall of learning?" He winked, a broad smile spreading across his face.

She reached in her pocket and withdrew the small jar. "I come bearing a gift from Aunt Ella."

Zeb grabbed the jar and turned it over and over in his huge hands. "I know all about that lady's apple butter. I accept." Then his brow furrowed. "By the way, how's she doing?"

Katie bit her lower lip. "Pretty miserable, I'd say. But she keeps up a good front. I'm not too sure that Baby'll wait until September."

Zeb ran his fingers through his hair. "Take good care of her. She's pretty special to the folks around here. And send for me if she needs anything." He reached for her hand and squeezed it between both of his. "I mean it."

"Thanks. I'll remember that."

He nodded, then strode off toward the door. The students followed, and by the time he rang the bell, most of them had already gone inside.

Katie started back the way she had come. Midway up the lane, she heard pounding footsteps behind her. Mike. He sped past her, yelling in her direction. "Quick. Gotta get help. Trouble at the school."

Cold fingers of dread raced up Katie's spine. Without hesitation, she did an about-face and sprinted down the lane.

Chapter 4

Zeb's heart pounded like a sledgehammer threatening to break through his chest. Every muscle in his body begged to tackle and subdue the man blocking the door with his presence. Zeb was perfectly capable. He'd done it before. But this time the schoolmaster stood motionless, weighing his options. There was no room for error.

"Give me the gun, Tank." He spoke in slow, measured syllables. Inching forward, he extended a hand.

"You come one step closer, and I'll blow Walter's head off." The rifle, trained on a teenager across the room, trembled in Tank's hands.

Zeb halted. He had to buy some time, find a way to distract the crazed man. His wide-eyed students sat rigidly at their desks, all in harm's way. He didn't dare instruct anyone to move.

Tank fingered the trigger. "He stole my horse, and I'm a'gonna shoot 'im."

Zeb's insides trembled, but he forced a calm, easy tone. "It's okay, Tank. Your horse is outside. Your brother just rode it to school. Let's go get it."

"I seen it." The man took a step forward and raised the rifle, shutting one eye and focusing through the sight. "And now I'm a'gonna kill that dadburned horse thief."

Zeb poised himself for what he knew was his only option. *Lord, help me.*

I'm right here. Those three words spoke loud and clear in his mind.

His body tensed for the plunge.

Something slammed against the side of the building, making a bone jarring thud. Startled, Tank jerked his head toward the sound.

In a heartbeat, Zeb was beside him. Grabbing the gun barrel, he angled it toward the ceiling and wrestled the rifle from Tank's hands.

The man clamored after Zeb, fists flying, but suddenly an overall clad form rammed Tank from behind, buckling his knees and sending him sprawling backward to the floor.

Duke stood. "Way to go, Katie!"

Luke followed suit. "Katie!"

The students cheered and clapped. All except Walter. He advanced on his big brother, eyes narrowed, lips pursed. Grabbing him by an arm, he jerked the man to his feet. "Come on. We're going home."

Shaking his head, his features drawn, Walter faced the teacher. "I'm real sorry, Mr. Harlow. You keep the gun here. I'll take him and his horse back home. Things like this happen all the time. He acts like he owns me—thinks he's forty years older than me, instead of a measly ten."

Zeb reached out and patted the boy's shoulder. "You can't take him home by yourself. You'll need an escort. I'll go with you."

Walter's entire body sagged, a resigned look on his face. "I'll be alright. Have been for sixteen years so far." Glaring at his older brother, he yanked him toward the door.

Zeb followed.

A large seedy-looking man emerged from among the trees.

Walter stopped. "Dad?"

The man approached Zeb. "I'm their dad." He nodded toward Tank and Walter. "I'm sorry for the ruckus Tank prob'ly caused in there. Hope he didn't hurt nobody. I seen 'im head out through the woods and follered 'im, but he's fastern me and I jist now got here."

Tank stiffened and stood silent before the big man.

Mr. Bailor bent and picked up a large stick, then turned to Walter. "Come on, boy. Let's drag 'im home."

The three shuffled off among the trees, Mr. Bailor prodding Tank with the stick.

Zeb turned back toward the school building. Katie

stood watching him. She brushed her hands together and smoothed her hair, then leaned casually against the door frame, hands in her pockets.

Zeb considered for a moment. No way could this gal be that relaxed after just tackling a would-be assassin. But she sure could look the part. He cleared his throat and stepped in front of her. "Wanna help?"

She straightened, the traces of a grin teasing the corners of her mouth. "Of course."

He handed her the gun. "Here, take this outside and make sure there's no ammunition in it."

She took it in one quick motion. "Can do."

He turned to the class. "After all that excitement, I think you guys could use a little breather." Actually, it was their teacher who needed the breather. "Kevin, how about you take everyone outside and get a baseball game underway?"

Kevin Walker, a trusted seventh grader, needed no extra prompting. "Let's go, kids."

As they beat a path to the door, Zeb sank into Kevin's big desk at the back of the room. He remembered sitting here in eighth grade. Was that only six years ago? It seemed like an eternity. He stared out the window, reliving those days as Miss Ella's student, recalling how he'd finally managed to attend enough days in one term to graduate.

"Zeb?" He turned to see his little brother stepping over the threshold.

"Come on in, Mike."

"I ran as fast as I could. Got Fred and headed back here, but he runs kinda slow. By the time we got here,

Katie was slinking around near the door. Looked like she was just waiting for a chance to make a move. She beat us to it."

"You did fine. Katie couldn't have done what she did if something hadn't startled Tank and given me the chance to rush him. She couldn't have risked tackling a guy with a rifle."

Fred came limping into the room, lugging a tire iron. "Doggone it. I tried my hardest. Was gonna hit him over the head with this here tire iron, but I tripped and it flew out of my hand. Hope it didn't knock a hole in the side of the building. I didn't see one. Anyway, by the time I could get up and grab it, Katie had moved in for the kill."

Zeb's tension drained away, at least for the moment, and he drew in a long breath and exhaled slowly. So *that* was the noise.

Thank you, Jesus.

"Fred, you provided the distraction I needed to get the gun away from Tank. That's the reason Katie was able to step in when she did."

Fred rared back and puffed out his chest. "You mean I helped?"

Zeb couldn't keep from liking the older man. "You made all the difference. We couldn't have done it without you." *And Jesus.*

Katie sauntered in, rifle in one hand, ammunition in the other. "It only had one round. I removed it. Here ya go."

Fred eyed the gun. "That thing doesn't need to be around a school. Why don't I take it back to the store for safekeeping?"

When Fred had gone, Katie eased onto a seat a couple rows from Zeb. "Do you think Tank really intended to shoot his brother?"

Zeb tried to stifle the dread that made his very soul ache. "It wouldn't have surprised me. That Bailor bunch is wild as they come, has no respect for anyone—not even family, and most of them act like they're a few bricks shy of a load."

Katie glanced around the empty school room. "What about Walter?"

Zeb stretched his legs out into the aisle, hoping against hope that his fears never became reality. "Walter's more levelheaded than the rest of them. I wish there was a way to get him out of there before something real bad happens."

Katie's eyes widened in understanding.

Zeb forced himself to his feet. "I guess I'd better call in the gang, even though I know they're out there havin' a ball."

Katie's tilted head and narrowed eyes told him his attempt at levity had failed. She stood and edged toward the door. "Guess I'll be heading on home then."

A strange urgency demanded that Zeb ask her to stay, but he pushed it aside. "Thanks for the help. I'll see you later."

She paused and glanced back, eyes sparkling. "At your service. Any time." Then, turning in the perky way to which he had become accustomed and took a hankering to, she was out the door and gone.

The rest of the day passed without incident, but Zeb's uneasiness robbed him of his concentration and kept him on edge. Walter did not return.

At dismissal time, Zeb opened the door to find Katie lounging against a tree trunk, casually watching the building.

~

"Katie. Katie." Duke and Luke pushed through the stampede of students exiting the schoolhouse and rushed into her outstretched arms. She knelt and squeezed them to her, knowing they were fine, but thankful to see it for herself.

Zeb stood behind the twins. "Come to walk the boys home?"

She plopped onto the ground, a kid clinging to each arm, relief flowing through her like a cool drink on a hot day. "Thought I might as well. I wasn't busy."

He placed his hands on his hips and looked down at her—a little too perceptively for her liking. "The rest of the day went fine. Nobody else showed up."

She faced Luke and tugged on a lock of his hair. "I wasn't worried."

Zeb squatted before her and gave her a sideways glance. "Yeah. Right."

Anxious to steer the conversation in another direction, Katie sprang to her feet. "Ready to go, guys?"

They followed her lead. Duke tugged at her pocket. "Can we stop at the store and get a soda?"

"Sure. Coke?"

Duke laughed. "Yeah! My favorite."

Luke nodded in agreement.

Zeb stood and cuffed Katie on the shoulder. "Could I come along and be one of your guys?"

She returned the punch. "Come ahead, School Teacher. It's a free country." But something about his idea made her insides smile a bit more brightly than she could have anticipated—or was sure how to handle.

The boys raced ahead, and Katie followed them at a brisk walk. Zeb stayed beside her. By the time Katie and Zeb reached the store, Luke and Duke already had their Cokes and were sitting on the porch engaged in deep conversation with Davey. A woman sat on a wooden chair nearby.

Zeb put his hand behind Katie's back and guided her up the steps. "Katie Gallagher, meet Davey's Aunt Lillian Wymore."

Davey, hearing the name, directed a bright-eyed stare at the woman. "Widdy!"

The slender, thirty-something brunette chuckled. "He can't say 'Lillian.' Glad to meet you, Katie."

The two shook hands, and Katie noticed a narrow scar extending from wrist to elbow on the woman's right arm. She wondered if the small, leather watchband irritated it.

Davey jumped up and ran to Zeb. He grabbed the man's pant leg and, tugging on it, shot him an imploring gaze. "Pway?"

Zeb reached into his pocket and extracted his harmonica. "You're in luck, pal. I just happen to have it with me."

As the strains of "Amazing Grace" filled the air, Davey climbed onto his aunt's lap and nestled into the soft folds of her blue cotton dress. She drew him close, and resting her head against his tousled hair, spoke softly to him. "That was your mother's favorite song before...before..."

The child reached up and put his arms around her neck. "Widdy."

She fell silent, rocking back and forth, cradling her small nephew in her arms.

When the song ended, Lillian stood and gently put Davey on the chair. "I have to go home now, Baby. But I'll be back, and I'll bring you something you'll like." Eyes pooling with unshed tears, she turned to Katie. "So glad to have met you. But I do need to get going. It's a long drive home."

"Glad to have met you, too, Lillian. Be safe." Katie sympathized with the woman. She was obviously Davey's aunt on his mother's side. But what had happened to his mother? And where was his dad? *Who* was his dad?

When goodbyes had been said all around, Lillian climbed into the old Model T parked near the gas pump. Zeb turned the crank, the motor coughed to life, and the woman pulled onto the road and drove away.

Hazel picked up Davey and took him inside the store. Zeb leaned on the porch post and faced Katie. "Lillian does her best, poor soul, but..."

"Zeb!" Boomer's grating yell interrupted him in mid-sentence, shattering the afternoon peace.

Zeb's mouth turned down in a grimace. "Duty calls." Resignation in his voice, he shook his head wearily and stalked across the lane, shoulders slumping.

Katie's heart ached for the man. "See ya." But he was already out of sight.

Something rammed her from behind. Her knees buckled and she hit the ground with a thump, seat first. Loud giggles erupted in both her ears as four small arms came around her neck.

"Great tackle, Luke."

"Tackle."

Katie suppressed a smile and put on her stern face. "Boys, that wasn't nice. You shouldn't go around tackling people."

"*You* did." Duke fell across her lap and gave her an upside-down stare.

"Yeah, but I had to. You guys were in danger."

Duke's expression became serious. "We know. Thanks, Katie."

Luke hugged her tighter.

The three of them got to their feet and headed home.

Aunt Nellie Banks stood in the open screen door, short black curls bobbing as she spoke. "Get right on in here, kids. I'm spending the night, and I've got supper on the table." The large woman's smile radiated warmth and compassion.

The boys dashed inside, but Katie paused beside the beloved lady. "Is something wrong?"

Chapter 5

Aunt Nellie drew Katie aside. "Everything seems to be fine, but it looks to me like that little one might want an August birthday. I'm going to stay, just in case."

A surge of calmness spread over Katie. "How can I help?"

"We'll know when it's time. You just sit tight, and I'll send you to get Hazel when that little baby decides to make an appearance."

Katie knew Hazel's reputation, and that she'd been the one to deliver the twins. "Okay." She headed for the supper table.

When the meal was over and the kitchen clean, Katie considered the sleeping arrangements. "Aunt Nellie, you can have my bed. I'll make a pallet on the floor."

The older woman glanced toward Ella and Marcus' bedroom door. "You all go ahead and get some rest.

I'm not sleepy just yet."

Katie retired to her room and snuggled deep in the soft featherbed.

Moonbeams were the only light in the room when a hand touched her shoulder. Suddenly wide awake, she opened her eyes. Her aunt spoke in a whisper. "Honey, it's time. Get on some clothes and go fetch Hazel for us."

Katie sprang out of bed, snatched her shirt and overalls from the back of a chair, and hastened to don them.

"We've got some time yet. Don't run. You might fall and break your neck." Aunt Nellie chuckled. "I'll be in with Ella."

But Katie *did* run. Gently closing the screen door so as not to wake the boys, she flew off the porch and sped along the lane toward Hollisters' store. She beat on the door with both fists, a rush of adrenalin causing her to ignore the fact that she might alert the entire household. "Hazel! Hazel, wake up."

A sleepy-eyed Fred, carrying a lantern, opened the door and peered out at her. "Hazel ain't here."

Katie wanted to scream, but she maintained a calm tone. "Not here? We need her. Now. Where is she?"

"Gone. That Bailor girl come a-runnin' through the woods a while ago. Said Tank shot their brother, and Hazel went with 'er to try to help."

Katie's heart pounded. Walter? But Hazel was with him. She could take care of him. And Katie had to concentrate on getting help for Ella. "Fred, Aunt Ella's in labor. We need help."

The man took a few steps backward. "Oh, no. Don't look at me. No way." He retreated further and shut the door.

Katie's thoughts collided over one another. She had to act fast. But how?

Zeb. He had said to call him if Ella ever needed anything. And he *was* a doctor. Sort of. Was it possible? Did she dare hope?

There was no other alternative. She ran across the yard and pounded on his door.

~

Zeb sat bolt upright in bed. What was that sound? Someone at the door. He swung his feet over the side of the bed, but hesitated when Boomer bellowed from the next room. "Who is it?"

The noise stopped. "It's Katie Gallagher. We need Zeb."

Katie. Something's wrong. He reached for his jeans.

"Get out'a here. It's the middle of the night. Go home and go to bed." The man's rude words grated on Zeb's every nerve.

Zeb didn't bother to put on a shirt. "I've got it, Boomer." Stumbling through the living room, he flung open the front door. "Katie. Come on in. Are you alright?"

"There's no time. Aunt Ella's in labor, and Hazel's not home."

Zeb's brain whirled. I'm a vet. A vet! An animal doctor. Oh, dear Jesus.

You can do this,--a small, calm voice spoke.

Leaning down, he found her in the darkness and lightly gripped her shoulder. "Run and tell them help's on the way. I'll be right behind you."

Her hand reached up and covered his in a gentle squeeze. "Thank you."

Dashing to his room, he slipped into his boots and a shirt, grabbed his vet bag, and whispered a quick explanation to his wide-eyed brother. In a matter of seconds, he was loping up the lane toward the Banks home.

The bedroom was dark except for a kerosene lamp on a small table and the first light of dawn peeping through a window. Aunt Nellie sat in a rocking chair beside the bed, holding Ella's hand. Ella. His beloved teacher. His responsibility. He breathed a silent prayer and approached the bed.

Mustering his brightest countenance, he brushed a hand across her damp forehead. "It's okay, Miss Ella. Everything's going to be fine. Zeb the Great has arrived."

Smiling, she reached up and trailed her fingers along the side of his face. "Yes, you are. I've always known you were great." Then, grabbing his arm, she clenched her fingers in an unyielding grip and emitted a sharp gasp.

The next two hours passed in a blur. Time hung suspended, motionless, yet flew at breakneck speed. Nellie assisted Zeb, Zeb assisted Nellie, and they both assisted Ella—but Jesus was in charge.

~

Zeb pushed open the screen door and squinted in the early morning sunlight. Backing up against the wall, he sank to the porch floor, his tired muscles screaming for relief. Four sets of inquiring eyes met his.

"Is it alright to go in now?"

Zeb leaned his head against the wood. "Go on in, Marcus. Ella's asleep. Nellie's holding Molly. Everybody's fine."

Duke beamed. "Molly. We got a little sister, Luke."

Luke vigorously nodded his approval. "Sister."

The boys followed Marcus into the house. Katie sank to the floor beside Zeb. "Close your eyes and lean your head back."

Too tired to argue, he obliged. Soft cool hands massaged his temples in gentle circles. His tension slowly began to ease. "Mmm. That feels good."

She never missed a beat. "I'm glad. You're a lifesaver."

"By the way, where was Hazel last night?"

Katie continued the massage. "Fred said Tank shot his brother, and the sister came and got Hazel to try to do something for him."

Zeb's gut clenched and his eyes flew open. "Which brother?"

"Fred didn't say. How many does he have?"

An icy dread gripped Zeb to the core. "Several. And you don't know if it was Walter?"

She gave him a direct look. "No, I don't. I just pray it wasn't."

Zeb was in the habit of praying daily for the young man. He could sympathize, *and* empathize. If it wasn't in God's plan to intervene and rescue him and Mike, and Mom—then maybe Walter. At least it was worth a prayer or two.

He stood. "I've got to be going. Nellie's here with Ella, and I still have a day of teaching ahead of me."

Katie hopped to her feet and sidled up next to him. Blue eyes shining, she leaned toward him and planted a light kiss on his cheek. His toes tingled clear up to his ears and begged him to return the gesture. But he stood frozen in place, savoring the moment.

"Thanks for coming, Zeb the Great."

To his dismay, he felt his face warm, alerting him that his cheeks had turned a deep shade of scarlet. "You heard?"

"I heard." She punched him on the arm. He didn't pull away.

Katie stepped back and raised a hand in a little wave. "I know you need to go. I'll have the boys at school before you can ring that bell."

Zeb stepped off the porch. "See you then."

He had barely started down the lane when Fred came lumbering toward him. "Hey, Zeb, I thought I'd come and see if there was anything you all needed."

Zeb didn't want to appear rude, though he *was* in a bit of a hurry, so he plastered on his best smile. "That's nice of you, but I think everything's under control back there. I'm headed home to get cleaned up for school."

Fred scratched his head. "Well, okay, you go ahead home. I think I'll mosey on up there and meet that new little youngun."

"It's a girl. They named her Molly."

Zeb resumed his trek, but his thoughts returned to Walter. Hazel must be home by now, or Fred wouldn't be traipsing around out here without Davey. Anybody, including Fred, would surely have better sense than to go off and leave a little kid alone.

Chapter 6

"Anybody home?" Fred's voice made Katie stop on her way across the front room. He opened the screen door and stepped inside. "I come to see the new baby."

"Just a minute." Katie peered into the bedroom, then turned to Fred with a finger across her lips. "Shhh. She's asleep. So is Ella."

Fred advanced. "Can I see her? I'll be quiet."

Aunt Nellie appeared in the bedroom doorway, holding the sleeping child, brown curls already covering the crown of the tiny head.

Fred stepped back, chuckling, and ran a palm across the top of his bald head. "She's a pretty little thing. Wish I had some of that hair."

Aunt Nellie smiled at him, then retreated with the still sleeping Molly. Fred eyed Katie. "Is there anything you need?"

Katie's thoughts returned to last night's episode and Fred's complete lack of helpfulness. *Not anymore.*

"No, I think we've got everything under control. But thanks for the offer."

The man nodded, then raked a forearm across his perspiring face. He glanced beside him, and plopped onto a wooden rocking chair, setting it in motion.

Katie stepped to the window and pulled back the curtain. "Which one of the Bailor brothers was shot last night?"

Fred stopped rocking and cleared his throat. "Couldn't say for sure. Don't know. Hazel ain't home yet."

Katie's brain jolted into high alert. She spun around to face Fred. "Then where's Davey?"

Fred sucked on a tooth. "Asleep, I guess. It was early, and I didn't hear any noise from his room. Hated to wake him up when he was sleepin' so good."

The fists of her consciousness clenched and unclenched. *The very idea. The very INSANE idea!* Her gut tightened as irritation gave way to fear. Fighting the urge to grab his shoulders and shake some sense into him, she only half tried to hide the urgency in her tone. "Go home, Fred. Go see about Davey. He shouldn't be left there alone—ever."

Fred grunted, dragged himself out of the chair and stalked across the room. He pushed the screen door wide and stepped through it, letting it swing shut behind him. Katie barely had time to grab it, preventing a sleep shattering-slam.

She shook her head as Fred tottered off down the lane, periodically glancing back at her with his "you insulted me" stare. She didn't care. Davey's face flashed across her mind, overpowered by the looming image of Bone's sneer.

No, he couldn't. Fred will be home soon. Nobody even knows the child is alone.

After whipping up a quick breakfast for Marcus and the boys, and giving the kitchen a lick and a promise, Katie stuck her head around the bedroom door frame. Ella still slept peacefully while Aunt Nellie sat rocking Molly. "Aunt Nellie, I'll take the boys to school and be right back to relieve you."

Nellie adjusted the little blanket and snuggled the baby to her. "Honey, there's no hurry. No hurry at all. I'm in the height of my glory right here just doin' what I'm doin'."

Katie leaned over, patted the older woman's hand, and mouthed a "thank you."

Aunt Nellie flashed her a warm smile and nodded. "Now, shoo. Get those brothers to school on time."

The boys were already in the front yard tossing a small gourd back and forth in a game of catch. Katie snatched their lunch buckets off the table. "Hey, guys. Let's go. You don't want to be late for school."

Katie set off down the lane with them at a brisk pace, thoughts of "what if" racing through her mind.

The store stood silent and still in the early morning mixture of sunlight and shadow. A shut door, closed curtains—peaceful, yet, what? Ominous? She shrugged at the unease that gnawed at her insides.

Fred had made it home. Hazel was probably back by the time he got there. Davey was fine. And that was that. Or was it? Invisible spiders of doubt crawled along her neck and down her arms, and she shivered in the eighty-degree heat.

As they neared the schoolyard, shouts and laughter reached her ears. The loud crack of wood against leather told her there was a baseball game in full swing. A ball whizzed through the air straight for her. She sprang up and snatched it midflight. Amid shouts of "Home run!" "No, out!" "Fly ball," she tossed it to Kevin who nabbed it from his perch on the pitcher's mound.

Leaning against a tree, she scanned the area in search of Zeb. Glancing behind her, she caught sight of him sprinting down the lane toward the schoolyard. Puffing, he stopped beside Katie and leaned forward with his hands resting on his knees. "Sorry. I'm. Late."

Giving him a fist tap on the arm, she cocked her head. "You're not late. We're early."

He raised his head and winked, one corner of his mouth assuming an upward curl. "All of you?"

Warmth rushed from behind her eyes and invaded her cheeks. She attempted a nonchalant pose. "Sure."

To her surprise, he reached an arm around her shoulders and squeezed tight, just for a split second. But it was enough to send a warm skittering sensation through the whole length of her.

He let go and winked again, a full-fledged smile enhancing his features. "Thanks."

Suddenly his smile disappeared, and his focus shifted toward the woods. Katie aimed a glance in that direction, and her eyes stung with tears of relief. Walter emerged from among the trees.

Hair tousled and clothes disheveled, he approached Zeb. "Mr. Harlow, you won't have to worry about Tank anymore for a long, long time. He shot Flat last night and killed him. Hazel came and tried to save him, but it was too late."

Katie's heart stopped. "What are you saying?"

"The law got Tank and took him to jail. The coroner took Flat's body away. Hazel stayed through it all. She just now went home."

Zeb clasped Walter's shoulder. "I'm sorry, Son."

Katie looked up at the teen's face and realized he was staring at her. "I'm sorry, too, Walter. So very sorry." Their eyes locked, his glistening.

Then taking a deep breath, more like a sigh, he looked away. "It's okay." Spinning around, he took a few faltering steps toward the schoolhouse, then straightened and crossed the playground, head held high.

"Katie, did Fred show up at the Banks' house this morning?" If Zeb noticed the change—the relief in Walter's demeanor—he was keeping it to himself.

Katie spoke past the bitter taste in her mouth. "Yes, but I sent him home. I couldn't believe he'd go off and leave Davey in that house alone. I guess everything's alright, though, because when we came by a few minutes ago, it was quiet and the door was shut."

Zeb rubbed his chin between his thumb and forefinger. "I suppose so. But sometimes poor old Fred uses no judgment whatsoever." Curling one corner of his mouth and shaking his head, he strode across the playground, waving an arm in the direction of the in-progress ball game.

By the time the school bell tolled, the kids were already heading for the door, some rushing, some strolling at a leisurely pace. But Kevin hung behind. He approached her, eyes looking up, then quickly averting downward as he stood before her, a toe nervously scuffing a pattern in the dirt. "Miss Katie, I know you're Miss Ella's niece. She can play the piano. Can you?"

Katie's heart warmed at sight of this barefoot, tousle-headed in-between guy in overalls, not really a kid, yet not quite a man. "A little."

He raised his eyebrows, keeping his head lowered. "Well, could you—I mean, would you—play for us?"

"Kevin, get in here." Zeb's voice resonated across the school yard.

The boy grabbed Katie's hand, dragging her along with him. "Mr. Harlow, could she play our opening song today?"

Zeb directed a questioning look at Katie. She nodded, holding back a grin, and shrugged. He gave her a sly wink. "Sure, bring the lady inside."

Pondering the wink, Katie followed Kevin but, out of the corner of her eye, she noticed Zeb jerk his head in the direction of the woods.

~

Zeb was sure he saw something, or somebody, lurking at the edge of the playground just beyond the tree line. Squinting, he continued to stare.

The familiar strains of "Down By the Riverside" in unison with his students' voices drifted across his consciousness, bringing thoughts of Miss Ella, bluebirds, and happier days front and center.

'It' moved again. A face peered through the brush, and Cryder Zarbone burst into the open. "Zeb. Help. Help." His mannerisms indicated he was sober, for the time being, but Zeb knew him only too well.

He warily approached the man. "What do you want, Bone? School's in session, and you know it."

Bone clutched Zeb's arm and edged close, their faces almost touching, the odor of stale whiskey making Zeb's stomach roll. Bone stared at him with huge, unwavering eyes. "I'm not here to cause trouble. Hazel's in a panic. Davey's gone."

Zeb trusted Bone, and anything he said, about as far as he could throw an iron cook stove. "That's not even funny."

"I'm not *tryin'* to be funny. He's gone, I tell ya. G-A-W-N. Gone. I went by the store just a minute ago, and Hazel and Fred was a-runnin' all over the place, and she was a-cryin', and a-screamin', 'The baby's gone!'"

A trickle of unease in the pit of Zeb's stomach surged to torrential proportions. Did Bone follow through on his threat? "What did you do with him, Bone?"

"I didn't do nothin' with him. Don't you understand? The kid has *disappeared*."

Zeb's imagination threatened to override his common sense. This couldn't be happening.

"Zeb!"

He turned to see his mother racing up the lane

toward them. He ran to meet her. What had Boomer done now? "What's wrong, Mom?"

The woman's skin was flushed, and perspiration streamed down her face. Her breath came in short gasps. "Something awful. Has happened. Davey's disappeared. Hazel got home. Fred was asleep. Davey's bed was empty. It's an. Emergency."

Bone stood with his arms crossed, a smug expression on his face. "See. I told ya."

Zeb ignored him. "Here, Mom. You sit down and catch your breath. I'm on my way."

He spun around and stopped short. *The students.*

He sprinted to the schoolhouse door and opened it a crack. Luke glanced around, and Zeb summoned him. "Luke, go get Katie."

The child nodded and slipped across the room. The piano music stopped, and Katie met him at the door. All eyes were on the two.

"Step outside for a minute." He shut the door. "Davey's wandered off, and I have to leave for a little bit. Would you stay with the kids till I get back? Walter can help you if they misbehave."

Katie squeezed his hand between both of hers, her eyes surveying the yard where Bone stood watching them. "We'll be fine. You just be careful."

He nodded. This girl was something special. No doubt about it. He cuffed her chin with his free hand. "Will do."

Zeb loped across the yard and up the lane. Maybe he'd find Davey already back at the store, safe and sound. Probably only wishful thinking, but he could hope.

And pray.

"Zeb, wait." Mike fell into step beside him, never breaking stride. But the schoolmaster pushed on, a sense of urgency propelling him toward the store.

Chapter 7

The scene at Hollisters' store was nothing short of chaos. Hazel scurried around the property, screaming Davey's name and tearing through bushes and ditches. Fred leaned against a front porch rail, trembling and wringing his hands. "It's all my fault. All my fault." Fearing the man would collapse, Zeb took him by the arm and guided him to a chair.

A small group of men had gathered on the parking lot, too far away for their words to reach Zeb's ears, but close enough for him to see them nodding to each other and pointing in various directions. Zeb wanted to join them and help plan their search strategies, but when he glanced down at Fred, he knelt by the older man's chair. "What happened, Fred?"

Fred's shaky voice made him hard to understand. "I shouldn't'a gone off and left him. Katie was right. But it's worse than that. When I come home, the house was quiet, so I figgered Davey was still asleep. I just went and laid down on my bed and went to sleep, too. I didn't even go look in his room. I don't know *when* he left. I just plain don't know. Davey's old grandpa is even worse than his dad." He rested his elbows on his knees and let his head droop.

Zeb thought he should try to comfort Fred, but at this particular moment, he agreed with everything the man had said. He half-heartedly patted Fred on the back. "We'll find him." And Zeb strode across the parking lot to join the other men.

"Did anybody see anything suspicious?"

"Nope. Not me. I was home eatin' breakfast when I heard about it." Rance Tillman patted his stomach and nodded toward his brother.

Zeb's nerves grew increasingly on edge. "Men, we need to develop a plan and get this show on the road. That little boy may be in danger, or worse."

Rance shaded his eyes against the sun climbing higher in the sky. "We don't know how long he's been gone. So he could have gotten farther away than you might think. I say the creek needs to be our first priority."

A momentary hush enveloped the little group. Zeb pushed aside the morbid picture taking shape in his mind. "Then let's get on it."

As the men fanned out in the direction of the meandering stream, Boomer sauntered toward the lane, scratching his chest inside his overall bib. "What's wrong?"

Zeb didn't want to waste any time in a conversation with his hateful stepdad. He continued toward the creek, yelling back over his shoulder,

"Davey's disappeared."

Not waiting for the man's reaction, he scanned every bush and cubby on the way, calling the child's name.

Mike trotted up beside him. "Let me help."

"Okay, you run back to the school and tell Katie to dismiss the kids for the day and send them straight home. To not hang around in the woods. It could be dangerous."

~

Katie's thoughts went into a tailspin when Mike burst into the schoolroom, red-faced and breathless. "Send 'em home. Send everybody home. Don't play in the woods. It's too dangerous. Go home *now*."

Katie, her heart pounding in her ears, steadied herself against his next words.

The child waved his arms frantically. "Davey's gone. You're all in danger." He looked wild-eyed at Katie. "Zeb said to dismiss school. Send 'em home. It's not safe."

Mustering up her best façade of tranquility, she faced the students. "Okay, Mr. Harlow wants everybody to get your things and go straight home now."

The classroom buzzed with excitement. Students grabbed books and lunch pails while they bombarded her with questions.

"What happened to Davey?"

"Is there school tomorrow?"

"Will it still be too dangerous?"

"Why are we in danger?"

Katie gave up trying to hide her impatience, so she ushered the group out the door and said, "I don't know. Just go on home for now."

With many backward glances, the students made their ways toward home.

A hand touched Katie's shoulder. "We'll help find him."

She spun to face the speaker. "Walter?"

The teen's eyes showed compassion. "Me and a few others."

A lump formed in Katie's throat at the group surrounding her. Walter, Kevin, and every big guy in the school. And the twins.

Duke's lips quivered. "He's our friend. We're helping, too."

Luke nodded, as did the entire menagerie.

Mike leaned close to Katie. "They're all gathered at the store."

Katie's heart broke for what might lie ahead. Pasting on the most determined look she could manage, she closed the door and smacked her fist into her other palm. "Okay, guys. Let's do this."

Walter forged ahead. "This way, men." The boys fell in behind him, as he led their small army up the lane toward the store to receive their instructions.

Mike hung behind. "Katie, do you have a minute?"

She slowed and allowed the child to walk beside her. "What is it?"

"This." Digging into his pocket, the child extracted a small blue object and held it out to her.

She turned it over in her hand, brushing the dust

off the soft fur and finding it pleasing to touch. "It's a little toy dog."

Mike's voice was thick with emotion. "It's Davey's toy dog. Its name is Roscoe. He cherished that toy. He would have never been careless with it."

Katie stopped. "Where did you get this?"

"I found it in the bushes just across from the store. In our yard." His voice broke and he turned away.

Katie put a hand on his arm. "Davey's only two. Sometimes two-year-olds misplace things, even if they *do* really like them."

Mike twirled to face her, his eyes brimming with unshed tears. "No, Katie. Not Davey. Not with Roscoe. Bone's been hanging around a lot lately. I think Bone kidnapped Davey. I'm afraid for him."

Katie's breath caught. Bone's threat rang in her ears as she relived the experience, "But when *you* sleep—beware." His evil sneer returned to the front of her mind and embedded itself there. They had to find Davey *now*.

"Come on, Mike." She grabbed the kid's hand and sped down the lane, dragging him with her.

A wagon was parked by the gas pump. Several men bearing rifles sat clustered in the back while Marcus stood before them gesturing and pointing. Walter and the boys were gathered beside Marcus, their eyes focused on him.

When Katie and Mike reached the parking lot, Walter broke from the group and met them. "Marcus is organizing a search party. Mr. Harlow already has one going in this area, but those guys in the wagon are gonna spread out all over the valley. They've brought guns, just in case."

"How can we help?' Katie indicated Mike at her side.

Walter glanced back at the assembly. "Don't know, but I'll tell Marcus you're here." With that, he turned to rejoin them.

Mike tapped Katie's arm. "Look at my stepdad over there. He doesn't even look like he cares. How can he not care?"

Boomer leaned against the fence and watched the activity, a blank expression on his face.

"Okay, move 'em out." Marcus's command prompted the man on the wagon seat to prod the mules and set the wagon in motion. Walter and his gang had climbed in and joined the mobile search party.

Marcus approached Katie and Mike. "Mike, why don't you search the outbuildings on your property and the woods around it? Then report back here."

"Sure thing." Mike trotted off toward home.

"Katie, if you don't mind, we could use you at the store. Fred's a basket case, Hazel's fit to be tied, and I believe my boys are in there. I intend to search along the highway west of here."

She could read her uncle well. "You think there's foul play, don't you?"

His face told the story. "I don't know, Katie. But I think it's possible. I'm hoping not."

Marcus had a job to do. She surveyed the expanse of highway. "I'll be in the store."

The screen door creaked in protest as Katie pulled it open and stepped inside. She shut her eyes momentarily to let them adjust to the store's dim interior.

The twins emerged from Davey's bedroom, Duke in the lead. "It smells like cinnamon in there. But Davey's not in there. Neither is Roscoe. But we smelled cinnamon."

Luke knit his brows, his expression somber. "Cinnamon."

Katie slid her hand in her pocket and felt the softness of Roscoe. Should she mention it to the boys? No, probably not.

Fred paced the floor. "My fault. My fault. Stupid old grandpa. All my fault."

"Shut up, Fred. Of course, it's your fault." Hazel sat on the pile of feed sacks just inside the door, twisting and untwisting a hankie. "Katie, what will we do? Marcus told us to stay here in case Davey comes home. If he finds nobody here, he might wander off again."

"Good idea." Katie lowered herself to a feed sack beside Hazel and draped an arm around the woman's shoulders, knowing full well the men just wanted Fred out of the way, and becoming more certain that Davey didn't just wander off.

By mid-afternoon, everyone in Bluebird Valley who was capable of trekking through woods and across fields had joined the search. Knowing Aunt Nellie was at the house with Ella and Molly, Katie felt free to remain at the store with Hazel.

The door creaked and Rance's big form appeared. He motioned outside, and stepping off the porch, guided her out of hearing distance of the store's occupants. He spoke in a guarded tone. "We've searched every well, field, forest, outbuilding, and every inch of that creek. He's gone, Katie. Vanished into thin air. I don't think he's even still *in* Bluebird Valley."

Katie's stomach churned. She fingered the bluebird pin, now secured to the inside of her pocket. *If bluebirds bring happiness, then this little guy has a lot of work to do.* "Uncle Rance, let's pray for him."

"Sure." Her uncle put an arm around her shoulders, and squeezing tight, drew her to him. They bowed their heads. "Dear Lord, we know that not even a sparrow falls to the ground without You knowing and caring. Well, Davey's worth a lot more than a whole flock of sparrows, and we need Your help in finding him. We sure would appreciate it if You'd keep him safe and lead us to him. Thank you, Lord. Amen."

"Amen." Zeb's familiar baritone voice made Katie jerk her head toward the sound. He stood behind her, his face drawn.

"Any news?" She knew the answer before the question left her lips.

Zeb closed his eyes and shook his head. "I think we'd better get the law in on this."

Katie's hopes plummeted as the man did an about-face, crossed the parking lot in long strides, and disappeared into the store.

Katie followed, her fear for Davey's safety rapidly

escalating to terror.

Chapter 8

Zeb had no sooner stepped through the screen door than Hazel was at his side. "Have they found him?"

He paused, wracking his brain to find the right words to soften the impact of his response. "Not yet, Hazel. I think I'll make a little run into the county seat and see about getting us some help with our search."

Fred raised his head. "I'll drive you."

Zeb shuddered inwardly at the thought of a man in Fred's present state of mind driving anyone anywhere. He glanced at Hazel for what? Support? He was surprised to see that Katie had silently made her way to Hazel's side.

She gave the woman's arm a reassuring pat. "The boys and I can stay with you while they're gone."

Zeb searched for a rebuttal, but none came.

Hazel placed her hand over Katie's. "Honey, that's awful sweet of you," she smiled at the young woman, "but it won't be necessary." Her smile morphing to a frown, she marched over to her husband and placed her hands on her hips. "Fred, you blitherin' idiot, just stay out of it. You've done enough. Heaven help us, you've done enough."

Fred stared at the floor, but no words came.

Hazel never seemed to suffer with that problem. Taking off toward the back of the store, she glanced over her shoulder at Zeb. "Just a minute, Sweetie, I'll be right back."

Katie raised her eyebrows, a slight grin on her face, and mouthed the word *sweetie*, her eyes making it more like a question.

Zeb's face grew warm. Shrugging, he averted his eyes.

Presently, Hazel reentered the room. "Hold out your hand, Sweetie."

Zeb, aware of Katie's ever-present stare, obliged.

Hazel dropped a key and some coins into his open palm. "Take Fred's car. He ain't goin' nowhere." She cast a glare in Fred's direction. "Katie can ride with you. The boys'll be fine. Marcus should be back in here before long."

Fred whimpered. "My car?"

"Shut up, Fred." Hazel gave Zeb a light push. "Go on, you two. Skedaddle. Time's a-wastin'."

On the porch, Zeb heard the screen door slap shut behind them. "Katie?"

She was already trotting across the parking lot. "Come on." She hopped into the passenger side of Fred's old Model A and settled in for the ride.

Beside her, Zeb started the motor and eased the car onto the road. "Not bad for a '29 model. Ford does alright."

"Zeb?" Her voice warmed his heart, even as the gravity of the situation demanded his mind remain on constant alert.

He kept his eyes on the road. "Yeah?"

"Do you think Bone did something to Davey?"

"I don't know. I hope not. But if he did, we're gonna need help from the law."

She was silent for a few moments. "Why does Davey stay with Hazel and Fred? What happened to his parents?"

Zeb glanced to his right for a split second. Katie's eyes were fixed on him, her face holding a mixture of compassion and curiosity. He weighed his response. "His mother has an affliction. She was fine when Davey was born, but then something snapped. The lady lost her mind and landed in the mental institution at Farmington."

"What about his dad?"

Zeb slowed the car and weaved across the road, dodging a group of cattle that had chosen to congregate there. "Davey's dad is Hazel and Fred's son. His name is Charlie Eugene. They love him dearly, but he never had a lick of common sense."

She gave a light chuckle. "Kinda like Fred?"

"Worse. He married Myrtle, and a year later Davey was born. After his wife was institutionalized, Charlie Eugene went out of control. He'd leave Davey with Lillian—you know, Davey's mom's sister—and disappear for days at a time."

"No wonder he loves his Aunt Widdy. She's the

only mother figure he's known."

Zeb stroked his chin and swallowed the lump in his throat, using the moment to steady his voice. "Yeah, and Lillian loves him, too. That's why she was so upset the day his dad came and picked up Davey and his things and left. Wouldn't say where they were going, so Lillian contacted Hazel and Fred."

A hawk swooped in front of the car, a little too close for comfort, and Katie drew in a sharp, noisy breath. Crossing her legs, she wrapped her hands around her knee and clasped her fingers. "So what happened?"

"Well, a few days later, Charlie Eugene showed up at the store with Davey and told Hazel and Fred, 'He's yours, but keep a watch out. He's in danger.' And they've had him ever since."

She studied Zeb's profile as he concentrated on the road. "Why was he in danger?"

"Charlie Eugene admitted he'd made a poker wager with a guy, and if he lost, his opponent could have anything of his he wanted. Well, ole Charlie was drunk and over confident, and he ended up losing the wager."

Katie sank back against the seat. "And the guy chose Davey?"

Zeb tapped the steering wheel. "Yep. So Charlie Eugene told Hazel and Fred not to let anyone know where Davey was and not to ask where he was going. He said soon as the guy found out Davey was gone, his own life would be in danger, and the guy would try to steal Davey if he could find him."

"So Davey's dad disappeared and left his little boy behind." Katie's voice broke.

"Right again."

Katie leaned forward. "But that's not even legal. You can't just lose your child on a bet."

Zeb slowed at the intersection. "No, but neither are any of those wagers."

"Who is this guy that won Davey? Does he have a name?"

Zeb signaled and turned the car south. "Piper. His name's Lyle Piper."

They rode in silence for several minutes. Suddenly, Katie clutched Zeb's arm, then as quickly withdrew her hand. "Where is he now?"

Zeb slowed the car and extended his hand, signaling a right turn. "Have no idea. But we need to find out. Fast."

Katie stiffened, bracing her hands against the dash. "We have to hurry."

The sweat on Zeb's palms made the steering wheel slip in his grasp as he pressed toward the center of town. He brought the car to a halt in front of the courthouse, a prominent four-story rock structure located in the middle of the center of the county seat.

Katie flung open her door and slid to the ground. Side by side they loped up the walk, ascended the concrete steps, and entered the building. More steps led them to the sheriff's office on the third floor. Zeb grabbed the doorknob and gave it a hearty twist. Nothing.

"It's locked. Look at the sign."

Hand still gripping the knob, his eyes took in the information painted on the door's glass.

SHERIFF
Office Hours
8-5 M-F, 8-12 Saturday, Closed Sunday

He pulled out his pocket watch. 5:20. *Rats.*

Katie leaned against the wall. "So, now what?"

"Whatcha need?" The shrill voice startled Zeb. Spinning around, he came chest to face with a tiny, elderly man in striped overalls. "I'm the jailer." He indicated a shadowy stairwell at the end of the hall. "Whatcha all need?"

"Could you tell us how we might get in touch with the sheriff?"

The little man hooked his thumbs in his pockets and nodded vigorously. "Sure, Son. You and the wife just mosey on over to his house. He'll be there."

Wife. Zeb shot a quick glance at Katie. She was leaning against the wall, same spot, grinning like a Cheshire cat.

Zeb knew Sheriff Barton, but had never had occasion to visit his house, nor was he aware of its location. He turned his attention back to the jailer. "Where does he live?"

"Go out the front door, other side of the street, three houses to your left."

Zeb extended his hand. "Thanks, buddy."

The man came to attention and saluted, an ear-to-ear grin adorning his wrinkled face. "Anytime." Then, pivoting in an about-face, he marched back toward the stairwell.

Zeb and Katie exchanged smiles.

Outside, they dashed to the car and Zeb parked it in front of the house the little man had indicated.

The wood door stood open, and a little boy peered through the screen. "Hey, Dad, we've got company."

A familiar dark-haired man in tan slacks and shirt pushed open the screen door and stepped out onto the porch. Shading his eyes, he stared toward the car. Moments later he brightened in recognition. "Zeb Harlow, is that you?"

The sight of his old friend calmed Zeb much like a light in a dark forest and planted a hint of hope among his frenzied thoughts.

At the same moment he and Katie flung their car doors open and hopped to the ground, meeting on the sidewalk. They rushed toward the house side-by-side.

"Sheriff, this is Katie Gallagher. We've got an emergency. It's urgent." Zeb faced Barton directly, struggling to keep his voice on an even keel.

The sheriff's expression grew serious. "Come in and tell me about it."

Seated in the living room, the two brought Sheriff Barton up-to-date on the events of the past few hours. The man listened intently, asking questions and writing notes in a small tablet. "You're right. This is more than urgent. There's an ongoing search for your Lyle Piper. He's considered armed and dangerous, and he's been evading the law for several weeks. He could be our man. We'll need to explore all possibilities, and we'll need your cooperation."

Katie reached over and squeezed Zeb's arm. "Whatever you want us to do."

Zeb nodded his agreement. *Bless her heart.*

The sheriff stood. "Let me call my deputy." He went to the phone and turned the crank. "Edna, this is the sheriff. Connect me with Deputy Fox pronto."

It seemed to Zeb as though his friend had barely hung up the phone when heavy footsteps sounded on the porch. Without knocking, a tall clean-cut man entered the room. Wearing cowboy boots and a tan outfit that matched Barton's, the pleasant, sandy-haired guy looked to be in his late forties, definitely no more than fifty.

The sheriff waved a hand in the man's direction. "Zeb, Katie, this is my deputy, Jesse Fox. He'll be going back to Bluebird Valley with you."

Katie stood. "Such a pleasure to meet you, Deputy Fox. Thank you so much for being willing to help us find Davey." She looked him up and down, eyes sparkling. "We'll do anything we can to help. Just say the word."

Jesse Fox took hold of her hand and patted it. "Just doing my job, ma'am. But if everyone were as cooperative and pleasant as you, we lawmen might soon be unnecessary."

Zeb watched the exchange, a sense of unease clouding his mind. Katie was friendly with this old guy. A little too friendly, in his opinion. But why should he care? He didn't like the sensation he was experiencing.

Jealousy? Nah. No way. It didn't concern him what she did. Or with whom.

Did it?

Katie's gaze followed as the sheriff and deputy stepped out onto the porch. Zeb avoided eye contact with her.

After a brief consultation, Deputy Fox stuck his head back into the room and beckoned the pair outside. "You two ride with me. You can leave your car here for the night."

Zeb's eyes drank in the sight of the deputy's 1937 Chevy, its shiny black paint with the word *Sheriff* prominently displayed on the front door in contrasting white letters. Better seats, better headlights, smoother ride. *Better man?*

Fox opened the front passenger door for Katie, who eased in, smiling. "Why, thank you."

Zeb grudgingly climbed into the back seat and shut the door. Deputy Fox settled into the driver's seat and started the engine.

Katie leaned back. "Nice car."

Fox shrugged. "It'll do. It's what the county provided." Swinging into a spot in front of the courthouse, he brought the car to a halt. "I need to make a quick run in here to double check some information and grab some equipment. Be right back."

As the deputy pushed the door shut, Zeb leaned toward him. "Robbing the cradle, aren't you?"

Fox gave him a questioning look, then turned and sprinted up the walk.

Chapter 9

Katie watched the tall, good looking dude take the steps two at a time and disappear into the courthouse.

"You can put your eyes back in their sockets, Little Girl."

Katie wasn't sure she'd heard correctly. She twisted in the seat and met Zeb's stony stare. "What?"

His eyes bore a hole through her. "Why did you play up to that guy?"

What's it to you? "I didn't *play up* to anybody."

Zeb thumped the back of the seat with his knuckles. "I saw how you sidled up to him and showered him with your sweet talk. Gimme a break, Katie. He's old enough to be your dad."

An unexpected tingle embraced Katie as a realization struck her.

He's jealous!

She brushed a stray hair away from her face. "Exactly. He'd be just the right man for my mother."

Zeb's mouth fell open, but no words came. His

Adam's apple bobbed up and down. "Your mother?"

Twisting around, she rested her chin on the back of the seat and faced him head-on. This was hard. This was always hard. "Yes. She's not been the same since Daddy died. And I want to help her find another man. One who'll be good to her like Daddy was. Besides, it's my duty."

Curiosity replaced Zeb's defensive attitude. And concern? "Why is it your duty? What happened to your dad?"

The kindness in his eyes tore into her soul, making the conversation twice as difficult to endure. She remained silent for several moments, swallowing the tightness in her throat, suppressing the stubborn tears that threatened to surface as her mind replayed those last terrible moments at Camdenton. She shut her eyes as the memory came flooding back.

"Ladies and Gentlemen, out of chute number three. Here comes Root Gallagher on Rocket, the orneriest horse this side of Texas."

The cowboys swung open the gate and the horse exploded from its confinement, Katie's dad on its back, waving a hand in the air. Each of the bronc's attempts to throw Root Gallagher was met by his own attempt to complete the ride.

With her heart in her throat, Katie relaxed as the whistle blew and Gallagher slid safely to the ground. The crowd roared approval.

Katie slipped from her spot on the sidelines, and started across the arena to congratulate her dad.

Suddenly the loudspeaker blared. "Get back,

everybody. Get back. Loose Brahma. Give 'im room. Get back."

Katie glanced up in time to see the Brahma heading straight for her. She froze. A shove from behind sent her sprawling on the ground out of harm's way.

She remembered the hushed crowd, the look of horror on her uncle's face, and her own paralyzing fear as the tragic nightmare became a reality. Her dad lay lifeless on the ground, trampled to death by the Brahma from which he'd saved his daughter.

"Katie?" Zeb's voice jarred her back to the present.

Blinking, she gave her head a shake and steadied her voice. "My dad was killed in a rodeo accident." She wanted to tell him more, but feared losing her already-wavering composure.

He placed a hand on hers, and his voice softened. "Katie, you can't blame yourself for a rodeo accident."

Reveling in the comfort of his touch, she drew in a deep breath. "We were only there because he wanted to give me a chance to participate in the barrel racing event. He wouldn't have been near that Brahma if it hadn't been for me. He wouldn't have even been anywhere near Camdenton."

Zeb squeezed her hand. "Katie, things happen. Sometimes tragic things. Don't blame yourself."

She glanced toward the courthouse, wishing Deputy Fox would return. This conversation was about to get the best of her. "Well, I just feel responsible for the whole thing. And I want to make it up to Mama."

Zeb withdrew his hand and leaned back. "Are you sure your mother wants to get married again?"

"That's just the problem. She says she doesn't."

"Then don't you think you should let it be?"

Katie sighed. *Hurry up, Jesse Fox.*

"Mama, Daddy, my sister Ruth, and I all lived with Daddy's brother in St. Louis. When Daddy died, that left us three women living with a single man—no blood kin to Mama. We couldn't continue to stay there under those circumstances."

Zeb pulled a bandana from his pocket and wiped the perspiration from his face. "What did you do?"

"The only thing we could do. We moved out and rented an apartment. That's where Mama and Ruth live now. But there are bills to pay. Mama has a job at a candy factory, and Ruth is out of high school and works babysitting. But it's too much. Mama needs a man around to support her and take care of her."

Zeb pressed a knuckle to his temple and shook his head. "Having a man around doesn't always make things better. I think you'd better back off and let your mother take care of her own affairs."

Out of the corner of her eye, Katie detected movement. Deputy Fox, carrying several flashlights and leading a beagle, approached the car.

Thank goodness.

Fox opened the back door and deposited the flashlights on the floorboard. "We may need these. Hop in, Rebel."

"Hey there, little guy. Whatcha doin', buddy?" The warmth in Zeb's voice made Katie wish he was talking to her instead of the little dog.

Deputy Fox settled into the driver's seat and directed a comment over his shoulder. "Rebel's our local bloodhound."

Zeb coughed. "He's a beagle."

Fox chuckled. "Wait'll you see him in action. He can out track the best bloodhound that ever sniffed."

As the deputy pulled the car onto the highway, Katie's eyes focused on an apparatus mounted on the left front fender. "What's that thing on your fender?"

"That's the siren. If I flip this switch," he touched the switch lightly, "the red light comes on and the siren sounds. It only works when the key's in the ignition. Pretty handy. Leaves no doubt I'm trying to get someone's attention."

Katie slid her hand into her pocket to make sure the bluebird pin was still there. She breathed a silent *thank you* when her fingers brushed its smooth surface. But as she started to withdraw her hand, she touched something else. Roscoe.

She slid the toy out of her pocket and held it up. "This is Davey's toy dog. It was found today by the lane near his house."

"Let me see that. We'll need it for evidence." The deputy reached for the toy. He flipped it over in his hand, then placed it on the seat between them. "We'll let Rebel have a go at this when we get there."

A loud whine from the back seat let Katie know the dog had recognized his name.

"Just hold on, Rebel. You'll get your chance." The compassion in Zeb's voice warmed her heart. His kindness extended even to God's little creatures. He'd make a great veterinarian. He'd make a great husband. *Whoa, Katie. Where'd you get that thought?*

Warmth crept up her neck and onto her ears. She turned to stare out the window. The iridescent glow of fireflies flickered across the fields, and Katie was thankful for the ensuing darkness. Her mind raced through a blur of Davey, Zeb, Jesse Fox and Mama.

"Look out!" The car jolted to a stop. Deputy Fox swung open the door and jumped out. Katie strained to see in the dim beam of the headlights. Fox bent over something in the road ahead. "Zeb, I need some help here."

Katie leaned forward, squinting until her eyes focused. A wave of nausea swept over her. A man's motionless form lay sprawled on the highway.

~

Adrenalin skyrocketing, Zeb exited the car in one flying leap and hit the ground at a run. The sight of Deputy Fox kneeling over the inert form made the hairs on his neck stand out like a porcupine's quills. "Did we hit him?"

"No, I saw him and got the car stopped in time." The deputy pressed his fingers to the man's wrist. "He's alive."

Zeb knelt and got a glimpse of the man's face— and a whiff of him. In protest of the foul odor that he could literally taste, he held his breath and leaned away. "He's drunk."

The deputy nodded. "Out stone cold. You know 'im?"

Zeb stood, hoping for fresher air six feet above the man's face. "Oh, yeah, I know the guy. It's Cryder Zarbone. Lives in our area and stays tipsy two-thirds of the time."

Fox shrugged. "I know the kind. Well, let's get *Mr. Debonair* in the car."

"Can we help?" Katie stood behind Zeb, Rebel in tow.

"Go back to the car and put Rebel in the front seat with you. We'll put this fellow in the back with Zeb." Fox grabbed Bone's shoulders, none too gently. "Zeb, you get his feet."

In the car Zeb stared over at the man lolled against the back of the seat, mouth hanging open, dead to the world. He yanked out his bandana and held it over his nose.

Oh, fine. Lovely seat mate. Just great. This ride'll take forever.

Deputy Fox eased the car back into motion. With every bump, Bone emitted something between a snore and a snort. Zeb couldn't tell which, nor did he care. The old codger. Here they were wasting time on him while Davey was out there—who knew where. Alone. In the dark.

The car jolted and Bone flopped against Zeb. He shoved the guy away, trying to ignore the loud snort that his shove enhanced.

"What?"

Zeb didn't answer.

Katie persisted. "Zeb, what did you say?"

Oh, good grief. "That was Bone. He made a noise."

Zeb's tension eased when Fox wheeled the car in at Hollisters' store. It had to be going on ten o'clock. The gibbous moon had risen high enough that he could make out the images of several men on and around the front porch. Kerosene lanterns glowed from the store's windows.

Zeb glanced to his left. "What should we do with Bone?"

"Nothing. Let him sleep it off in here. This car's not going anywhere for now, and we've got more important things to worry about." The deputy opened the door and, grabbing the key and Rebel's leash, headed across the parking lot.

Katie yanked open her door and took off after him. Zeb followed a few paces behind.

Katie paused near the group of men. "Any new developments, Uncle Rance?"

"None yet. There're still several men out with lanterns. We're waitin' to hear from 'em."

Deputy Fox flung open the screen and led Rebel inside. Zeb eased in behind him and stood near the counter.

Fox approached Hazel. "Hello, Ma'am. I'm Deputy Jesse Fox and this is my dog, Rebel. We're here to help you get your boy home safe and sound."

Something slammed against the door. It flew open and Bone lunged in, bumping against the door frame and catching a toe on the threshold. Losing what balance he had, he flailed his arms and pitched forward. "Woo-oo-oo."

A small blue object flew out of his hand just as he

did a belly buster on the hard wood floor. It bounced off Rebel, who yelped and jumped sideways. Then it landed on the floor at Hazel's feet.

"What's this?" She bent and picked up the item. "Why, it's Davey's little toy dog. Wait a minute. How did Bone end up with it?"

Fred clenched his fists. "I'll kill 'im." He tottered over to Bone, who continued to lie prostrate in front of the counter.

Fred used the toe of his shoe to flip the man onto his back. "You took Davey. Where is he?"

Bone uttered a low groan and attempted to sit upright, but fell backward. "I ain't got Davey." He covered his eyes with his hands and groaned again. "What I got is a powerful headache."

"Good." Fred folded his arms in front of him and stalked across the room toward the feed sacks.

Zeb bent and put his arms under Bone's shoulders, dragging him to a sitting position and leaning him against the counter. This was ridiculous. What was the matter with these people? It was time to cut out all the conversation and keep the search going.

Disgusted and frustrated, he stepped out onto the porch. Katie broke from the group and made her way to him. She lightly touched his arm.

A breeze ruffled his hair and cooled his face. "What did you find out?"

She sat on the step. "Nothing much. They plan to go in shifts and search all night. Walter's out there with them. Are you gonna call off school tomorrow?"

He rubbed his palms along his jawline. Fatigue

threatened to seriously impair his ability to function. "I guess I'd better."

"I'll tell those men. They'll get the word out in plenty of time." She got up and bopped back to the group.

Doesn't that girl ever run out of energy?

"Thanks," he said to no one. Stifling a yawn, he leaned against a porch post. Two nights in a row with virtually no sleep. That couldn't be a good thing. He stepped back inside.

Bone still sat on the floor, propped against the front of the counter. Deputy Fox was talking to Hazel. "...too dark to see anything tonight. Soon as it's daylight, we'll combine forces and get those search parties organized. We'll use Rebel to..."

A commotion outside made Zeb spin around and Deputy Fox halt mid-sentence. The door swung open and Katie dashed in, almost slamming into Zeb. "They've found something!"

Chapter 10

Flattening herself against the counter, in front of which Zeb stood, Katie stared at the three men who came bustling through the door. Boomer, his clothes and hair in disarray, and another guy—Walter?—dragged a struggling man between them. Tall and lanky, shirtless, with a mop of filthy dark hair that matched his equally grimy overalls, the middle guy emitted a string of expletives that made heat creep up Katie's neck until it engulfed her entire head.

Catching a glimpse of the man's face in the lamplight, her breath caught. There was something familiar about those eyes, that attitude. *Oh, Lord. He looks like Walter's brother, Tank. Not another one. Oh, Walter.*

Katie's mind spun, and her body swayed against Zeb. She didn't pull away when his arm came around her shoulders.

Hazel took a step backward and placed a hand over her heart. "Tip Bailor?"

Boomer gave the man's arm a violent jerk. "One and the same." His voice was a growl. "Caught 'im tryin' to sneak in one of your side windows just now. I wrestled him to the ground and hollered at Walter here to help me bring 'im in. He took Davey and now he's tryin' to destroy some evidence he left behind."

Walter glanced toward Katie and Zeb, then lowered his head but maintained his grip on Tip's arm. Katie's heart ached for the young man, trying so hard to make something of himself, and faced with opposition at every turn.

She stepped past Walter and stood in front of Boomer. Her heart pounded, but she stood firm. "You can't know that, Mr. Slocum. The Bible says we're not to judge another person."

Boomer's eyes shot daggers at Katie. "Oh, so now you're the expert, Girlie?"

Zeb was standing beside her. His light touch on her arm made her swivel toward him, and their eyes met. She got the message and stepped away, the rest of her thoughts remaining unvoiced.

Zeb ushered her back to their spot near the counter. Placing his mouth next to her ear, his whispered words told her what she already knew. "It's not a good idea to mess with Boomer. He's dangerous."

She nodded, feeling secure in the warmth of his nearness.

Deputy Fox approached, Rebel at his heels. "Just who is this guy?"

Walter's drooping shoulders and still lowered

head made Katie wish for a way to comfort him, somehow make his life more bearable. The young man drew in a long breath, then raised his head to meet the deputy's eyes. "I'm afraid he's my big brother, Sir."

Fred harrumphed from his perch on the feed sacks. "Brother, schmother. You can't trust none a'them Bailor boys."

"You can trust this one." Zeb stepped beside Walter and placed a hand on his shoulder.

Deputy Fox nodded at Zeb, then turned his attention to the younger Bailor. "Okay, Son, suppose we escort your brother on home tonight, and we'll get back with him for questioning later."

Boomer released his hold on Tip's arm and stalked away, muttering. "We had that kidnapper dead to rights, had 'im caught, and they just turned 'im loose. I'm goin' home." Stomping across the floor, he caught his foot on Bone's pant leg. Bone drew up both legs and flattened his back against the front of the counter. Boomer glared down at him. "Move!"

Bone struggled to his feet and grabbed Boomer by the hair. "Make me." With his other fist he swung at the hateful man and missed.

Boomer pushed him away and stormed out the door, letting it slam behind him.

Bone scratched his head and leaned against the door frame, examining his fist. "Well, I'll be." Then he stumbled out into the night.

Katie's uncle Rance poked his head into the room. "Come on, Walter. Let's get your brother home." He patted the young man on the shoulder, then took his place on the other side of Tip, and they escorted him toward the door together.

Tip, becoming calm in Boomer's absence, leaned toward his brother. "It's not what you, think, Walter. It's not what you think at all."

Walter nudged him through the door. "Save it. Let's just go."

As the door closed behind them, Katie's heart broke for Walter. Just a teenager—a kid really. One brother dead, another in jail for the murder, and now this. How much more could a kid stand?

Deputy Fox pulled out a pocket watch. "It's after midnight. We can't see much now. What say everyone get a good night's sleep, and we'll get things organized and continue this search in the morning?"

Katie's skin crawled, and something akin to rage built in her brain, threatening to escape. Just leave Davey out there tonight and do nothing? But she'd just heard the local guys say they planned to search all night. Was the deputy planning to throw a monkey wrench in their plans? She wanted to reprimand the man and remind him of the seriousness of the situation. What was wrong with this guy? Didn't he call himself a lawman?

Fred yawned and stretched. "Yeah, I guess we do need to rest. That way we'll be all ready to get out there in the morning and find our boy." He got up and headed for the back of the store.

Hazel hesitated. "Isn't there anything we can do tonight?"

"No, Ma'am. Just go on to bed. By the time you

wake in the morning, we'll have the search in full swing." The deputy reached down and patted his dog. "Won't we, Rebel?"

Katie was shocked when Hazel offered Deputy Fox Davey's room for the night.

The man thanked her, but declined. Pausing near Katie and Zeb, he turned back toward Hazel. "Get some sleep, now. See you in the morning." Then he stepped out onto the porch.

Zeb put a hand behind Katie's back. "Let me walk you home. It's late and I'd like to see that you make it safely."

Still dumbfounded at the deputy's behavior, she nodded consent.

As they passed the small group of men still gathered in the parking lot, Deputy Fox's voice drifted to her ears. "Okay, boys, there's not a moment to lose. Listen up."

Zeb guided her across the highway and onto the lane leading to the Banks' home. They walked a few moments in silence. Then Katie could contain her curiosity no longer. "I can't understand that deputy's behavior. What do you think he has in mind?"

Zeb took her hand. "He's gonna search all night. He just told Fred and Hazel to go to bed to get them out of the way. You can bet he won't let this thing rest until it's solved."

The warmth of his hand brought a peacefulness she couldn't understand. She embraced it. "Do you think Davey's still around here?"

He squeezed her hand and slowed their pace. "I

don't know. In a way, I'm beginning to doubt it. But we have to search everywhere, follow every lead."

"You suspect foul play, don't you?" She was loath to utter the words, the same words she'd asked Marcus hours before, still fearing the response she knew was inevitable.

The moon illuminated the Banks' house, now in plain sight. Zeb stopped in the middle of the shadowy lane and faced her, taking both of her hands in his own. "I wouldn't put anything past Bone, Piper is a definite threat, the Bailors don't have any sense and might try no tellin' what, and there's always the possibility Charlie Eugene decided to drop by and secretly reclaim his son."

The warm August air turned to a December blast. She raised her face toward the heavens. Toward God. "You don't think they've harmed him, do you?" To her dismay, her voice quivered. As her tear-filled eyes overflowed, silent rivulets streamed down her cheeks. She was thankful for the darkness.

"I don't know. I hope not." He pulled her to him and gently raked a thumb over the wetness on her face. He was too perceptive. But she laid her head against his chest, and let his arms surround her.

Lost in the steady rhythm of his heartbeat, her body relaxed. His sturdiness, the warmth of his nearness, comforted her. His hand stroked her hair. Her arms, as though they had a mind of their own, crept up and around his neck.

Head lowered, he cupped her chin in his hand, and she stood on tiptoe as their lips met. Heaven engulfed her. Her arms held on tight, as did his.

Gently drawing his lips from hers, he hugged her as though his life depended on it. Then, trailing a hand across her face, he whispered. "Thank you."

She leaned into him, her heart pounding. *Thank YOU.*

His arm around her shoulders, her feet seeming to float six inches above the ground, Katie let Zeb escort her the remaining distance to her front porch. "Try to get some sleep, Katie, girl. I'll see you in the morning." He bent down and kissed the top of her head, then retraced his steps across the yard and into the darkness.

Katie carefully pulled open the door so as not to disturb anyone, and entered the silent house. Aunt Nellie lay asleep on the daybed in a corner of the front room. Katie closed her bedroom door and lit the coal oil lamp on her bedside table. Reaching underneath the bed, she retrieved a small wooden box and placed it on the comforter, then removed her shoes and sat cross-legged by the pillows. She popped open the brass-hinged lid and removed the box's only contents, a silver belt buckle with the name *Root* engraved across it—the only tangible memory she had of her father. A country boy locked in a city world—except for that blasted rodeo that killed him. She was sure Mama would like a country boy. Mama didn't know it yet.

Running a finger across the smooth surface, she held it to her. *Daddy, I'm so sorry about what happened to you. We should have never gone to Camdenton. It was all my fault. I'd give anything to have you back.*

What do you think of Zeb, Daddy? What do you think of Deputy Fox? Do you think Mama needs another man to take care of her and Ruth? Would you want that?

She lay back across the bed, cradling the belt buckle. She could never really talk to her dad again, not until they met in heaven. But she could talk to God. Anytime, anywhere. Sitting up, she replaced the belt buckle in its box and slid it back into its hiding place.

She undressed, blew out the lamp, and crawled into bed. Her eyelids drooped shut.

Dear God, please take charge of this situation. Help us find Davey safe and sound. And help me know what to do about Deputy Fox and Mama. And about Zeb. I like him. A lot. You know my heart, but I want Your will to be done. Thank You, Lord.

Katie opened her eyes to the sound of a rooster crowing. Wednesday. A full day since Davey's disappearance.

After assisting Aunt Nellie with breakfast and giving Molly a cuddle, she headed for the store in hopes of hearing good news about Davey. The early morning sunlight cast shadows across the lane, giving her an odd sensation of foreboding. Upon reaching the highway, she checked for traffic and crossed to join the crowd of people already gathered on the parking lot of Hollisters' store. Deputy Fox was talking to a group of men, and Zeb, his hand looped through Rebel's leash, stood to the side.

Katie stepped silently beside Zeb and caught the

last of the deputy's words. "...so the situation has become even more urgent."

~

"What's happened?" Katie's words whispered in his ear made Zeb turn around. Blue eyes alive with concern and curiosity bore into his heart, his soul.

He wanted to spare her the details. The what-ifs. But he had to be honest with her. He ushered her away from the group and around the corner of the store. "One of the men found something last night." He paused, searching for the right words.

Her eyes pleaded with him to continue.

"They found one of Davey's shirts stuffed in Fred and Hazel's mailbox. There was a note pinned to it. They've put the items with Davey's toy dog for evidence."

She leaned forward. "What did the note say?"

How much should he tell her? How much would be considered classified information? Well, all those guys had already seen it—and handled it. And she had as much right to know as they did. "It was a threatening note. I think Davey's life may be in danger."

Katie's eyes flashed, and she grabbed his shirt sleeve. "What did it say?"

"It said..." Rebel cut short his words. The hair on the back of the dog's neck stood up, and a low growl rumbled from his throat. Zeb glanced in the direction the dog was staring.

Oh, no. Boomer, wielding an ax, advanced toward them.

He stopped, so close to Zeb that their shoulders almost touched. "I heard the news. He's probably in cahoots with that no-good Tip Bailor. I'll catch 'em and bash in both their heads."

Without waiting for a response, the man shouldered his ax and strutted off toward the parking lot.

Zeb watched him go. Since when did *he* care what happened to a little kid? He just wanted the drama and the power. Deputy Fox could handle him.

Katie folded her arms in front of her. "Well?"

Zeb sighed, wishing Boomer would move to another country. "The note said, 'I took what belongs to me. Quit searching, and nobody won't get hurt. Lyle Piper'."

Her face scrunched into an unreadable expression. "He signed his name? That seems odd."

Zeb nodded. "Yep. That he did." But his thoughts churned. Piper *was* odd. He'd never met the guy, but who in their right mind would choose a child as payoff for a poker wager? Odd, yes. But there was a fly in the ointment somewhere. And he meant to find out how it got there.

"So, do you think they'll call off the search?" Katie stuck her hands in her pockets.

He watched her slide the right one up and down inside the pocket and thought of the cherished pin she kept inside. *I could use a bluebird right now. We all could.*

The men had gathered into a tight cluster on the parking lot, Boomer and his ax among them, and were nodding as Fox waved his arms and pointed in various directions. Bone leaned against a porch post. Here to help—or here for the show? Who could tell? *Good luck, Deputy Fox.* Zeb punched a fist against his palm. "Not on your life. This fight has just begun."

Katie snatched Rebel's leash from Zeb's wrist. "Okay then, let's go help." And she and the dog bounded off toward the gathering.

Zeb closed his eyes and raised his face toward the morning sun. *Lord, help us. Lord, help us all.* Swiping a forearm across his already perspiring face, he followed Katie and Rebel.

SLAM! The screen door vibrated on its hinges as Fred came plodding across the porch rubbing the sleep out of his eyes. Stepping down onto the gravel, he nearly plowed into Zeb, who sidestepped to avoid a collision. Fred stopped. "You got my car key?"

Zeb tried to hide his impatience. "We had to leave your car in town last night. It was late and we rode back with the deputy. The sheriff has your key, and the car is fine."

The man glared at him. "The sheriff! I need my car. Go get it."

Hazel appeared out of nowhere. "You don't need the car today. You hardly ever use it anyway. They'll bring it back when they can." With a disgusted huff, she rolled her eyes at Zeb, then turned her attention back to her husband. "Now either help with the search or go back in the house."

Fred retreated, muttering under his breath. "First they take my car off somewhere and don't bring it back. Then I wake up and they ain't no breakfast cooked. I oughta just steal that fancy PO-lice car."

Hazel shook her head and followed her husband inside.

Zeb walked over and stood beside Katie. She bumped against him with her shoulder and pointed at Fox. He had stepped to an open space away from the group and squatted, balancing his weight on the ball of one foot. In one hand he held Davey's toy dog. He nodded to Katie, who released Rebel's leash.

The deputy waved the toy in the air and looked the dog in the eye. "Rebel."

The little beagle trotted over and Deputy Fox unhooked the leash from his collar, then held out the toy for him to smell. The canine sniffed and nuzzled the object. Then Fox pulled it back. "Rebel. Go find."

Rebel, nose to the ground, circled the parking lot, then made a beeline for the front door of the store. Pawing frantically at the screen, he raced through it the second it was opened. Zeb and Katie eased in the door behind the deputy and his would-be bloodhound.

Chapter 11

Once inside the store, Rebel made a mad dash for Davey's bedroom.

Fred, munching on a biscuit, leaned against the wall. "That's nothin'. Naturally that room smells like Davey. It's his room. Don't take a professional to tell ya that."

Zeb, a veterinarian at heart, sympathized with the dog. Poor little guy. That *is* Davey's room. Of course, his smell's in there. He began to question the validity of Deputy Fox's claim regarding the little critter. He poked his head inside the bedroom door to watch.

But Rebel didn't linger in the room. He pawed at the window frame. The deputy slid the pane up, and the beagle flew through it and out into the yard, nose scraping the ground, hot on the trail.

Deputy Fox raised the window the rest of the way and climbed through, so as not to lose sight of the dog. Katie raced back through the store, out the door, and around the corner of the building. Zeb was right behind her.

In the middle of the lane Rebel had paused, spinning in circles. He scooted his nose along the ground, sniffing loudly, and stopped beneath a bush on the other side. He turned around and sat, facing Deputy Fox and wagging his tail. "Well, he does that instead of pointing when he locates his quarry. He likes to please." The deputy gave a sheepish grin.

Katie grasped Zeb's arm. "That's the spot where Mike found the toy yesterday."

Zeb placed a hand over hers and squeezed to acknowledge the statement. But the temperature of his blood dropped to iceberg level. This was on his property, practically in his yard. Had the kidnapper been that close? Would he return? Was Mom safe? Was Mike? Boomer would be no protection against an assailant. He was sure of that.

Rance walked up and handed Fox a paper bag. He removed a little shirt from it—Davey's shirt, and waved it in front of Rebel's nose. Again, the dog sniffed and nuzzled. The deputy drew the shirt away. "Rebel. Go find."

The dog trailed to the parking lot, stopping to give Bone a particularly long sniff. The guy took a step backward. He put his hands in the air, palms out. "Hey, I didn't take the kid, I tell ya. I'm here to help find him."

The door opened, and Fred stuck his head out. "Oh, sure, Bone. Sure. Here to help find him. That's the perfect cover up. Everybody who believes that, stand on your head. I seen the dog look you over. He knows.

Dogs ain't no dummies."

But Rebel had moved on, as had Deputy Fox. The beagle went to the Hollisters' mailbox, into the road, looped around, and headed back to the bush across from Davey's window.

Several of the men followed. Zeb and Katie brought up the rear. When Rebel repeated his previous behavior, Deputy Fox faced the group. "We're going to need to expand our search area, and we'll need a way to communicate our whereabouts. Do any of you guys own fox horns?"

Boomer, leaning against the fence, quipped in a loud voice. "Fox horns? What'd you do, *Mister* Fox, invent 'em?"

Hateful old smart aleck, Zeb thought.

The deputy ignored the question.

Men bobbed their heads, commenting to each other. "Yeah, I've got one."

"Me, too."

"Sure, we've got one at the house."

"I think we've all got one."

Deputy Fox raised a hand for attention. "Okay, boys, go get your fox horns and meet me back here as quick as you can."

Katie tapped Zeb's arm. "What's a fox horn?"

"It's a hollowed-out cow horn. It's blown like a trumpet, and each one produces a unique sound, depending on its size and the manner in which it's made."

She bit her bottom lip. "I think Uncle Marcus has one of those."

"They'll use them to identify the owners and keep track of their locations during the search."

As the group dispersed, Fred approached Deputy Fox. "I've got a nice big one in the house. Let me go in there and get it, and I'll show it to you."

The deputy nodded, and Fred, grinning from ear to ear, headed toward his back door.

Deputy Fox sank to a sitting position in the grass, leaned back against a fence post, and closed his eyes. The man was exhausted. The other guys had worked in shifts. Fox had gone nonstop.

He opened his eyes and gave Zeb and Katie a furrowed-brow look. "I'm worried, kids. Real worried. We've got to find a trail, a clue—something. Soon." He rubbed a palm across his forehead.

Zeb knelt in the grass beside the man. "What say we go in the store and get you a bite to eat and maybe a Coke or some coffee? It won't take your crews long to get back here."

Deputy Fox nodded and pushed to his feet, Rebel in tow. "Sounds like a good idea, Son. I could use a little nourishment."

Zeb stood and faced the little beauty beside him. "You comin', Katie girl?"

She didn't answer, but when the deputy and Rebel were a few feet away, she wrinkled her nose and tilted her head toward the bush. "No, you go ahead. I think I'd like to do a little investigating of my own."

Zeb's throat tightened. "Katie…"

She shooed him away with the back of her hand. "I'll be fine."

~

Katie dropped to all fours and pushed her head into the bush Rebel had recently vacated. They had to have missed something. She raked her fingers through the cool, grassless earth underneath the brambles. Nothing.

Shifting her body into reverse, she crawled out and popped to a standing position. Brushing the twigs from her hair, she surveyed her surroundings, and her eyes paused at Davey's still open window.

She cut across the lane and dropped to her knees in the grass beneath it, combing her fingers through the tall blades. Bingo. Something in the shape of a pencil, only sticky, lay against the building. Grasping it between a thumb and forefinger, she carefully drew it out to examine. A cinnamon stick.

Reaching into her pocket, she retrieved a handkerchief and wrapped it around the dirt-and-grass-covered candy. Stuffing the entire bundle into a back pocket, she grasped the windowsill and started to rise.

Suddenly an arm came around her from behind and a hand roughly clapped over her mouth. She tugged at it with both hands, but it remained unyielding. Kicking back, she dug a heel into the top of a foot.

Her assailant drew in a short gasp of air and yanked her backward, slamming her head against a face covered in stubble. A man.

Katie swung one leg in the air and gave her body a quick twirl. Both she and the man slammed against the side of the house, Katie's head striking the windowsill with a loud crack. The world spun as black spots popped in and out of her vision.

A hand grabbed the back of her overalls. The fabric tore in a loud rip.

Attempting to gain her equilibrium and keep from passing out, she closed her eyes and rubbed her hands across them. Footsteps pounded on the lane, then all was quiet. Who *was* that?

She scooted to a sitting position, taking deep breaths until she gained her bearings. *He attacked me. And ripped my best overalls. Hope they're not beyond repair. Scumbag.*

But her mind didn't rest. She leaned to the side and felt behind her. The overalls seemed to be intact—except for one back pocket. It was hanging in shreds off the rest of her outfit. Why would he do that?

Then a new thought dawned on her. The cinnamon stick. It was gone. *He ripped off my pocket and stole the cinnamon stick.* He had to have been watching her. And he wanted it badly enough to attack her for it. Weird. Or maybe not. Her head pounded, but not from the recent blow.

There was probably nothing more to find here for now. And, anyway, who knew if he, whoever he was, would be back. She'd go on inside the store and join Zeb and Deputy Fox, if they were still there.

Deputy Fox sat on the porch step eating a bowl of biscuits and gravy, a coffee cup sitting on the floor beside him. Zeb, his lanky body stretched to its full length, reclined against the DeKalb sign nailed to the wall.

Zeb eyed her suspiciously. "You look a little roughed up. Everything okay?"

She wasn't ready to share her information with anyone, at least not until she'd done more investigating on her own. "I'm fine. Tore my pocket."

The sound of voices made Katie glance up the highway and ended the conversation for the time being. *Good.*

The men were arriving, fox horns in hand. Deputy Fox swallowed the last bites of his breakfast and hastened to meet them. Zeb got to his feet, giving her an *I want to talk to you later* look, and followed the deputy.

Katie took the opportunity to slip inside the store. Hazel stood behind the counter, while Fred lazed on the feed sacks, eyes half closed. He opened one eye and cocked his head sideways at Katie. "Looks like you backed into a bramble bush."

Hazel's face scrunched up at the sight of Katie's overalls. "What happened?"

Katie weighed her words. She didn't want to lie, but... "Guess I got a little too rambunctious and ripped my clothes."

The look that passed between Fred and Hazel told her neither one of them was buying that story, but Hazel gave Fred the evil-eye and no more comments were offered.

Katie peered into the candy case with its glass front and bins of assorted sweets. "Hazel, do you have any cinnamon candy in there?"

Hazel smiled. "Sure, honey. I have these cinnamon drops right here." She pointed a finger in the direction of one of the bins. "Would you like one?"

"Do you have any cinnamon sticks?" Katie surveyed the counter and surrounding shelves as she spoke.

Hazel chuckled. "No, we don't carry those, but the cinnamon drops are the same thing, as far as flavor is concerned."

She pushed further. "Does Davey like those drops?"

Hazel's brow furrowed, and her chin quivered. "I'm sure he would have. He loved cinnamon sprinkled on his toast and applesauce, but I never gave him any of those drops. We never let him have any hard candy. Two years old is way too young. He was," tears pooled in the older woman's eyes, "*is* just a baby. It would have been too dangerous." The woman straightened her posture. "But you're welcome to one if you want it."

"What about cinnamon sticks? Did you ever let him suck on one of those?"

Fred rared up off his feed sack couch and slapped his hand against his leg. "For corn sake, girl. Are you deaf? We don't carry cinnamon sticks, so he wouldn't have had any. He didn't eat cinnamon drops. I don't even know if he'd a-liked them cinnamon hard candy drops if he'd a-got 'em—which he didn't. But you're welcome to one of the blame things if you want it!"

Hazel blushed. "Fred!"

Katie's heart pounded. She'd learned what she

wanted to know. And it wasn't good. "It's okay, Hazel. He didn't mean anything by it."

"Yes, I did." Fred got up and stormed off into the kitchen.

Hazel stirred the chocolate drops at lightning speed. "Katie, you need to fix that pocket. Go in there in the bedroom and use that needle and thread to sew it back on. Nobody'll come in there, and if you don't fix it, I'm afraid it'll just rip further and fall completely off before you can get home."

Katie started to refuse, but thought better of it when she considered the possibility of finding another clue. "Okay. Thanks."

Behind the closed door, Katie slipped out of her overalls and sat on the edge of the bed with Hazel's sewing basket beside her on the patchwork quilt. Voices from the adjoining room drifted through the thin wall. She sat stone still, straining to hear.

"If Piper took Davey, why didn't he just take him and skedaddle? Why would he bother to leave a note—and sign it?" Hazel's voice held agitation.

Fred's tone dripped with sarcasm. "'Cause Piper's ignorant."

"Not as ignorant as Charlie Eugene for letting the whole thing happen in the first place." She could envision the woman standing before Fred, hands on her hips.

There was silence for a few moments before Fred spoke again. "Well, somethin' just don't add up."

"Nothing adds up when Charlie Eugene is involved."

The man's response was low, making Katie strain to hear. "Maybe he's not involved."

"Bet your bottom dollar he is."

"Woman, that's an awful thing to say. Charlie Eugene's our son."

"Maybe so, Grandpa, but if you weren't so much like him, you'd see I'm right."

A few heavy footsteps and a slamming door ended the conversation. Katie finished reattaching her pocket and returned Hazel's sewing kit to its spot on the dresser. She paused in front of the mirror.

Could it have been Piper that attacked her? Or Bone? Or Charlie Eugene himself? She wished she'd seen his face. At least, then, she could have identified the guy. And she would have recognized him if it had been Bone. But she hadn't, so the questions remained. Who did it? And why? She had to find answers and, in doing so, she might locate Davey.

She slipped through the bedroom door, thinking it best not to approach Hazel right now.

Zeb stood on the front porch when she emerged. He surveyed her up and down. "I see you got your pocket repaired. Just how did that happen anyway?"

"I told you. I tore it." Why couldn't he let the whole thing alone? For now. "What have you learned since the search parties went out?"

He shook his head and propped himself against a post. "Nothing. If you listen, you'll hear the guys announcing their locations with their fox horns every so often. They're spread out all over the valley and beyond, but Fox is being pretty secretive. I'm thinking something's up that he isn't sharing yet."

The afternoon was passing too rapidly. Another night approaching—with no answers, no Davey. Why couldn't they find him? Where was he, and with whom? Tragic scenes flashed through her mind, and her less rational self prayed for daylight to linger. "I need to get home."

Zeb caught her by the arm. "You going to church tonight?"

Her heart skipped a beat. Would he be there? "Planning to. How about you?"

"Yeah, I'd like to. I thought I'd bring Mike with me, and Mom if Boomer'll let her go."

Boomer must be an even more domineering man than she'd thought. "Hope all three of you get to come. I'll be looking for you."

Chapter 12

Zeb and Mike, the first ones to arrive for the Wednesday night service, walked across the grass toward the little building, and Zeb breathed a bit easier. A sense of peace, if that were possible considering the turmoil of the last few days, flowed through Zeb's mind, causing his entire body to relax. But even then, his thoughts raced to what might have been—what still could be.

Why had Boomer been so against Mom attending a church service? This would have done her so much good, and what was it to Boomer? He didn't have to come if he didn't want to. Well, at least Mike had been allowed to come. This was where Zeke Harlow had walked the aisle with Zeb eleven years ago, when Zeb had given his heart to the Lord. *Oh, Dad… Dad… Dad."*

"Hey, Mike!" Duke ran up and bumped the boy from the side.

Luke followed. "Mike."

Mike wrapped an arm around each twin's neck

and started to wrestle them toward the ground.

"No." Katie scurried across the yard toward them. "Stay off the ground. We just got you cleaned up."

Mike grinned at her and let the twins go. Marcus headed into the church, but Katie lingered beside Zeb, who stood near all three boys.

Zeb did a double take. In her blue print dress with the bluebird pin neatly attached to the white collar and blond hair flowing softly over her shoulders, this girl was a sight for sore eyes. He suppressed a strong urge to take her in his arms.

She doubled up a fist and, eyes sparking, gently punched him on the arm.

That's my Katie girl, Zeb thought.

Katie glanced over at the boys, now standing in front of the church sign. "Where's your mom?"

Zeb's heart plummeted. "Boomer wouldn't let her come. Said her first business was to stay home and tend to her husband."

Katie brushed a hand across his arm, making his insides turn to jello. Her eyes showed what looked like genuine sympathy. "I'm sorry."

Zeb managed the words, "Thanks. I'm sorry, too."

Then she pointed toward the kids and brightened. "I'm glad you were able to bring Mike."

The church bell rang, and the boys dashed inside. It was good to see Mike at God's house and enjoying himself. But poor Mom. Boomer had turned on the charm in the first few months of their acquaintance. But Zeb had seen through it. His mother had not. If Zeb ever married, he'd make sure his wife would never have to suffer like that.

Katie took him by the arm. "Shall we go in?"

The church yard had filled, and a steady stream of people entered the building. Brother Deren greeted each one with a smile and a handshake. When Katie and Zeb reached him, he grasped Zeb's hand between both of his. "Glad to see you tonight. I'm praying for your mom and Boomer—and you."

Tears welled in Zeb's eyes, but he managed a "thank you".

Brother Deren gave his hand a reassuring squeeze and let go. The warmth in his kind eyes touched Zeb's heart.

Blinking away tears that no one ever needed to see, he ushered Katie to a seat near the aisle, halfway to the front. The boys had already taken seats two rows in front of them, between Katie's uncles Rance and Everett Tillman.

Zeb squeezed onto the pew next to Katie. Bits and pieces of conversations drifted to his ears.

"It's just a shame about that little Hollister boy."

"I don't know what happened."

"They say that old Cryder Zarbone made threats right before the boy disappeared. Hope he didn't kill 'im."

"I heard tell somebody run off with 'im. I mean *off*."

"His mother's in the asylum."

"I know it."

Brother Deren made his way to the front and

faced the congregation. The chatter stopped, as all eyes turned toward him. "Looks like it's about time to start. Rance, get your choir together."

Rance Tillman stepped into the aisle and headed for the front of the church. Duke, Luke, and Mike followed. When the choir, the pianist, and a man with a guitar had taken their places, Rance held up a hymnal. "Come on up here, Zeb. We can use a strong baritone."

Brother Deren's eyes met Zeb's, silently encouraging, almost pleading. Zeb felt safe here, secure, loved. He stepped out and joined the choir, taking a seat in the back row.

Rance announced the page number, and strains of "The Old Rugged Cross" filled the chapel. It felt good—no, it felt great—to lift his voice to the heavens and sing words of praise and thanksgiving to the only One who could make everything alright. The One who could keep Davey safe and lead them to him.

The song ended much too soon, and the choir and musicians returned to their seats. Zeb, noticing Mike, Duke, and Luke weren't in sight, craned his neck in an attempt to locate them.

Katie gently nudged his shoulder and pointed a finger. The boys had taken seats on the front row. Oh, no. He could envision a scuffling match during the service, with Mike as the instigator.

Katie nudged him again and mouthed the words, "It's okay."

Brother Deren stepped to the podium. After opening with prayer, the gentle pastor placed both hands on it and leaned forward. "Our hearts are heavy tonight, due to the alleged kidnapping of our young friend, Davey Hollister. Let's all be constant in prayer, placing the situation in God's hands, and trusting Him for the outcome."

Heads nodded, and several Amens sounded throughout the congregation.

Brother Deren indicated the wooden cross mounted on the wall behind him. "The title of our message for this evening is Refuge in the Cross."

"Now, if you'll turn with me in your Bibles to the book of John, I'd like to share a few verses with you."

After reading the scripture aloud, Brother Deren moved away from the podium to his right, directly facing the boys on the front row. "The idea of being kidnapped is a scary thought. If you were kidnapped, the first thing you'd want to do is find a refuge, a place where you would be safe from the person who took you away. You'd want to find a way back home."

Zeb scooted closer to Katie so he could see Mike. All three boys were sitting stock still, heads lifted toward the preacher's face. Duke and Luke leaned into each other, their heads touching. Davey was their friend and a victim.

Brother Deren returned to the podium and continued. "But there's another kind of kidnapping that is even more dangerous. There's a kidnapper that can take not only your life, but also your soul. It's called sin."

A thought surfaced in Zeb's mind and took hold. Boomer was a victim as well, but his kidnapper was the second kind—the deadliest.

Zeb turned his attention back to the preacher's words. "So when you're kidnapped by your own sin, you need a refuge, the refuge of Christ's sacrifice on the cross, to bring you back home to God."

As the sermon ended, Brother Deren stepped in front of the pulpit, facing the congregation, and spread his arms in a sweeping motion to encompass the entire group. "Beloved, if you have any doubts, any doubts at all, don't be afraid to come. I'll be glad to pray with you. Bring your burdens to the foot of the cross and give them to Jesus. There's safety in Jesus. He will be your refuge if you'll just come to Him."

Zeb detected movement on the front row. Duke had stepped away from the others and was making his way toward Brother Deren. Zeb tensed. Duke was not quite five years old. Did he know what he was doing?

Brother Deren bent over to welcome the child, who grabbed him by the neck and whispered something in his ear. The man nestled Duke's head and whispered something back. The child nodded and smiled.

The pastor stood, placing a hand on Duke's shoulder. "Brothers and sisters, this young man has come tonight with a very important request. He wants to know if we could all join hands and have a special prayer for his friend, Davey, before we go to our homes."

As people filled the aisle, locking fingers, Zeb reached for Katie's hand. He bowed his head and closed his eyes while Brother Deren asked the Lord to deliver Davey from whatever danger threatened him and bring him home safely.

Zeb breathed a silent prayer of his own for Boomer, for Mom.

Amens resounded all around the room, and Zeb released Katie's hand. Kevin approached the two. "School tomorrow, Mr. Harlow?"

Zeb stepped aside to help clear the aisle. "Yes, we'll have school, Kevin. Hope to see you there."

"Wouldn't miss it." The boy clapped his hands and people jerked their heads toward the sound. "Hey, everybody, there's school tomorrow."

A man's voice bellowed across the room. "Okay, Harlow, go ahead and have school, but don't you let nothin' happen to any of them kids."

The room fell silent.

Zeb's sense of tranquility threatened to disintegrate before his eyes. How would he answer that? How could he be sure everyone made it to and from school safely?

His answer was provided in the form of their pastor. Making his way to the center of the crowd, he raised his arms. "It's simple. Just make sure nobody walks alone. Bring your kids to school yourself if you need to, and come get them in the afternoon. I'll be available to help. I'm sure others will as well."

"Sure, I can do that." One of the men patted Zeb on the back.

"Me, too. I can help."

"I've got a turn on a search crew in about an hour, but I can help ya tomorrow afternoon."

Well, that was that. Offers came from all over the room. He knew the kids needed to be back in school, but Davey's situation weighed heavily on his mind. "Come on, Mike. You ready to go?"

"Almost." He leaned over and cuffed each twin gently on the top of the head. "See ya tomorrow at school, Banks and Banks."

"We'll see ya tomorrow." Duke dodged and punched Mike on the shoulder.

Zeb rolled his eyes. *Wonder where he got that habit.*

Mike headed for the door and Zeb followed a couple paces behind, hesitant to leave this haven for the familiar turmoil awaiting him at home.

Brother Deren had positioned himself inside the foyer, and as Zeb passed by, their eyes met. Zeb reached out and gripped the man's hand. "Thanks, Brother Deren."

The preacher responded with a warm handshake and a pat on Zeb's shoulder. "It's gonna be alright, Son. Just keep believing and trusting. Faith in God can move mountains."

Zeb nodded and attempted a smile, then hightailed it out the door. It was hard to keep that mountain-moving faith when he couldn't even figure out how to move Boomer to another state. Or planet. He wanted to protect his mom and little brother. He wanted to find Davey safe and sound. He needed a bluebird.

A hand touched his arm, then lightly cuffed him just above the elbow. Katie.

"Gotta go, but I'll walk the boys to school tomorrow. You go on home and get some rest."

Zeb stared across the field and down the road. Where was Davey? Why couldn't he be here and Boomer be gone?

Zeb, vengeance is in MY hands.

His head reeled as the familiar Bible verse blared through his consciousness. "It is Mine to avenge, saith the Lord." Attempting, unsuccessfully, to ignore the thought, he turned his attention back to the vision of loveliness standing at his side. Could she keep the boys safe tomorrow, or would she be in danger as well? He needed answers before other children were kidnapped, maybe killed. Sweat droplets formed on his temples, and he hoped she didn't notice.

Blue eyes bore into his, and her expression softened. She grabbed his hand, gave it a quick squeeze, and let go of it. "See you tomorrow, Harlow."

"Yeah, see ya. Uh, Gallagher." He wheeled around with Mike in tow and started the trek to the Slocum household, his personal prison.

Katie watched Zeb and Mike walk away. Aunt Ella's words came back to her. *Poor Zeb.* If only she could do something to help him. But what? How? The lanky schoolmaster was getting dangerously close to edging his way into her heart.

"Hey, Katie. Whatcha starin' at? Where's your brain, out in the north forty?" Duke took her by the hand and swung himself around.

Luke giggled and grabbed her other hand. "North

forty."

Katie put an arm around each twin and pulled them to her. A strong urge to protect them, keep them close, gripped her insides and she hugged them tighter.

The walk home took only a few minutes, but the gathering darkness made Katie thankful her Uncle Marcus was along.

That night she dreamed of Davey standing just outside her bedroom window, calling her name.

"Katie. Katie." Daylight streamed through her window. When she opened her eyes and the blur disappeared, she looked into the lidded eyes of a terrapin. Sitting up with a start, she bunched the blanket to her chest. Laughter erupted on either side of her. Duke and Luke, of course. They peered up at her, hands covering their grins.

Duke leaned into her. "Look what Luke found. Can we take it to school?"

Katie backed away. "Not as long as I'm the one walking with you. Put it back in the yard, or wherever you found it, and leave it alone. It has feelings, too."

The boys shrugged, but offered no argument. Duke placed an arm around his brother's shoulders. "Looks like we gotta make another trip out behind the chicken house."

They, at least, had the decency to close Katie's bedroom door as they exited. Good grief, waking up to a terrapin in the face. She slid out of bed, slipped into the comforting softness of her well-worn overalls, and pinned her bluebird brooch securely in her pocket.

Aunt Ella sat rocking Molly in a corner of the front room, while Aunt Nellie prepared biscuits and gravy for breakfast. "Morning, Katie. Sit yourself down and get you some of this while it's hot." The older woman's presence was like a ray of sunshine on a cloudy day. Katie hoped her stay in the Banks' home would last for several more days—or weeks.

The tantalizing aromas made her mouth water. "Aunt Nellie, can I do something to help you?"

Before she could answer, the twins bustled through the door. "We put the terrapin back." Duke slid onto a chair at the table. Luke took the chair beside him. Aunt Nellie chuckled and winked at Katie. "Yeah, help me serve these wild guys, and then eat a bite yourself before you head 'em off to school."

Heavy footsteps sounded on the porch, and a loud knock rattled the screen door. Ella and Aunt Nellie exchanged startled looks. Marcus's voice boomed from somewhere outside. "Hey, there. What do you need?"

A gravelly voice, unfamiliar to Katie, responded immediately. "I ain't meanin' no harm, Mister. I was just a-wonderin' if maybe you could spare me a bite to eat."

Katie got up and crossed the floor to sit on a hassock near Ella and Molly. From her vantage point, she could see clearly through the front window. The man's scruffy thick brown hair looked like it had never known a comb, and his tattered clothing hung loosely on his slight frame.

Marcus circled around the man. "You wait here. I'll see if I can find you something."

The man eased onto the edge of the porch, and Marcus stepped inside. "It's a hobo, Nellie. What say we give him something to eat, and then send him on his way."

The woman nodded and dished up a serving of biscuits and gravy in an enamel bowl and handed it to Marcus. Duke and Luke slid off their chairs, looking expectantly at their mother.

Ella shook her head. "You two stay in here for now."

They pressed their faces to the screen while Marcus sat a few feet from the man as he ate. Between bites the guy told his story. His voice carried easily through the open window. "Oh, thank you, sir. Ya see, I'm a little down on my luck right now. Times is hard, and I ain't got no place to go and nothin' to eat. Ain't got no money neither."

"I'm sorry. Wish I could help, but we don't have any money to spare." Marcus's voice held genuine sympathy.

The man scraped the bowl with his spoon. "Aaah. That there was some awful good eatin'. Say. Do you have any odd jobs that need doin' around here?"

Marcus repeated, "We couldn't pay you anything."

The man persisted. "I'd work for food. If I just had a place to bed down for a few nights and some nourishment, then I'd be on my way."

Katie's heart pounded. She glanced at Ella and Molly. *Don't agree to anything, Uncle Marcus.*

But alas, Marcus cleared his throat. "Well, there

are a few jobs where I could use some help, and maybe you could sleep in the barn for a few nights. Be right back."

The man leaned against a porch post and laced his fingers behind his head. "Bless your heart, sir. You won't be sorry. I'll not take advantage of your kindness."

Marcus returned the bowl and utensil to the kitchen, and cringed when he saw Ella. "Uh, I..."

Ella sighed audibly. "We heard."

Marcus didn't answer, but slipped out the door and ushered the man in the direction of the barn. Aunt Nellie sank into a kitchen chair. "He's a hobo. I feel sorry for him, but I hope Marcus hasn't done something we'll all regret."

Katie couldn't keep her misgivings to herself. "I don't know about that man. There's no telling who he is."

Aunt Nellie put her arm around Katie's shoulders. "Honey, he's probably just what he said—a man down on his luck that needs a little help getting back on his feet. But if it'll make you feel any better, we'll be real careful to keep the doors locked. I think Marcus'll watch him close and not let him cause any trouble."

But Katie remembered Aunt Nellie's earlier words—"something we'll all regret."

She could envision the guy making off with one, or both, of the twins. Especially Luke. Without Duke he probably wouldn't even yell. That could even be the person who took Davey. And if he did, what had he done with the child?

The walls were closing in on her, yet the outdoors seemed way too big with too much open space surrounded by too many hiding places.

"Let's go, Katie. We're ready." Duke waved his lunch bucket in front of her.

Luke swung his bucket back and forth, then spun in a circle. "Ready."

Katie snatched a jar of apple butter from the cabinet. "I think the teacher might need a present today. Come on, guys."

On the way down the lane, Katie could see Marcus and the hobo doing something to the gate in the fence that surrounded the barnyard. The boys saw them, too.

Duke pointed toward them. "He's nice. We like him."

Katie tried to hide her concern so as not to alarm the kids, but she also didn't want them to get too familiar with strangers. "What makes you say that?"

The child swung his lunch bucket back and forth a few times, then turned to her, but kept walking. "'Cause he's nice. He was out there behind the chicken house when Luke found the terrapin, and he was nice to us. And when we took it back, he said he'd take care of it for us. Right, Luke?"

Luke skipped a circle around his brother. "Right."

Katie had misgivings about them even talking to someone they didn't know. Their safety could be at stake. But, she told herself, most hoboes were harmless. *Most hoboes.* She couldn't get that phrase out of her mind. Most of them meant not all of them.

"Boys, you shouldn't hang around with someone you don't know."

Duke halted in front of her, forcing her to either stop or step around him. She stopped. "But we *do* know him, Katie. Remember? We met him. And besides, he told us his name. It's Manfred Olsen."

Katie gave Duke her sternest expression. "Just because you know his name, doesn't mean you know him."

She put her hands on Duke's shoulders, spun him around, and gave him a gentle nudge to get him started down the lane again. He giggled. It wasn't funny to Katie. Just what had this Manfred Olsen been doing that far onto their property, hidden from view?

Fred's car was parked on the gravel road near the store. The door stood open, and the back side of Fred protruded from the driver's side space.

The boys bopped over to the car and Duke tapped a hand against Fred's leg. "Hi."

The man scooted the rest of the way out and faced the kids and Katie. "Oh, hi. The sheriff brought my car back this mornin' and I thought I'd come out here and make sure that scalawag didn't do any damage to it." He wiped perspiration from his brow, braced a hand on the fender, and pushed to a standing position.

Katie stared at the sweaty man, hands hooked in his galluses, and couldn't help but wonder if Fred was more concerned about the car than about finding Davey.

The boys were taking in every word, every

mannerism that Fred dished out before them. That couldn't be good.

Fred rared back and rocked on his heels, wiping his brow again. "Yup, I've had more attention from Hazel these last few days than I've had in all the time since Davey come to live with us." He harrumphed a couple times. "Now, don't get me wrong. I don't want anything to have happened to him. But I just think Charlie Eugene, our own son—wherever he is, needs to take some responsibility and be a real dad to his boy."

Weird fingers of dread crept across Katie's scalp and into her brain. *What did Fred know? What's he not telling?* Then relief took dread's place. *If he took him, then Davey must be safe. Fred wouldn't hurt his own grandson. Would he?*

A sudden urge gripped her—she must get the boys away from Fred.

"Boys, how about a Coke before school?"

Their eyes widened in disbelief. Then a smile crept over Duke's face. "A Coke *before* school?"

Katie flipped him lightly on the ear. "Yeah, let's go in the store for a little bit."

The twins raced ahead of her. She glanced back to see that Fred had already poked his head back inside the car, examining whatever.

Inside the store, the boys were already at the soda box. Hazel fixed questioning eyes on Katie. Katie nodded, and Hazel extracted two cold Cokes, opened them, and handed one to each twin.

Deputy Fox, Rebel at his feet, sat on the feed sack couch next to Sheriff Barton. Boomer and Mike sat in cane-bottom chairs by the kitchen door.

Sheriff Barton reached down to pet Rebel and spoke to Deputy Fox. "So you say the dog keeps doing the same thing over and over?"

The deputy nodded and scratched his canine behind the ears. "We're working with him, but he's persistent. He keeps returning to that same bush, then dashes to the highway. Then he stops and looks confused. Then right back to that bush."

Deputy Fox rubbed his eyes with his palms. "We've a mind to slow down this local search, or halt it altogether. We're almost positive Davey was taken away in a vehicle."

Boomer stood and sauntered across the room, taking a cocky stance in front of the two lawmen. "Well, that lets out everybody around here except Marcus and Rance and Fred. Nobody else has a car that'll go that far."

Deputy Fox's eyes clouded. "*How* far, Boomer?"

Chapter 13

Katie's stomach knotted. She exchanged glances with Mike.

Boomer spit on the floor. "Far enough to get out of this dadburned valley."

Fred pushed open the screen door and shuffled inside, flopping down on a feed sack. He eyed Boomer. "I heard that, and I don't appreciate it. Maybe *you* took him, Boomer. Maybe you carried him off on that old rattle trap tractor of yours."

Katie knew of the tractor in question. Zeb had told her it sounded like a gas-operated Maytag washing machine on it last leg, and if she'd understood him correctly, it hadn't run in over a month. But the words still set her nerves on edge.

Boomer approached Fred. "You accusin' me of somethin'?"

Fred, fists doubled, pushed to his feet. "You guilty of somethin'?"

The men advanced toward one another and came

to a standoff, blocking the exit. Trapped, Katie drew the boys to her and guided them toward a far corner of the store.

Deputy Fox grabbed Fred's arm, but he jerked away and stormed toward the back room.

Boomer stalked toward the exit, slamming into the door frame with his forehead.

Mike stifled a giggle.

Boomer emitted a guttural snarl, turned around wild-eyed, and headed for Mike. "Make fun of me, boy. I'll show you fun."

No longer smiling, Mike backed up, arm raised in front of his face. Sheriff Barton stepped between the man and boy. Grasping Boomer's wrists, the sheriff initiated a 180-degree turn and ushered him outside.

By this time, Mike was standing at Katie's side, his head pressed against her shoulder.

Deputy Fox approached them and faced Katie. "Mind if I accompany you and these three guys to school this morning?"

Mike brightened. "A police escort?"

The deputy patted Mike's shoulder. "Sure, you could call it that. How about it?"

All three boys bobbed their heads up and down, as did Katie.

A weight lifted from her shoulders. A police escort. She didn't trust Fred. It made her shudder to think what Boomer might be capable of doing, and now there was that hobo to complicate things.

"Okay, guys. Let's hit the road." Deputy Fox marched out the door. The boys formed a line and followed, while Katie brought up the rear. The deputy's pistol hung in plain view at his right side, and he walked erect and with purpose. He could, and would, protect them.

Deputy Fox. Deputy Jesse Fox. Jesse Fox. Dad?

Halfway down the lane, the little group became more informal. The twins fanned out and meandered through the dried roadside stubble, drinking their Cokes and "looking for clues."

Mike fell into step beside Fox, and Katie moved to his other side. Mike gazed up at the man, admiration in his eyes. "Deputy Fox, thanks for walking with us. I usually walk with Zeb, but today Dad said he wanted to bring me to school himself to be sure I was safe, so I waited. But then he threw another fit, and here I am."

Boomer protect Mike? A likely story. Katie glanced at the boy's outfit—overalls and a thin, long-sleeved shirt. Too hot for this time of year. But the boy never rolled up the sleeves. Was he attempting to hide bruises, or cuts? She remembered the red mark on Mrs. Slocum's face, and warning signals blared through her mind.

The deputy cut to the chase. "Son, does your dad ever hurt you?"

Mike didn't answer right away, but slowed his pace. Finally, he stopped altogether. "Nah, not much. Sometimes he..." The boy hesitated and bit at a fingernail.

Deputy Fox stepped in front of him, facing him. "Sometimes he does what?"

Mike averted his eyes. "Nothin' really. I'm tough."

Katie's heart was breaking. Boomer might not be a kidnapper, but he was a mean man, and no way should innocent people have to live in fear because of him.

The conversation was apparently over as far as Mike was concerned. He jogged ahead and joined the twins in the grass. Katie and Deputy Fox walked side-by-side down the lane, keeping the kids in view.

Several parents and other volunteers milled around in the school yard as Zeb herded students into the building. All eyes turned toward the deputy, and questions bombarded him.

"Any news yet?"

"Have they found the kid?"

"Is the kidnapper in custody?"

While poor Deputy Fox tried to satisfy the agitated crowd, Katie stepped to the schoolhouse door to join Zeb. "How's it goin'? Everything okay?" She pressed the jar of apple butter into his palm.

He mouthed a silent "thank you," but his drawn features told the story. "It's a nightmare. We're surrounded by woods, and I'm the only adult. These kids are in my care, and to be honest, I'm worried."

Katie wasn't sure how to answer because she was scared to death, but she put on a brave face and jabbed him in the arm. "I'll stay if you want."

He didn't respond to her offer, but took her by the hand and pulled her out of the range of listening ears. "We're having recess inside even though it's hot, but there's the issue of the outhouses. I just can't watch every kid every minute. Lord, help me."

She leaned into him and pressed her mouth

against his ear. "They said they think the kidnapper took Davey out of the area by car or some other vehicle. I think they plan to pull the search teams and concentrate their efforts in a wider area."

Zeb's eyes closed. "But the kidnapper could be anywhere, even in that group of volunteers over there. And...and Davey could be *dead*."

She couldn't leave him like this. Walter was here, and the other big boys, so she knew there was teen-power available. But what she didn't know, and what worried her tremendously, was the location of the kidnapper with whom they were dealing. "Zeb, I'm staying."

He touched her hair and drew in an audible breath. "No, you go on home. We'll be fine. We'll have to be. Just pray for us."

Every muscle in her body willing her to stay, Katie backed away and started toward the group still questioning poor Deputy Fox on the playground. Turning around for one last glance, she met Zeb's eyes and gave a wave and the best smile she could muster.

He nodded and waved back, then stepped inside the schoolhouse and closed the door.

~

"Mr. Harlow, do you have your harmonica?" Memories of Davey's *Pway* shattered his heart at Duke's plaintive words.

Luke squirmed sideways in the seat he and his twin shared and stared at Zeb. "Harmonica?"

He almost always carried it with him. "It's in my pocket."

Kevin stood and faced Zeb. "Mr. Harlow, they want you to play "Amazing Grace" for the opening song today. You know, in memory of..." The boy hesitated and his Adam's apple bobbed up and down. "I mean, in *honor* of Davey. They tell me it was, uh, *is* his favorite song."

A wail broke out from a small girl in the front row. "He s-s-said *in memory*. Don't that mean somebody's dead? Is Davey dead, Mr. Harlow?" She looked at him imploringly, tears glistening in her eyes.

Kevin was at the child's side in seconds. He knelt by her desk and placed an arm around her shoulders. "We can pray for Davey to be home soon, safe and sound. Jesus knows where he is, and He can protect him."

The little girl raised her head. "Really?"

Kevin smiled. "Really."

If only Zeb could have the confidence and faith this young teen displayed. Jesus knew where Davey was alright, and He could protect him. But things sometimes happened—bad things that no one could explain. What was God's will in all this?

Duke persisted. "Wouldja play?"

Luke's familiar echo, "Play?" was almost too much for Zeb. He envisioned Davey on his lap, waving the harmonica in his face and begging him to *pway* a song. His stomach tightened, and a burning sensation invaded the backs of his eyes. He blinked.

Pulling the harmonica from his pocket, he perched on the edge of an empty desk, resting one foot on the wooden seat. He drew in a deep breath and placed the instrument against his lips.

"Wait." Kevin stood and raised a hand. "Everybody bow your heads and pray while Mr. Harlow plays Davey's song."

The students, in a single motion, bowed their heads. Kevin glanced around the room and nodded, then lowered his own head. "Okay, Mr. Harlow."

Through trembling lips, Zeb made strains of "Amazing Grace" swell from the worn harmonica. For Davey. For Jesus.

Lost in the music, he closed his eyes. It was so easy to desire a way to find and punish the lowlife who made away with his little friend. For that matter, it was easy to want to punish Walter's brother, Tank, for shooting and killing Flat. And Boomer for abusing and terrorizing Mike and his mom, and yes, even himself at times. But vengeance was up to God, not people.

That's right, Zeb. Give it all to Me. I can handle it for you.

When the song ended, the class stood for the Pledge of Allegiance. Then Walter led in prayer, and the school day began.

"Can I go to the toilet?" A small boy, wiggling in his seat, raised his hand.

Uh-oh. Zeb had to let him go, but he wasn't about to send a child outside alone. Partners, that's what he'd do. He'd send them out with partners. But still.

"Mr. Harlow, I gotta go." The wide-eyed child wiggled and danced in the aisle.

Walter's eyes met Zeb's. "I'll take him."

Zeb wilted in relief as the teen got up and headed

for the door. On the way past the teacher's desk, he leaned down and whispered, "You helped me. I'll help you. Nobody's gonna steal one of these little 'uns whilst I'm around."

Throughout the day, Walter was everybody's escort, one or two kids at a time.

By three o'clock, voices drifted through the open windows of the schoolhouse. Zeb glanced out at the group of adults gathering in the yard, here to walk the students home as promised.

He scanned the crowd for Katie. Sure enough, there the pretty little gal stood, leaning against that same old tree, looking like she hadn't a care in the world. Deputy Fox stood nearby, engaged in conversation with her.

Zeb stepped away from the window and faced the students. "Okay, everybody. It's almost time to go home, and I see several of your parents out there. When I open the door, I don't want any of you to just take off. If you don't see an adult to walk home with you, then come back to me. I'll make sure you get home safely."

"We get it. We'll be good." Mike picked up his books, secured by a leather strap, and rose to stand beside his desk. The other students followed suit.

Zeb was proud of his little brother. Why couldn't he figure a way to let this kid have a childhood like he deserved? He was a good kid. A real good kid. "Alright, line up along the side of the room. I'm going to open the door now. Remember what I said. See you tomorrow."

He swung open the door. People rushed toward the building, calling children's names. Zeb's tension eased as, one by one, his students paired up with their adults and headed up the lane.

"I love you, Mr. Harlow." Hands came around him from behind and hugged him tight. He knew that voice.

"Mike, what are you doin' back there callin' your own brother *Mr.* Harlow?"

The boy eased around in front of him and grinned. "Okay. I love you, Harlow."

"I love you, too, buddy." Zeb grabbed his little brother's hair and tousled it worse than it already was. It felt good to lighten up a little—do something silly, if only for a moment. Mike ducked under his elbow and bopped out the door, grinning.

Deputy Fox stuck his head inside the room. "Everything go okay today, Zeb?"

"Yeah, it all worked out fine. That Walter Bailor is an alright guy. He was a lot of help watching the little ones. Any news to report?"

The deputy frowned and shook his head. "Not yet. We've got more patrols out in the surrounding areas, and people are being questioned. But so far we've come up with a big fat zero. We're reasonably sure, though, that he's not in this area."

"Where's Rebel?" Zeb had taken a liking to the little self-proclaimed beagle turned bloodhound.

Fox smiled. "Take a look out in the yard."

Rebel, surrounded by Katie, Duke, Luke and Mike, sat peacefully under the tree, his leash looped around Katie's wrist.

"Let's go." Zeb locked the schoolhouse door, and he and Deputy Fox joined the little group.

Pushing to her feet and brushing the dry August grass from her overalls, Katie handed the little dog's leash back to his owner. The trio-times-two plus dog made their way up the lane toward Hollisters' store.

A familiar car in the driveway came into view. Oh, no. Lillian. *What'll we tell her? She probably doesn't even know Davey's gone.*

Setting his pace to match that of Deputy Fox, he walked beside the man, then gradually slowed. "That car belongs to Davey's aunt. She comes to see him periodically and is attached to him. She'll be hysterical."

Fox slowed even more, allowing Katie and the children to move ahead. "Did you people not notify her of his disappearance?"

Zeb rubbed his fingers against the side of his face. "It would have been Hazel and Fred, and I'll bet they didn't."

The deputy's jaw tightened. Placing a hand over the pistol in his holster, he quickened his pace. Zeb followed, and they walked into a nightmare.

Duke and Luke huddled at one end of the porch, Katie's arms around them.

"Hurry, Mr. Policeman. There's a fight, and Aunt Lillian's a-winnin' it." Duke huddled closer to Katie and pointed toward the door.

Inside the store, Fred lay back against a pile of feed sacks with his hands covering his face. Lillian pounded his head with her fists, while Hazel tried unsuccessfully to pull the woman away from her husband. Lillian's voice elevated to a scream. "I'll kill you. If Davey's been hurt, I swear, I'll kill you."

Deputy Fox clasped Lillian's arms and, in restraining her, wrapped his fingers around her watchband. The woman's screams mingled with sobs. "Ow! That's my bad arm. Let go of me."

"Calm down, ma'am, and I will." He led her to a chair and eased her onto it, her shoulders shaking as she rubbed the long scar on her right arm where the watchband crossed it.

When she calmed down, the woman eyed the deputy. "I came here to visit my little Davey like I always do. And when I walked in, they told me he was gone. Hazel said it was Fred's fault." She pulled a hankie from her purse and wiped her nose. "If anything's happened to that baby, I just can't go on. I just *can't*. He's my baby. You've got to find him." Tears streamed down her cheeks and she covered her face with the hankie.

Deputy Fox squatted in front of the distraught woman. "We're doing all we can, ma'am. May I ask for your name and your relationship to the missing child?"

Lifting her face to look him in the eyes, she answered through hiccupping sobs. "My name is Lil-Lillian Wymore, and I'm Davey's aunt—on his mother's side."

"Are you from around here?"

"No, that's why I don't get to see him often." With shaking hands, the woman stuffed the hankie back inside her purse and twisted and untwisted the purse's handle.

Zeb, his heartstrings taut to the breaking point, observed the woman. He'd been a nervous wreck ever since he'd learned of Davey's disappearance. How much more so a woman who had taken care of the child and nurtured him as her own until his dad brought him here to live because her beloved sister was in the asylum.

It was times like this when a sense of helplessness shrouded Zeb's body, and he wished he could be the one to disappear. There was nothing he could say, nothing he could do to bring the child back.

You can pray.

A sudden light-headedness made Zeb touch the wall for support, and goose bumps pricked his arms.

Hazel slipped to Lillian's side and placed a hand on her shoulder. "Lillian honey, wouldn't you like to stay here for the night? It'll probably be dark before you can make it home, and there's a nice bed in the back room. You're welcome to sleep there."

Lillian reached up and gave Hazel's hand a pat. "Thank you for your kindness, but there's no point in me staying here with Davey gone. No, I'll drive on back tonight. I'll be alright."

Hazel tried to protest, but Lillian braced her hands on her knees and got up slowly, then turned to face Deputy Fox. "I'm sorry if I offended anyone. It was all just such a shock. Excuse me. I need to go." Her face puckered. "But, Deputy, please find my baby."

Zeb stepped onto the porch and held the screen door open for Lillian. As she passed in front of him, he glanced across the highway and saw Katie and the twins walking hand in hand up the lane toward the Banks farm.

Rats. He'd wanted to talk to her some more, maybe walk them home—maybe spend a little time alone with her. *Shoot.*

Oh, well, tomorrow was another day.

But tomorrow came and went, with no glimpse of Katie. Deputy Fox had walked Mike and the twins to school that morning, dropped them off at the door, and left.

By the time school was finished for the day, Zeb was more than ready to turn his charges over to their escorts for the trek home.

Friday afternoon. Hallelujah. He could use a couple days' break. If not for Walter and his watchful eye, Zeb's sanity would have already taken a vacation.

He scanned the school yard. Parents and volunteers had arrived for a second day as promised. As his students ran to join them, Zeb's heart pounded in his temples. Leaning against her tree was Katie, nonchalantly running a hand through her hair. He wanted to run to her, throw his arms around her, tell her how much he'd missed her. But the twins made a dash for their pretty cousin. She knelt and embraced them, burying her face in Luke's, then Duke's hair.

With butterflies going wild in the pit of his stomach, Zeb locked the door and strode toward the tree. Mike was beside him in a flash. "Feelin' a little nervous, brother?"

The kid knew him too well. He made a fist and

gently bopped his little brother on the side of his head. "Shut up, boy."

Mike grinned. "She *is* cute, ain't she?"

Heat crept up Zeb's neck and slapped him on the cheeks. He knew his face had to be flaming red.

Katie wrinkled her brow and looked at him sideways. Then, popping to a standing position, she twirled a strand of golden hair around her index finger. "You look hot. Hard day?"

"Stressful."

She nodded in understanding. "Still no word on Davey. They have units out all over the place, but Deputy Fox has stationed himself and Rebel right here. Something's up. I'm not sure what, but I intend to find out."

Chapter 14

Katie knew something was wrong. Sure, the kidnapping or whatever it was was wrong. But it was more than that. Too many suspects. No concrete evidence. No progress. She was confident Deputy Jesse Fox knew it, too, or he wouldn't still be here in the valley.

A huge—and vital—piece of this puzzle was missing. And it was the piece that held the answer. Of that, she was sure.

"Katie." Zeb's hand lightly touched her shoulder, making her swivel to face him. "A penny for your thoughts?"

The almost forgotten phrase now surfaced in her memory, sending a half warm/half edgy sensation fluttering through her insides. "Thoughts come and go. So do pennies."

He grinned. "You already said that. A few days ago."

Hooking her arm through his, she followed the

boys up the lane toward the store, pulling Zeb with her.

He fell into step beside her and leaned close. "I missed you."

"I missed you, too, Zeb the Great."

He pulled his arm from hers and placed it around her waist. "I'm glad."

Mike's head popped out from a nearby bush. "So, brother, looks like your day's takin' a turn for the better."

"You get out of here and mind your own business." Zeb playfully made a run for his little brother, who disappeared into the weeds. A few yards ahead he emerged and joined Duke and Luke on their trek up the lane. One last backward glance, accompanied by a huge grin, earned him a mock fist shake from Zeb.

This time his arm came across her shoulders and squeezed tight. She wanted to stop on the spot and plant a kiss on that kind, troubled face. But she suppressed the urge. "Truly, how *was* your day?"

With the store now in sight, he dropped his arm to his side and matched her pace. "It was good, and it was bad. The kids gave no trouble, and Walter was on escort duty all day again today. But the stress, the not knowing, has me jumpin' at every little sound."

Katie wanted to embrace him, tell him everything would be alright.

But would it?

Her mind raced as they passed what she had mentally begun to refer to as *Rebel's bush*.

The little dog was nowhere to be seen, but Boomer stood inside the gate glaring at Zeb. "Grab that no good kid you call a brother and git over here. The cow's out."

Zeb cringed. "I'm sorry, Katie. If I don't do it, he'll take it out on Mom and Mike when I'm not home."

Katie had hoped to spend some more time with him, maybe discuss the kidnapping—and other things. "It's okay. You gotta do what you gotta do."

He shook his head and gave her arm a light cuff. "Thanks for understanding."

She cuffed him back. "See ya later."

Glancing around, she faced an empty lane. The twins. Her heart leaped into her throat. A door slammed.

Relief flooded through her veins as the screen door of Hollisters' store bounced open, and Duke's face peered out at her. "Hey, Katie, come on in here. Hazel's givin' out free Cokes."

Luke's small hand, waving a full soda bottle, extended through the opening underneath his brother's arm. "Cokes."

"Don't drop it." Katie's warning was met with giggles, as both boys ducked back inside with another door slam. Katie sprinted across the driveway and onto the porch.

Hazel pushed open the door and beckoned her inside. "Here ya go. Today the treats are on me." She handed Katie the cold drink.

Katie took a swig of welcome relief as the fizz tingled the inside of her mouth. "Aaaah. That tastes good. But you didn't need to do that."

The woman straightened her apron. "Wanted to. Had to do it before Fred got back. That old worm's so tight he squeaks."

The mention of Fred's name made Katie's skin crawl. Had he played a part in Davey's disappearance? Was he a threat to the twins? Or was he just an innocent guy with a bad attitude?

The clunk of footsteps on the porch brought her speculation to a halt. Fred threw open the door and faced Hazel. "Who you callin' a worm, woman?"

Hazel retaliated. "If the shoe fits, wear it."

Fred hooked his thumbs in his galluses and rared back, sticking out his stomach. "I wouldn't be talkin' about shoes if I had feet the size of runnin' boards."

Hazel didn't miss a beat. "Well, you started this whole mess. At least, I didn't let our grandson get run-off-with."

Fred glowered. "I didn't start nothin'."

While the argument escalated, Katie caught Luke's eye and mouthed, "Let's go." Luke nudged his brother, and without a word, the two followed Katie out the door.

Placing their empty soda bottles in a box near the door, the three crossed the highway and made their way toward home. The boys meandered from one side of the lane to the other, examining rocks, sticks, and anything else they considered clue-worthy.

Katie, glad for their distractions, made no effort to hurry them along. Her own slow pace was no match for the breakneck speed of her thoughts. She was missing something. They all were. But what? She began to list the suspects in her mind.

Fred was such a jerk. But would he, could he, go so far as to make sure Davey was out of his way? Permanently?

"Katie, what's this?" Luke held a smooth white oblong object in front of her, but Duke asked the question.

Taking it in her hand, she examined it. "Looks like some kind of animal bone to me."

"Okay." Duke took the bone and handed it back to Luke, who stuck it in his pocket.

Katie followed behind her charges. A bone. Bone. What about Bone? He was certainly free with his threats. But did he really have the nerve to carry out any of them? Of was he just a bunch of hot air?

And Boomer. Hateful old buzzard. But what could he have had against Davey? And besides, he was too busy mistreating his own family to worry about causing grief to another.

Then there was Lyle Piper. He was a mystery. How could he have gotten that note in the Hollisters' mailbox, and then disappeared without being detected? And if he did, where did he go?

The twins had squatted in the middle of the lane, examining a kildeer's nest. Duke poked Luke in the chest. "Ya see, the mother killdeer pretends to be hurt. She flops around away from the nest, so the enemies will follow her and not bother the eggs. She's protectin' the kids. You know, like Walter's been protectin' us at school."

Luke nodded, then stood, and the boys walked on.

Walter Bailor had been such a help to Zeb these last two days. He was the only one of that clan that acted like he had good sense. But what about his brothers? Tank was in jail, and Flat was dead. Did Tip have a reason to want to hurt Davey?

Wait a minute. Maybe it wasn't Davey the kidnapper wanted to hurt. Maybe it was Fred and Hazel. Or maybe it was just Fred.

Her mind spun. The seclusion of the trees that lined either side of the lane gave way to the Banks' fence row and open field. Out of habit, Katie focused her gaze toward the barn. Manfred Olsen, their newly acquired resident hobo, lurked near its door.

What was he doing? He glanced up, and for a split second, their eyes met. The man ducked his head and twisted away.

"Boys, come on. Let's get in the house and wash up for supper."

As they trotted past her, Katie shot another quick look across the field. Manfred Olsen stood leaning against the side of the barn, staring at her. When their eyes met, he hastened through the open door.

She dashed onto the porch, but paused momentarily. It seemed to her a coincidence that the hobo would show up at this time. But then if he had anything to do with the kidnapping, wouldn't this be the perfect cover-up? Just come around acting like nothing had happened?

Yes, she was going to have to do a little investigating on her own. Definitely. She entered the house, a plan taking shape in her mind.

"Well, the dickens." Aunt Nellie tapped the flour tin on the kitchen table. "If I shake it loose, we've got enough flour for supper, but there won't be any left for us to use in the morning. I knew there was something I forgot to pick up at Hollisters. Katie, honey, would you care to run down there and get some before the store closes for the night?"

The dear woman's very presence gave the house a warm, cozy atmosphere, and Katie would do anything for her. "Sure. I'll be back in a jiffy." She spun on her heel and headed for the door.

Once outside, Katie looked straight ahead and tried to ignore the ever-present barn with its eerie new occupant. But as she entered the tree canopy, perspiration trickled down her back, and not from the August heat. She was being watched. She could sense it as sure as bluebirds were blue. She stroked the smooth enamel of the pin securely attached to the inside of her pocket.

Maybe one quick glance. She peered through the trees' lengthening shadows. and standing mere feet away was Manfred Olsen, his gaze fixed intently on her. Unwavering, she met his stare. The man averted his eyes, then ducked his head and rushed off toward the barn.

Katie's heart pounded as her easy gait turned to a trot. By the time she reached the highway, her canter had become a run, and she paused for only a moment before racing across.

"Hey, there, what's the rush?" Zeb stood in his

front yard, leaning on a fence post.

Her heart soared with pleasure, and relief, at the sight of the familiar face, his soft eyes radiating kindness and friendship. *Or something more?*

She leaned on a fence post to catch her breath. "We're out of flour. I need to get some before the store closes."

Zeb patted her on the back. "You're out of breath, Katie girl. That sack of flour must be pretty urgent." He chuckled. "There's no hurry. They'll stay open for at least another hour. Visit with me a little bit. We've got Boomer satisfied for the time being, and Mom's in there making supper. I think Mike's out back in what garden we've got."

"I'd better get my errand run first. I'll be back in a minute." Truth was, Katie wanted to get in and out of that store as quickly as possible. Olsen staring at her through the trees, and Fred lurking no telling where made it seem that she was walking out of the frying pan and into the fire.

Zeb straightened and stuck his hands in his pockets. "I'll be here."

Hazel was alone in the store, thankfully. Katie purchased the flour and had the woman add it to Marcus's tab. "Thanks. See you later."

Zeb stood at the edge of the porch as Katie emerged from the store. He reached out to take the load from her. "Don't guess you'd like an escort home?"

She released the sack to Zeb, hoping he couldn't detect the relief she felt at not having to navigate that lane alone. "You wouldn't believe how much I'd appreciate that."

He flung the sack across a shoulder, his eyes twinkling, and winked at her. "Oh, I don't know. I might."

Once they were across the road, Zeb turned to her, the joviality gone from his eyes. "Okay, give. What's up?"

"Nothing really, but that hobo keeps staring at me. He was watching me again this afternoon as I was going after the flour. He just gives me the willies."

Zeb didn't answer immediately, but took her hand and intertwined his fingers with hers. When his words came, they were husky, almost a whisper. "I don't want you to be alone with him around."

Rainbows danced in her head. *He cares. He DOES!* So as not to betray the ecstatic trembling welling inside her, she answered in an easy tone. "Okay."

Zeb stopped and faced her. "I'm serious. Stay away from him. Please."

An uneasy feeling in the pit of her stomach made her want the schoolmaster to stay beside her every second. To protect her. And, together, they could find Davey. "I'll be careful."

Midway up the lane, Zeb stopped again, and pointed to an opening among the trees.

"Look." Manfred Olsen and Marcus, their backs to Katie and Zeb, were walking toward the creek, buckets in hand. "They'll be gone for awhile, and besides, Marcus is with him. Let's relax a little."

He led Katie to a grove of trees on the other side

of the lane, laid down his bundle, and lifted her to the top of a weathered gate. Perching beside her, he put an arm around her waist and placed his other hand over hers. He pulled her close and bent down until his head rested lightly on hers. His slow steady breathing soothed her and the tension in her body gave way to peace, even in the troubled days they were facing.

His breath was soft against her ear. "Listen. Whippoorwills, tree frogs, nature's symphony."

Katie closed her eyes and snuggled against him, drinking in his gentle scents of chalk dust and hay, intermingled with the lingering aroma of Aunt Ella's apple butter. This man, the shelter of whose arms afforded a satisfaction she'd never known, could easily become her world. Easily.

Zeb withdrew his arm and traced a finger along the side of her face. "It's getting late, Katie girl. It'll be dark soon."

Sliding from his perch on the gate, he reached up to assist her. She could have hopped down on her own, but Katie, savoring the moment, allowed him to place his hands around her waist and lift her off the gate to the ground.

As her feet touched solid earth, he wrapped his arms around her and drew her to him. Tilting her chin with a sturdy but gentle hand, he lowered his face and pressed his lips to hers. Stars exploded in her head. Bells pealed. Threads of pleasure raced from her head to her toes and back again.

When the kiss ended, they remained in each other's embrace for what Katie wished could be an eternity.

Zeb drew back and ran a caressing hand over her hair. Hoisting the flour sack to one shoulder, he took her by the hand and led her back to the lane.

When they reached the Banks' yard, Zeb started toward the house. Oh, how Katie wished this evening didn't have to end, but she reached for the sack of flour. "I'll take it from here, Zeb the Great. Aunt Ella was right, you know. The title fits you well. And thanks. For everything."

He kissed the tip of his index finger, then touched it to her lips. "We *will* do this again. Count on it." And his long strides carried him away from her. For now.

She wanted to shout for joy. She wanted to cry— for Davey, for Mama, for what could yet might never be.

That night, Katie lay in bed listening to the tree frogs and whippoorwills, and thinking of Zeb. In her dreams he came to her and wrapped his arms around her, bringing a peace she hadn't known since Davey's disappearance. They sat on a teacher's desk, surrounded by beagles and deputies, and the schoolmaster held her tight, assuring her that everybody was safe, that everything would be alright.

Katie awoke to the silence of a sleeping household. The first one up, and not wanting to disturb her family's Saturday morning sleep, she slipped into a shirt, overalls, and her brogans, and crept to the front room to sit until the others woke.

Aunt Nellie was snoozing away on the daybed at the far end of the room. Katie tiptoed to the rocker and eased herself into it, so as to let their aunt get as much rest as possible.

Bless the woman's heart. She said she liked staying here, and Katie hoped she did. Aunt Nellie lived alone, and Katie made up her mind to talk to Ella about inviting her to stay until the end of September, at least.

Suddenly Marcus and Ella's bedroom door flew open and Ella rushed into the room. "Molly's gone!"

Chapter 15

Ella sailed out the front door in her nightgown.

Marcus dashed into the room, pulling on his shirt as he ran. "Duke! Luke!"

No answer.

Katie and Aunt Nellie, who was wide awake by now, hurried to the boys' room and found it empty. Katie skidded through the house, calling the twins' names. But only silence greeted her.

Her heart pounded. Where was Manfred Olsen?

She ran to the front porch, letting the screen door slam behind her. Ella was already out of sight. Marcus loped toward the barn, frantically yelling over his shoulder. "Run! Look everywhere. Duke! Luke! Molly!"

Aunt Nellie tore around the corner of the house in the opposite direction.

Katie headed for the woods on the other side of the lane. As she crossed, she glanced to her right. Zeb was sauntering up the lane toward her.

She waved her arms. "Zeb, hurry. We need your

help."

Without waiting for a response, she rushed into the woods.

~

Zeb's breath caught at Katie's words, and he broke into a run.

Dashing into the forest at the spot where she'd entered, he dodged low-hanging branches and leapt over logs and debris on the forest floor. "Katie, wait."

He finally spied her, bent over, one arm outstretched with her hand against a tree for support, her breath coming in short gasps. Stepping to the tree and kneeling before her, he watched her wipe her face with the back of her hand, her chest heaving in and out.

"What's wrong?"

She straightened up and leaned back against the tree trunk. Moving to stand in front of her, he grasped her shoulders and searched her face. She returned a wordless stare, a mixture of pain and horror radiating from those heavenly blue eyes.

"What is it?"

Taking a deep breath, she pulled away. "There's no time to lose. The kids are gone. All three of them. Sometime during the night. We woke this morning to find them all missing."

She turned and appeared ready to bolt, but Zeb grabbed her hand. She struggled to free it, but he held it fast, pulling her in the direction from which she'd come. "Quick, where's Marcus's fox horn?"

Bouncing back and forth from one foot to the

other, she scanned the area as she talked. "We have to find the kids."

He tried not to let the fear inside him surface on his face. "I know. I'm gonna alert Deputy Fox. He'll be right here. Now, where is it?"

Already dashing back among the trees, Katie called over her shoulder. "In the front room. On the wall inside the door."

Zeb turned toward the house and met Aunt Nellie coming across the yard carrying the horn. "I heard. Here it is. Oh, Zeb, what'll we do?"

Snatching the apparatus from her hand, and hoping against hope, he put it to his lips. He blew like there was no tomorrow. He blew till he was dizzy—long, loud blasts on the instrument. And again. And again.

Placing the horn back in the woman's hand, he recognized and understood the panic etched across her features. "Thanks. Help's on the way. Deputy Fox should be here any minute. Wait for him at the house and fill him in on what's happened. I'm going to help them search."

Aunt Nellie twisted her apron in her free hand.

An answering call split the morning stillness. Zeb recognized the sound. "That's him. He's coming. Hold on tight."

Zeb raced toward the woods, and Katie. Who could have taken the kids? And how long ago? And why hadn't they made any noise? The kids had not been alone in the house. And the doors had to have been locked. So how did the kidnapper get in, and how did he keep all three children quiet?

Oh, Lord, help us. Don't let them be hurt—or dead. Will this nightmare never end?

Zeb joined Katie and they searched every nook and cranny that side of the lane. Their voices echoed through the morning stillness. "Duke! Luke!"

But there was no answer.

No giggles.

Nothing.

Katie sank to the ground beneath an old oak tree. Zeb knelt beside her and laid a hand on her knee. "Let's calm down and decide what to do. Deputy Fox and Rebel are on the way. What say we head back to the house and get this search organized?"

Katie swiped at an eye with one finger. "You're right. Let's go talk to the deputy." She pushed to her feet and started back through the woods. He stepped beside her and put an arm around her shoulders. She was trembling.

"You don't have to be strong. This is serious. It's okay to be upset. Lean on me,

Katie girl."

She didn't answer, but she let him guide her back to the lane.

When they reached the yard, Deputy Fox was already there with Rebel. Marcus, Ella, and Aunt Nellie stood facing him. He beckoned to Zeb and Katie. "Marcus said he found Manfred Olsen asleep in the barn. Or at least he *said* he'd been asleep. But Marcus wants him questioned, and that's exactly what I plan to do."

Zeb's mind replayed the events of the day before—the hobo's obsession with Katie. He edged nearer to her. Exactly what was the man capable of doing, and to whom? He pulled her to him. No one protested.

Deputy Fox squatted on the ground and slapped his leg. Rebel sidled up to him expectantly. "Ready to get to work, boy?"

The beagle's bright eyes glistened in the sunlight. With a woof the dog put both front paws on the deputy's leg and wiggled in anticipation.

Deputy Fox addressed everyone, and no one in particular. "We need to get something that belongs to Molly and let Rebel sniff it. He'll track her. We'll give that little nose a workout. Won't we, boy?" He scruffed the dog's head.

Aunt Nellie started for the porch, then paused. "What about the boys?"

The deputy stood. "One scent at a time, or we'll confuse Rebel. If we find Molly, I'm saying we'll find the boys, too. I'm guessing one person was responsible for this whole thing, and that all three kids are together."

"Sit down, Aunt Nellie. I've got this." She sank into the porch swing, while Katie scurried into the house and returned with a baby quilt. She handed it to the deputy, who knelt and allowed Rebel to sniff it up and down.

Leaning against Marcus, Ella stared at the deputy and dog. "Do you think they're hurt? Or worse?' Her voice broke on the last word.

The deputy kept his eyes on his dog. "We won't even think like that. We're going to find them and get them back to you, safe and sound."

Pulling the quilt away, he locked eyes with the dog. "Rebel. Go find."

The little dog trembled and strained at the leash, then darted off around the house and across the field, nose to the ground. Deputy Fox loped along beside him.

Manfred Olsen staggered out of the barn, rubbing his eyes. "Guess I musta dozed back off. What's up?"

Marcus planted his feet in front of the man. "Why don't *you* tell us, Olsen?"

The hobo scratched his head, befuddled. "Tell you what? What's goin' on here, man?"

"The kids are gone. I don't suppose you'd have any idea where they'd be, would you?" Marcus's tone indicated his patience was wearing thin.

The man rubbed his chin. "Nope, can't say that I would."

Marcus's voice rose. "Did you take those kids?"

Mr. Olsen looked hurt. "Of course not."

Marcus's eyes blazed. "If you didn't take them, then help us look for them."

The hobo lifted a hand to shade his face from the morning sunlight. Zeb watched his eyes travel around the small group, momentarily resting on Katie, but quickly moving to center on Marcus. "Sure I'll help. I like those little guys. Don't wanna see any harm come to 'em."

The hobo's face clouded with—what?

Compassion? Either this guy was innocent or he was one great actor.

Deputy Fox and Rebel were nearing the creek when Katie nudged Zeb. "Let's follow them. We can catch up with 'em if we run."

Hand in hand, Katie and Zeb covered the distance in a flash, and reached the pair just as Rebel made a beeline for the foot log spanning the creek's width. Fox barreled through the water while the dog pushed on across the little bridge, nose to the ground—or in this case, the log.

Once on the other side, Rebel made a flying leap and dashed across the next field. His human counterparts ran to keep up, while the little dog pursued his quarry.

"Look." Katie yanked on Zeb's arm and pointed.

Chapter 16

Rebel was racing straight toward Bluebird Valley Church, but that wasn't what drew Zeb's attention. Brother Deren, carrying a large picnic basket, emerged through the open front door. Flanking the pastor on either side, heads down, were Duke and Luke.

Rebel, nose snuffling the ground furiously, made his way to Brother Deren-and stopped, stretching on his hind legs and whimpering and pawing at the basket.

"Duke! Luke!" Katie let go of Zeb's hand and rushed to the twins.

The boys raised their heads in acknowledgement, but immediately lowered them again and said nothing.

Deputy Fox eyed the preacher. "Let's see what you've got in that basket."

"Sure." Brother Deren smiled and pulled back the cloth to reveal a sleeping Molly.

Fox extracted a treat from his pocket and offered it to his beagle turned bloodhound. "Good boy."

The deputy, his brows furrowed, turned his attention back to the preacher. "I'm afraid I'm going to need some answers from you, Reverend Grayson."

Brother Deren, kindness radiating from his very being, handed the picnic basket to Katie, then patted the deputy's shoulder. "Of course, you will. And we have answers for you." He indicated the subdued twins with a sweeping motion of his hand. "Don't we, boys?"

Duke, head still lowered, muttered. "Yes, sir."

Luke drew in a quivering breath and sniffled loudly.

Brother Deren knelt and pulled the boys to him. "It'll be alright, guys. Let's go home."

The two leaned into him and buried their faces against his shirt. His arms still around the boys, the pastor peered up at his dumbfounded observers. "We need to get these kids back home. I know their folks're crazy with worry. I'll go with you to the house, and we can talk there."

It was a quiet procession that made its way back to the Banks' property. The boys hung close to their pastor, and Katie carried Molly in her arms. Zeb swung the empty picnic basket at his side, his thoughts flying higher than the bluebird that lit on a fence post, then spread its wings and ascended toward the heavens.

How in the world did Brother Deren end up with all three of the Banks kids? Where did he find them? Surely he didn't take them. No, that's ridiculous. Maybe that hobo, Manfred Olsen, stole them, and Brother Deren caught him in time to rescue them. But then, how did Olsen get them out of the house without making any noise? How did he even get *in* the house in the first place?

There were no logical answers. Nothing made sense. Zeb's temples ached, and light-headedness made his steps waver.

"Hey, buddy. You okay?" Fox, his eyes showing concern, had fallen into step beside Zeb.

"Yeah, I'm alright. Just lost in my own thoughts, I guess." But he appreciated the man's concern, so much. If only Boomer would show a bit of compassion. If not for him, at least for his mom, and Mike. Hot tears stung the backs of his eyes, and he turned away.

Fox clamped a hand on his shoulder and squeezed. "Okay then. Long as you're alright. Take it easy, buddy." And he walked on ahead.

When the house was barely in sight, Ella came flying across the field to meet their little menagerie. Snatching Molly from Katie's arms, she showered the child with kisses and tears. Marcus, close behind, grabbed a twin in each arm and hugged them like Zeb remembered Zeke Harlow hugging him—a long, long time ago.

I hope they appreciate it. Oh, Lord, I hope they realize what they've got.

Inside the house, the questions began.

"Where were they?" Aunt Nellie sat on the daybed beside Katie, hanging onto the young woman's hand as if her life depended on it.

"Did anybody hurt you?" Marcus directed his question at Duke and Luke, sitting at the kitchen table and drinking glasses of milk.

Ella rested in the old rocker, cradling Molly in her arms.

Brother Deren sat in a cane-bottom chair near the front door and Deputy Fox squatted on the floor across from him, leaning back against the wall, Rebel at his side. "Let's let Reverend Grayson tell us what happened. That okay by you, Preacher?"

Brother Deren crossed his legs and eyed the twins. "I'll tell you our story the best I can, but I'll need Luke and Duke's help. Okay?"

Two white-mustached faces solemnly nodded.

"Well," the preacher began, "I went to the church early this morning like I do every Saturday to tidy up a bit and get ready for the Sunday services. But today when I got to the front of the chapel, I found those two sitting on the floor at the foot of the cross with that picnic basket between them. Naturally, I asked what they were doing." He nodded toward the boys. "Your turn."

Duke wiped his upper lip with his shirtsleeve and slid off the chair. He began in a low voice. "We... uh, we..."

Luke slid off his chair and stood beside his brother, putting an arm around him and whispering something in his ear.

Duke returned the hug, and they stood side-by-side. He tried again, Luke nodding encouragement. "We was scared that Molly'd get took like Davey did. So we took her to the cross, so in case she did, she'd have ref... uh, ref..."

Luke whispered in Duke's ear again. Duke smiled.

"Refuge."

Marcus's eyes widened. "You mean you boys..."

"Tell the rest of it, Duke." Brother Deren leaned forward.

The child shuffled his feet. "Well, there's ref... ref..."

"Refuge!" Luke blurted.

"Refuge at the cross, so we put her in the basket and we carried her to the cross. Davey's safe 'cause of the cross. We know. But we can't see him. But he's safe. So we wanted our little sister to be safe, too. So we took her to the cross." Duke took a deep breath and leaned against his brother.

Deputy Fox got up and squatted in front of the boys. "Do you know where Davey is?"

They both shook their heads. Duke bent to pet Rebel. "But we know he's safe. We seen the cross."

Brother Deren stood. "That's exactly what they told me. I'm not sure what it all means, but I wanted you to hear it from them. I need to be going, but let's have a word of prayer first."

Everyone joined hands and bowed their heads. "Almighty God, thank You for blessing our lives even in these troubled times. Thank You for keeping these children safe, and bringing them home to their parents. Be with Davey, wherever he is, and protect him and bring him home safely to us, too. We thank You for the blood. In the name of Jesus Christ, our Lord, we pray. Amen."

The dear man stepped to the door. "I'll be checking in from time to time. Take care."

And he was gone.

Zeb glanced at Katie. Her gaze was focused on the twins. He wondered. What did it mean—they saw the cross, and they knew Davey was safe? *How* did they know? What had they seen? *Who* had they seen?

~

The cogs in Katie's brain spun into overtime. She needed to talk to her little cousins. In private. And she needed to talk to Zeb. Also in private. She glanced at the handsome schoolmaster, who just happened to be glancing at her. "Do you have a few minutes? Would you mind waiting for me on the porch?"

His smile lit up the room. "Take your time. I'll be there." He stood and sauntered out the door.

Marcus had followed Zeb outside, and Aunt Nellie and Ella had taken Molly into the bedroom, so Katie and the boys were alone. She nabbed a chair and pulled it up to the table. "Guys, would you tell me your story again? The one about why you took Molly to the church? That was a long way to walk."

Duke drained the last drops of milk from his glass. "We had to do it. We had to find the cross. If you see the cross it means the little kid's safe from the bad man."

An invisible vise gripped Katie's brain and made her eyes hurt. "What bad man, Duke?"

Luke chimed in. "The bad man."

Katie licked her index finger and held it in the air. Each boy did the same. "Promise time. Be honest."

They nodded solemnly.

"What do you mean? Did you see a bad man?"

Luke shook his head.

Duke responded to the question. "No. But we seen the cross."

"Where?" Katie was on the edge of her seat. "Where did you see the cross?"

The boys didn't answer the question right away.

Duke squeezed his eyes shut. "Davey's fine, and he's safe from the bad man. But we had to promise not to tell, 'cause if we did tell, then the bad man might get him. We got cinnamon sticks. And we seen the cross."

These little guys were hiding some vital information. She had to find out what they knew. She scooted her chair until it touched Duke's, and spoke in low tones. "Duke, please tell me where you saw the cross. And who gave you the cinnamon sticks."

The child leaned away from her, his eyes huge. "But we promised. Dad said you never break a promise. You know that, Katie."

She persisted. "But this is important. Please, Duke."

He shook his head vigorously. "Uh-UH. A promise is a promise."

Luke slapped his brother on the back. "A promise."

Drat.

There was no use pursuing this any further. Their minds were set, and this was crucial. Doggone that Marcus. Well, she'd just have to tell this to Deputy Fox. Let him handle it. But first she'd discuss it with Zeb.

She pushed her chair back and stood. "Okay, guys. If you change your mind, come tell me."

They shot her looks that plainly said that wasn't about to happen.

She turned her back on them and opened the door.

Zeb stood leaning against a support post, his arms folded. Katie sank to the porch step and patted the spot beside her. He sat, scooting close and causing that familiar warm tingle to surge through her. "What's on your mind?"

Hooking her arm through his, she sighed. "Those boys know something. Something important. I think they have the key to Davey's disappearance, but they're not telling."

His eyes darkened, and he turned to face her. "Oh?"

She told him every detail of her conversation with the twins. "So, who would have access to cinnamon sticks?"

They sat in silence for a moment. Katie's vision became a blur as she stared into the trees across the road. Then something clicked in her brain. Swiveling to face Zeb, she snapped her fingers and opened her mouth to speak, as Zeb did the same. In unison, they voiced identical thoughts. "Fred!"

The store didn't carry cinnamon sticks, but Fred could order anything he wanted from the supply man, and as long as he paid, no one would ever have to know.

But why? And what had he done with Davey?

The sound of bare feet on packed dirt drew Katie's attention. Mike raced up the lane and stopped in front of them. "Zeb, Dad said to come a-runnin.' The cow's out."

Zeb wilted before her very eyes. "And what if I don't?"

The preteen's lower lip trembled. "You know what'll happen. He'll give me another lickin' if you don't."

The man got up and brushed off his jeans. "I know he will. Run home and tell him I'm on the way."

"Thanks, brother." The kid staged a 180-degree turn, and raced off down the lane.

Zeb, his mouth set in a grim line, took Katie's hand in his. "I'll have to go. Blasted cow. Blasted Boomer. But I'll be back."

Katie stayed on the step and watched Zeb until he was out of sight. Then, placing her elbows on her knees, she cradled her chin in her hands. She had to tell Deputy Fox about Fred as soon as possible. Other lives could be in danger. The old coot was crazy.

The crackling sound of footsteps on dry grass startled her. She sprang to her feet.

"Katie." Manfred Olsen stood at the end of the porch.

Chapter 17

Shards of panic shot through her veins. A scream threatened to erupt from her throat. She ran to the door, and yanked it open.

"Katie, wait."

Darting into the house, she didn't look back. As she crossed the front room, the corner of her eye caught a movement at the open window. Olsen had rounded the corner of the house and was peering in at her. She dashed into her bedroom, slammed down the window, and pulled the curtain shut. Shaking, she sank to the bed and buried her face in the pillow.

Katie wasn't sure how long she'd slept, but Aunt Nellie's soft caress on her forehead made her open her eyes. "Honey, wake up. Zeb's in the front room. He wants to see you."

Swinging her legs over the edge of the bed, she brushed her hair away from her face. "Thanks, Aunt Nellie. Tell him I'll be right there."

"Okay, I'll let him know." The woman stepped out

of the room, closing the door behind her.

Katie splashed her face with water from the enamel basin on her washstand and ran a brush through her hair. Then she opened the bedroom door.

"Well, it's about time you got in here. Remember, we had a date." Zeb, one ankle propped on the opposite knee and hands laced behind his head, leaned back against the couch, a mischievous grin adorning his wonderful face.

He considers it a date. Oh, yes.

Katie's heart sang, her ordeal with Olsen forgotten for the moment. "Here I am." She plopped down beside him, giving him a punch on the shoulder.

He laid an arm across the back of the couch and let it drop to her shoulders. "I've got it all planned out. We'll go by the store and get some comma-doodles and something cold to drink, then head for the hills." He chuckled as she took it all in.

Katie eyed him, trying to appear suspicious. "What's a comma-doodle?"

"I'll tell you when we get there. But you'll like it." He stood and pulled Katie up by the hand. "Ready?"

Hand in hand they strolled down the lane without saying a word. Zeb broke the silence. "A penny for your thoughts?"

Katie considered. She liked, maybe loved, this guy. "Okay."

Delight shone in his eyes, and he squeezed her hand tighter.

"I'm afraid of Manfred Olsen. He gives me the heebie-jeebies."

Zeb turned serious and slowed his pace. "What's he done now?"

"After you left, he approached me at the porch and tried to get me to talk to him." She watched for a reaction.

Zeb stopped and gripped her shoulders. "Don't do it. We don't know him, and I do not like how he's always starin' at you."

"But what do you think he wants?"

Zeb's eyes narrowed, and a grimace crossed his lips. "You know what he wants. What does any man want? Now stay away from him." He threw his arms around her and hugged her tight. Then he drew back, his voice softer. "Stay away from him."

At the intersection of the lane and highway, Zeb pointed. "There's Fred."

The man sat in one of the cane-bottom chairs on the front porch of Hollisters' store. Katie edged closer to Zeb. "What's he doing?"

A rifle across his knees, Fred was running an old piece of cloth up and down the barrel that glinted in the late morning sunlight. A bowl sat on the floor by his chair.

Zeb put a hand behind Katie's back, and guided her to the gravel parking lot. Davey's pup, unnoticed by Fred, crept onto the porch and stuck its face into the bowl. "Choo." The pup sneezed. Startled, Fred jumped to his feet, the rifle clattering to the wooden floor. "Get outta here, you ornery mutt. Get outta my Cream of Wheat."

The pup made a dash for the end of the porch.

Fred, shaking his fist and muttering, tottered after the little terrier.

Zeb, grinning, nudged Katie. "Let's take the opportunity while it's here." He hooked a thumb through her gallus and tugged her toward the store.

Stifling a chuckle, she followed. Sometimes Fred was scary, but at times like this, one wondered if he was perhaps a few apples shy of a bushel. Her thoughts sobered. If his mind did have on and off moments, wouldn't that make him even more dangerous?

Hazel stood behind the counter, lines of weariness etching her face. Her eyes brightened at the sight of them. "Mornin,' you two. What can I do for ya?"

Zeb stepped forward, placing both hands on the counter. In mock seriousness, he lowered his head and looked sideways at Katie, then addressed Hazel. "Hazel, would you believe this lady here has never heard of a comma-doodle?"

The older woman slapped her own face, feigning horror. "No! Well then, she's in for a treat. How many would you like?"

Zeb moved to the soda box and extracted two icy Cokes. "Oh, I guess two'll do for starters. And we need them to go."

Hazel snorted. "You don't think I'd let you eat those things in here, do you? Last time you did that, I was sweepin' crumbs off the floor for a week."

Katie's curiosity got the best of her. She leaned across the counter, watching Hazel's every move. The woman spread a piece of butcher paper on the smooth surface. She laid two nice big four-section saltine crackers on it side by side. Then, butcher knife in hand, she soon covered each cracker with a thick slice of bologna, topped by a slice of cheese. The whole concoction was covered with yet another cracker, amply spread with mustard.

The tantalizing aromas drifted to Katie's nose, and her mouth watered.

Hazel wrapped each sandwich separately, dropped them into a bag, and handed the bag to Zeb. She winked at Katie. "So there you have it—your first official comma-doodle sandwich."

Zeb paid the woman. "Thanks, Hazel."

She took the money and popped open the cash register drawer. "You two have a good time with those."

The sun was high in the sky when they stepped outside, and Katie's stomach rumbled. Zeb bumped her with his shoulder. "Hungry?"

Her face grew warm, and she clutched her stomach in hopes of warding off another outburst. "A little."

"Then let's head for the hills."

He led her down the lane, past Rebel's bush, and through the field in back of the schoolhouse. Beyond the creek, a narrow trail led them upward to a grassy knoll overlooking—everything. The view was breathtaking. Her house, Zeb's house, Hollisters' store. A view of the whole valley was there.

"It's beautiful."

"Glad you like it." He ushered her to a shaded spot

underneath a huge elm at the edge of the clearing. "Have a seat."

She slid to the ground and sat cross-legged, drinking in the peacefulness of this spot above the world.

Zeb handed her a sandwich and a Coke. "Mind if I say the blessing?"

Katie's heart surged at the nearness of this kind-hearted man. "I'd be honored."

They bowed their heads. "Thank you, Lord, for this food, and this ray of sunshine sitting here beside me. And watch over Davey. Amen."

Pulling a metal bottle opener from his pocket, Zeb popped open the soda caps, then unwrapped his sandwich.

Katie took a bite of hers, and cracker crumbs flew. They both laughed. Tensions lifted.

When they had finished, Zeb stretched out on his back, hands behind his head. A bird chirped. Zeb closed his eyes. "I'm glad comma-doodles are crumbly. That way we can leave something for the bluebirds."

Katie slid a hand over the enamel pin in her pocket. Bluebirds were supposed to bring happiness. Mama and Aunt Ella had said so. *Little enamel feathered friend, do your work.*

"What do you think? Do you think we'll ever see Davey again?"

She stretched out on her stomach beside him on the cool grass. "I think we'll find Davey, and I think God will take care of him till we do. I've been praying every day, and I think everything's gonna be alright."

Zeb opened one eye. "I've prayed, too. You don't know how much."

She had a pretty good idea how much, and for what. "I want to investigate Fred and some others. Are you game, or am I in this alone?"

The schoolmaster sat bolt upright. "What others? And what do you mean by investigate? I don't want you in any danger." He rubbed his temples and ran his palms down the sides of his face.

"I'd just like to do a little looking around—unobserved, of course, and maybe ask a few questions." She pushed to a sitting position and pulled her knees to her, wrapping her arms around them. From this vantage point, with the valley spread out before her, she could envision any number of hiding places for a kidnapper to stash a child. Or a body. Her gut tightened.

Zeb rubbed his eyes. "You want us to spy. That's what you want, isn't it?"

"You want us to find Davey, don't you?" She had him there, and she knew it.

Zeb leaned forward and covered his face with his hands. He squeezed his eyes shut, and an audible sigh escaped from his lips. "I'm game."

Chapter 18

Katie shaded her eyes and surveyed the valley. "You won't be sorry. The Katie and Zeb Detective Agency always gets their man." Then she sobered and tucked a few flyaway strands of golden hair behind her right ear. "Thanks for being willing to help."

Zeb surveyed the expanse of their little community and the unending woods surrounding it. Bone, Manfred Olsen, Fred, and the elusive Lyle Piper paraded through his mind's eye, and mental warning sirens blared.

What had he gotten himself into? What was he thinking? "You're welcome." *I guess.*

She scooted back and leaned against the tree trunk. "Okay, we'll need a plan, doncha think?"

He joined her, a mixture of dread and excitement pulsing through his veins. Maybe they *could* solve this case. Maybe they just could. Boomer wouldn't call him stupid then. He wondered what it would be like to receive a compliment from Boomer. The possibility was too far-fetched to even imagine. *Oh, well.*

"Well?" Katie tapped him on the knee. "Wouldn't you say we need a plan?"

Zeb jumped, startled out of his daydream. "Oh, yeah. Absolutely. We have to have a plan."

"Okay, then." She grabbed the empty paper bag and smoothed it against her leg. Then she set about checking her pockets. "We need to list the suspects—and our strategies. Do you have a pencil?"

"No."

Her tongue clicked a "tsk-tsk" and she shook her head. "A teacher without a pencil. My, my, what's this world coming to?"

Feigning offense, he put his hands on his hips. "Well, it *is* Saturday. I'm off duty, you know."

Katie replaced the bag on the ground between them. "That's okay. I have some at home. How about I write out a list tonight and bring it to church tomorrow?"

Church! Surely she wasn't thinking of doing any of her sleuthing at church. "Yeah, I'll be there unless Boomer decides to throw a monkey wrench in my plans. But, Katie…"

She cut him off mid-sentence. "Okay then, I'll get our list ready tonight and give it to you in the morning at church. That way, you'll have a chance to look it over before we meet tomorrow afternoon."

Zeb didn't bother to respond. This spunky little gal was slowly but surely worming her way into his heart—and taking up residence. He waited.

"I thought we could both go home after church,

eat dinner, and change clothes. Then maybe we could meet back up here again around two o'clock." She flashed a quirky smile that engulfed her whole face. "And plan our next move."

An aura of uneasiness descended on Zeb. He bit the inside of his jaw until it hurt. "So what do we do now?"

She patted his hand. "Nothing. We haven't planned our strategy yet. We can't go into this blind or we're likely to slip up somewhere, and tomorrow should be soon enough to start. Let's just relax for now and enjoy the rest of the afternoon."

She leaned against him and laid her head on his shoulder. Zeb slipped an arm around her and drank in the beauty of God's creation, both spanning the valley and resting on the ground beside him.

But somewhere out there, maybe not far away, lurked a kidnapper. An overwhelming urge to protect this feisty little gal invaded his mind. He pulled her closer and draped a hand over her shoulder.

Katie reached up and placed her hand over his. "This is nice. Such a peaceful place."

He leaned forward, wrapping his arms around her. She returned the embrace, and their lips met. As he held her close, her heart beating out a rhythm against his chest, he was sure he was experiencing a taste of what heaven would be like. Beauty everywhere, and an angel in his arms.

Sunshine gave way to lengthening shadows, and whippoorwills' calls filled the evening air. "Guess we'd better be going. It'll be dark before you know it." Zeb gathered up their empty soda bottles and stuffed the crumpled sandwich wrappers in the paper bag. Pushing to his feet, he gave Katie a hand up.

Single file, they descended the narrow forest path, then retraced their steps up the lane. Just outside the fence surrounding the Slocum property, Zeb deposited the bag in a patch of grass near the bush Rebel had so diligently investigated days before. "Let's return these bottles to the store now, and I'll pick up the bag later after I walk you home."

Bottles in hand, he and Katie started across the yard to Hollisters and met Fred stepping off the end of the porch, wielding a hammer. The older man grunted a hello and headed around back of the building in the gathering dusk. *That's odd,* she thought.

Katie grabbed Zeb's arm and jerked him back. "Oh, my word. Look, Zeb. He's killed Bone."

Sure enough, Bone lay face down in the gravel in front of the store, one leg awkwardly lodged against the bottom step. In the evening shadows the man lay completely still and did, indeed, give every indication of being dead.

While Zeb's brain wrestled with how to handle the situation, the screen door opened, and Hazel's face appeared in the waning daylight. Shaking her head, she glanced their way and spoke in a disgusted tone. "Is Bone still out there? I'd a'thought Fred woulda got rid of 'im by now."

Katie's body went rigid against Zeb, and he cleared his throat. "Uh, Hazel, I think he did."

The woman stepped out onto the porch. "No, he

didn't. I can see him from here. I told Fred to drag 'im off somewhere. We'll lose business if people see him a-layin' there that way."

Fred stumbled back onto the porch, still carrying the hammer. He thrust it into his wife's hands. "Here. I think I've jammed the handle back on for ya to where it'll stay this time. If you wouldn't use it so rough, it wouldn't keep a-comin' off like that."

Hazel grabbed the tool, then flipped Fred on the ear. "I thought I told you to drag Bone's useless ol' body off somewhere."

Fred slapped her hand away. "You want it drug off, you drag it. He's heavy. Leave 'im right there till he sobers up, and then he can drag hisself away."

Sobers up? Zeb backed away a few steps, pulling Katie with him. "We thought he was dead."

Fred plopped onto a chair. "Dead? Shoot no, he ain't dead. Wish he was. He's dead drunk, is what he is."

Hazel gave a snort and went in, slamming the door behind her, followed by the sound of a lock clicking into place.

Fred tilted his chair back on two legs. "Humph, she's locked me out again. Oh, well, I can always climb in a window. I've had to do it before."

Zeb's eyes met Katie's, and their gazes locked. He wondered if they were both thinking the same thing. He extended the bottles to Fred, who lazily indicated a spot near the door. Zeb bent over and placed them there.

When he turned around, Katie, wide-eyed, was

standing stock still out by the gas pump. He was beside her in seconds. "Let's go."

He took her hand, and they crossed the highway.

"Whew, that was one weird situation." Katie's fingers locked more tightly with Zeb's, then, releasing his hand, she shoved an arm through the bend of his elbow. "Do you think Fred is actually capable of climbing through a window?"

Zeb tilted his head and gazed up at the rising moon casting eerie shadows through the trees, and his thoughts traveled to Olsen and his strangely obsessive stares. The thought of him possibly lurking inside the tree line, within a few feet of Katie, set his nerves on edge. He shook off that visual as best he could.

Katie gave his arm a little jerk. "Well, do you?"

"Do I what?" His thoughts jarred back to the present. He found comfort in Katie's voice, an added reassurance that she was still beside him.

She huffed. "Do you think Fred is capable of climbing through a window?"

"I'm beginning to think that man is capable of doing just about anything."

The silhouette of the Banks' house rose in the evening twilight, letting him know he had seen the gal safely home and simultaneously reminding him that his time with her had almost come to an end—for now.

He placed a hand on her elbow and guided her up the porch steps, then sank onto the wooden swing, pulling her down beside him. Willing her to stay a bit longer, he slid an arm behind her shoulders and drew her closer. Cupping her chin in his hand, he turned her head to face him and gently pressed his lips to hers.

"Woo, woo. Go, Mr. Harlow!" The screen door flew open and Duke appeared in front of them, clapping his hands and hopping from one bare foot to the other.

Zeb jumped back and sprang to his feet. Katie bounced up as well, sending the swing wobbling and creaking on its chain. She shook a finger at the grinning child. "Duke, you get in the house right this minute."

The little boy bopped back inside, giggling.

"I'm sorry, Zeb." She squeezed his hand.

Zeb's face grew warm—no, hot. He took a step or two backward and almost fell off the porch. *Good grief.*

Grabbing at a post, he made contact and caught himself before causing an even more embarrassing situation. "It's okay. Kids are crazy. He didn't mean any harm. Uh, I'll see you tomorrow."

Katie raised a hand and wiggled her fingers in a wave. "See you at church."

What did she think of him now? He'd tried to do something nice, show her she was special, and... He didn't even want to think about it. He hurried across the yard, certain she was watching him, and thinking no telling what. *Fiddlesticks.*

The screen door clacked shut, and Zeb hightailed it toward home, wishing he could convince himself none of this had ever happened. The trees' leafy branches shrouded the lane in early evening shadows, the gathering darkness providing a welcome haven for his wounded pride.

Slowing his pace in the seclusion of darkness, he trudged along feeling sorry for himself, and suddenly became aware he was not alone. Something moved in the bushes the other side of the fence. When he walked, footsteps or paws—big paws—rustled the dry grass. When he stopped, the noise stopped. His muscles tensed.

Taking slow steps, then fast, then slow again, he thought of bears, pumas, wolves. It could be anything. He'd have to try to outrun it. He geared himself up for the chase.

"Zeb?" A familiar voice penetrated the darkness.

"Mike, is that you?" Zeb peered into the shadows.

His younger brother emerged through the tree line and climbed the fence, grabbing one of Zeb's arms with both hands and hanging on tight. "Something's going on at the Hollisters. I saw Fred sneak out to the mailbox and slip something in it. Then he went and climbed in Davey's window. I went out there and got it out of the mailbox."

"Little brother, you have to go put that back. You've tampered with the U.S. Mail. That's a federal offense." Zeb used his stern, schoolmaster voice.

The boy clung to his brother. "Doncha wanna know what's in it?"

Of course, he wanted to know. But this wasn't right. "No. It's none of our business."

Mike tugged on Zeb's arm. "Okay, I'll put it back. But it's in my room, and it got a little torn. Will you help me tie it back up?"

"Mike, you beat all. You know that?" Zeb grabbed

him by the galluses and gave a tug of his own. What was the matter with Mike? He had better sense than to mess with someone else's mail. But still.   He resumed his trek down the lane at a bit faster clip than moments before. "We'd better get a move on and see if we can repair the damage."

Reaching their yard in record time, they rounded the house and slipped in the back door. The house was quiet, and Mom and Boomer's bedroom door was closed. Good.

Inside their bedroom, Zeb lit the lamp on their small wooden table and sat on the edge of his brother's bed. A wrinkled piece of butcher paper and a length of twine lay on the quilt. Mike pulled a little cardboard box from under his pillow.

Before Zeb could stop him, Mike opened the box and took out a folded piece of paper. He handed it to Zeb. "Open it."

"I will not. It isn't ours." He thrust the paper back into Mike's hands and picked up the brown wrapper. Three one-cent stamps were haphazardly glued to the outside, and an address was printed below them in bold letters:

TO THE POLICE DEPARTMENT
CAPE GIRARDEAU, MISSOURI

Mike opened the note and read in a hushed voice. "Dear Police, Here is fifty dollars. If you can find my boy and send him home, it's yours. His name is Charlie Eugene Hollister, and I know he ain't much good, but we need him here. His boy is kidnapped, and some people think I done it. I didn't. Just send him to

Hollisters' store in Bluebird Valley, Missouri. Enjoy the money. Thank you, Fred Hollister. (Charlie Eugene's dad)."

Zeb's brain cogs turned double time. Deputy Fox needed to know about this, but they couldn't admit tampering with the mail. They'd put it back in the mailbox. Maybe Hazel would find it before it was picked up. After all, tomorrow was Sunday, so it would sit there over twenty-four hours. He needed to discuss this with Katie. But how far could he trust her to keep a confidence?

"Mike, we shouldn't have this. You need to forget you saw it, and tell no one. Let's tie it up and put it back where you found it."

Repair work done, Zeb eased out of the house and crept to the Hollisters' mailbox and replaced the parcel, thankful that Aunt Nellie, happy in her temporary home with the Banks family, had opened her house to Deputy Fox and Rebel for their stay in Bluebird Valley. At least he could be reasonably sure they weren't occupying a vantage point anywhere near the mailbox.

Breathing a sigh of relief, he made his way back to the house and flopped on his bed. "Mike, don't do that again. Don't *ever* do that again."

"But you're glad I did?"

Zeb sighed, wondering if it was all a lie. Was Fred guilty or just odd? He kicked off his boots, pushed to his feet, and blew out the lamp.

~

Katie woke early Sunday morning and slipped on

179

her powder blue dress with the white lace collar and the pocket sewn onto the skirt. Attaching the cherished bluebird pin to her collar, she retrieved the slip of paper from under her pillow where she'd placed it the night before. Her suspect list. Sliding it deep into her pocket, she breathed a silent prayer that Zeb would be able to make it to church.

After breakfast she lodged herself into Marcus's Model T, along with Aunt Nellie, the twins, Marcus, and Ella cradling Molly on her lap.

The Model T coughed to a stop. Marcus helped Ella to the ground while Katie scanned the crowd of people for Zeb. Where was he?

A tug on her hair made her turn around. Zeb stood behind her, a sheepish grin on his face. "Sorry about last night."

She feigned confusion. "What about last night?"

He stuck his hands in his pockets and lowered his eyes. "Thanks."

Inside the church, Katie slid onto the pew beside Zeb and slipped the folded paper into his hand. This wasn't exactly the place to discuss crimes and investigations, but she wanted to be sure the transfer of alleged evidence was made without the threat of prying eyes.

He took it and slid it into his shirt pocket. "Are we still on for this afternoon?"

She nodded.

After the singing of hymns and some opening announcements, Brother Deren stepped to the pulpit. Placing a hand on either side of the podium, he leaned forward and let his gaze sweep silently over the faces of his parishioners. "Brothers and sisters, this morning I want to talk to you about love. Not the *I think she's cute, infatuation for the moment* type of love."

Katie glanced at Zeb. His face was bright pink. He shifted on the pew and cleared his throat.

Brother Deren held up his Bible. "I'm talking about *real* love. The kind in which our Heavenly Father was willing to sacrifice His Son for miserable, unlovable, ungrateful people like you and me. In spite of our mistakes, our sins, He loved us so much that He built a bridge with His Son, Jesus Christ—a bridge that will lead us to Him if we confess our sins and trust Him to forgive those sins."

The pew directly across the aisle made a popping sound. Katie peered in that direction. Hazel sat, arms folded, staring straight ahead. Fred squirmed, crossing and uncrossing his legs.

"Beloved, if God cares that much for us, ought we not to love each other? Even the wretched, the unlovable, those who mistreat us?"

Zeb raised a hand to his face. A tear trickled down his cheek, and he brushed it away with one quick motion. Katie pretended not to notice.

The pastor reached for his handkerchief and wiped perspiration from his face. "God doesn't *need* our help. He *desires* a relationship with us because of His great love for us. But *we* need *Him*. Desperately." He held up both hands, thumbs together as if framing a picture. "The sign on heaven doesn't say *Help Wanted*. It says *Help Available*. Beloved, receive that help today.

His arms are open and waiting. Like it tells us in the book of Matthew, Jesus wants us to come to Him."

The familiar words of Matthew 11:28 eased into Katie's mind. Jesus' invitation offered His rest to all who were weary, burdened, and heavy laden. That included Katie. A peace settled over her.

Across the aisle, Fred fidgeted, leaning forward and clutching the pew in front of him with a white-knuckled grip.

Brother Deren stepped from behind the pulpit and came to stand in front of it. "So, brothers and sisters, we *can* love even the most undesirable among us, but only with God's help. As we sing a hymn of invitation, I'm here to pray with you, but God is here to save you."

After the final amen, Fred elbowed his way through the crowd and rushed out the door. Hazel gave Katie a forlorn stare and shook her head. Katie's heart went out to the woman.

The ride home was peaceful, though bumpy, and Katie thought the noon meal would never end. The grandfather clock in the corner reminded her that two o'clock was rapidly approaching.

Katie helped clean and tidy the kitchen, then donned her overalls and plaid shirt. "I'm going for a walk. Be back later."

Aunt Nellie flashed a knowing smile. "Have a good time. Here, take this with you. It might come in handy this afternoon." She held out a little cloth bag.

"Thanks." Katie gave her a peck on the cheek and took the bag without opening it. Once on the lane, she peered inside. Apple butter and biscuits. Dear lady.

Allowing her gaze to travel across the field, her insides tightened at the sight of Manfred Olsen using a sledge hammer to pound on a fence post at the far end of the property. At least he had his back to her. She quickened her pace, thankful for the midsummer sunshine.

Zeb stood waiting at the corner of his yard. "Boomer's gone off with a couple guys to look at a mule. Let's get outta here before he comes back."

"Good idea." Katie handed him the bag. "Aunt Nellie sent you a surprise."

He peeked inside and his face lit up in a brilliant smile. "Let's get this show on the road."

As they passed Hollisters, he touched Katie's arm and pointed across the lane. "Davey's window's up. Wonder if that's still how Fred's getting in and out, or if Hazel's decided to let him use the front door today." He eased around her, placing himself between her and the Hollisters' building.

"Probably so. He didn't look too disgruntled in church this morning. At least not until the time of invitation." She chuckled, but her insides clenched as she recalled last night's episode.

At the edge of the clearing, Zeb took her hand and guided her to their spot under the elm tree. He gently placed Aunt Nellie's bag in a patch of grass and slid to the ground, tugging Katie's hand and making her land softly beside him. "First things first. I believe we have a little unfinished business—which suffered an unexpected interruption last evening." His eyes glistened as his arms came around her.

Her whole body melted at his touch. Was this a taste of what heaven would be like? Beauty everywhere and strong arms to make her feel safe forever?

He pressed his lips to hers, and contentment flooded her consciousness like a cooling shower on a sultry day. She took a deep, satisfying breath, cupping the back of his head with one hand, and the world stood still.

Chapter 19

Slowly, tenderly, he drew back, grasping her shoulders and locking those intense brown eyes on hers. "I care about you, Katie. A lot."

Fiddles—no, violins—played in her brain, and bluebirds sang. Did she dare tell him she felt the same way? Probably better to stay on the cautious side, at least for now. She wrapped her arms around him in a tight embrace. "Oh, Zeb, you're something. You know that?"

He didn't answer, but returned the hug.

She released him and leaned back against the tree beside him. "So, what did you think of my list?"

Pulling the paper from his pocket, he unfolded it and spread it on his lap. "I think it's a good idea. And I'm not saying that just because I lo... uh, like you." He fumbled with his shirt collar and swallowed with a loud gulp.

Katie's heart sang.

I think I love you, too, Zeb.

But she allowed her thoughts to remain unvoiced, fearing that uttering them aloud might shatter the dream.

He picked up the list and held it before him. "I think every one of these characters could stand some investigating. You call the shots, and I'm in it with you for the long haul."

She scooted over until she was leaning against Zeb's side, so they could survey the list together. *And because she liked it there.* "Okay, the first name on here is Cryder Zarbone. What do we know about him?"

Zeb scratched his head. "Well, he gets drunk, passes out, and makes threats. And he *did* actually snatch Davey the other day."

Katie extracted a pencil from her overall bib pocket and drew an empty circle by Bone's name. "Check. Now what do we know about Lyle Piper?"

Zeb's brow furrowed. "Not much. We know he allegedly won Davey in a wager, and that he's elusive. Good grief, we don't even know what he looks like. We know the Hollisters say Charlie Eugene is afraid of him."

"Check. And speaking of Charlie Eugene, how about him?"

Zeb snorted. "We know he doesn't use good sense, he's a terrible dad, and he dumped his kid on his folks and then disappeared."

Katie drew her circle by Charlie Eugene's name. "Okay."

And we also know his wife landed in a mental institution, leaving him with a young child to raise.

She wondered just how desperate the young man had become.

She read the next name aloud. "Manfred Olsen. Whatcha think?"

Zeb frowned. "We know he showed up at a weird time, and we know he has an obsession with staring at you. *And* he made friends with Duke and Luke early on."

The thought of the hobo made shivers chill the back of her neck. "Alright. Check. Now the Bailor guys. Opinions?"

"I'm not sure they're a threat at all." Zeb patted her knee. "Tank and Flat are out of the picture, and Tip is mainly out for himself. I'm not sure he'd have any reason to bother Davey, unless he had a score to settle with the Hollisters—or one of the Hollisters." He pursed his lips and cocked his head at her.

"Check." Almost done. "What about Fred?"

No answer. Zeb, stiffening his back and sitting upright, gripped his chin between his thumb and forefinger and stared above the expanse of Bluebird Valley into the afternoon sky.

"What about Fred?"

Slowly, mechanically, he turned to face her. "We know he's Davey's grandpa, Charlie Eugene's dad, and Hazel's husband."

This was getting nowhere. "Cut the small talk. What do we know about Fred?"

The man gripped her hand between his and spoke rapidly. "We know he's rude to his wife, flies off the handle easily, is self centered, and..."

Threads of unease invaded Katie's previous sense of calm. "And what?" She dreaded his next words.

"Can you keep a secret?"

Tingles of excitement, coupled with fear, rendered her speechless. She nodded.

"I mean it. If I tell you this, you have to swear to keep it to yourself, no matter what it is, unless you and I agree to share it. Are you willing to do that?"

Her imagination ran wild. She nodded again, hoping against hope that he'd choose to trust her. Lost in Zeb's rich brown eyes, seeing the pain in his drawn features, she found her voice. "I'm willing."

~

Zeb steeled himself against Katie's possible reaction. After all, he and Mike had committed a federal offense—sort of. Mike's crime was committed through ignorance, and he *was* a minor. And Zeb had done all he could to *uncommit* Mike's crime by repairing Fred's package and returning it to the mailbox. But would Katie see it that way? And, even if she did, could she really be trusted to keep his secret until the time was right? There was only one way to find out.

Zeb leaned toward her and spoke in a hushed voice to make sure his deep baritone did not resonate through the valley. "Last night..."

BOOM! A rifle shot rang out, immediately followed by a loud CRACK, and a large squirrel fell to the ground less than two feet from them. Zeb whirled in the direction of the shot, as a blow to the top of his head sent him crashing into Katie.

Black spots, intermingled with bright rainbow hues, flashed across his vision, and the world spun. He tried to sit up, but fell backward, his head lolling against the tree's mighty trunk. His stomach churning like the rapids in a spring flood, he closed his eyes as everything went black.

"Zeb? Zeb! Are you okay?" Soft hands caressed his face.

He reached to touch the crown of his head. Ouch. Opening his eyes to slits, he made out two fuzzy forms kneeling before him.

"Zeb, don't pass out on us." Katie ran gentle fingers along his jaw and placed her other hand on his knee.

I think I just did.

He tested the waters. "What happened?"

He struggled to comprehend Katie's words. "Looks like that rifle shot made more than a squirrel come tumbling down. You just got walloped on the head by a good-sized limb."

A familiar voice—very familiar—penetrated the fog in his brain. "I didn't mean to do it."

Tip Bailor.

The man was sobbing! "I jist needed a squirrel fer supper, and Old Man Hawkins won't let us hunt on his land no more. So I come up here. Didn't mean nobody no harm."

Zeb pressed his palms to his eyes and shook his head to clear it. Ouch again. He decided against any more sudden movements.

Taking a deep breath, he dared to open his eyes

wider. The world had stopped spinning. So far so good.

"Don't cry, Tip. I'll be alright." *I hope.*

He felt like an idiot, stretched out against a tree, regaining consciousness, consoling a bawling man in front of the girl he loved. Yes, loved.

Tip blew his nose on the tail of his shirt. "I'll go get Hazel to come see about you."

Katie stepped in. Bless her heart. "We're fine. It was an accident. Just get your squirrel and go on home."

The distraught man laid his rifle on the ground next to Zeb. "Here, take it. It's yours. We got plenty more ta home." He grabbed the squirrel and stumbled down the hill and out of sight.

More rifles at home. Oh, fine. That's just what they needed, a bunch of Bailors armed with rifles, shooting up in trees and knocking limbs on people's heads—or worse. He groaned.

Katie cupped his chin in her hand and stared into his face. "Open your eyes wide."

He obliged. Why? 'Cause she was Katie, and she asked him to.

"Your pupils look fine. I'm sure there's no concussion. But you're gonna have a big ole punk knot on the top of your head."

He reached up and slid a finger across the now tender area on his scalp. Ouch.

"Katie girl, sit here beside me and let me finish my story." He pulled her against him, head pounding in pain, heart pounding in pleasure at her nearness.

She turned a wary glance his way. "You gonna be

alright?"

He forced a grin. "I'm always alright. I'm Zeb the Great. Remember?"

Her knit brow and pursed lips told the story. "Yeah, right."

He squeezed his eyes shut, willing the pain to subside. "Last night after I took you home, I was going down the lane, minding my own business."

He was met with silence. Not opening his eyes, he proceeded to relate Saturday night's events in detail, from finding Mike on the lane to returning Fred's package to the Hollisters' mailbox. "And that's it. That's the secret."

More silence.

He opened one eye. Thankfully his headache had progressed from excruciating to bearable. *Thank you, Jesus.*

Katie stared into his face, almost nose to nose. "So, do you think Fred had a hand in Davey's disappearance, and wants to use Charlie Eugene as an alibi?"

Smart girl.

"That's what I was thinking. But Charlie Eugene would be a miserable alibi, in my opinion. And, besides, the only way he could prove Fred's innocence would be to point a finger at the guilty party. And we both know that's not gonna happen."

Katie laid a hand on his arm. "It's getting late. You think we need to go?"

"I guess maybe we should. Sorry the afternoon turned out like this. I know it wasn't what you'd intended." He pushed to his feet and put a hand against the tree for support.

She slid an arm around his waist. "It was *exactly* what I intended, except for the part about you getting clobbered." Then she jabbed him in the arm, causing him to relax. To a degree. "Do you need some support walking back to your house?"

He pushed away from the tree. Nothing whirled. He was fine, but why waste a good opportunity. "It wouldn't hurt. I might get a little unsteady on my feet."

Her raised eyebrows told him she'd caught him in his charade, but she said nothing. Sliding the suspect list into her pocket and retrieving their burlap bag, she sidled against him. "Put your arm around my shoulder."

Gladly.

Her left arm around his waist and her right hand toting the gun, they made their way down the narrow path and onto the school property. Katie tightened her grip on his waist and slowed.

"What do you think about Tip?"

Zeb considered. "I don't know. I think he's full of himself and a few bricks shy of a load, but I don't really think he did anything to Davey. What do *you* think?"

She coughed and cleared her throat. "I think I don't know, either. But while you're in school tomorrow, I plan to do a little investigating. Then after school I'll report to you, and we can take it from there."

Torn between Davey's dilemma and Katie's safety, he hesitated, perhaps a little too long.

She tapped the rifle, barrel down, on the ground. "Well?"

He spoke in measured syllables. "I guess go ahead. I can't stop you. But, for goodness sake, be careful."

At the edge of Hollisters' property, loud voices interrupted the late afternoon stillness. Zeb's teacher instincts took over, and he pulled Katie into the shadows behind the store. "Shhh. Listen."

Katie, eyes wide, stashed the gun and treat bag in a tuft of weeds, slipped to the corner of the building and leaned forward.

Pressing against Katie from behind, Zeb strained to hear the angry words coming from inside Davey's open window.

"...and this is his little quilt. He lay on it just a few days ago, and I read him a story. I can't stand it, Fred. Our little grandson out there, maybe in danger. What if we never see our baby again?" Hazel's voice was thick with tears.

Fred's high-pitched reply held agitation. "All I can say is, it'd prob'ly be better for him to be dead than to grow up like Charlie Eugene."

"You old buzzard. Get out of my house. Get out of my life!" A door slammed, making the boards rattle. A leg pushed through the window opening, and Katie and Zeb watched from the shadows as Fred fell in a heap on the ground.

Grabbing the window ledge, he pulled himself to his feet and tottered off around the house, muttering.

Katie grabbed Zeb's hand and faced him, eyebrows raised expectantly.

Her message hit home, and a tinge of uneasiness coupled with the thrill of the chase made his legs tremble. This was as good a time as any to start their sleuthing operation. He tightened his fingers around hers. "Let's go."

Pressing against the wooden slats of the frame building, the two slinked far enough behind Fred that they wouldn't be noticed. He rounded the corner of the house and stepped up onto the front porch. Katie and Zeb waited.

"Fred!" Hazel's yell was enough to alert all the Freds for miles around. "Get in here."

"Make up yur mind, woman."

Zeb peered around the corner as Fred staggered across the porch and through the front door. Zeb eyed Katie. "The store's fair game. You thirsty?"

She grinned. "I thought you'd never ask."

The instant they stepped into the store, Zeb wished he'd never suggested a drink. Boomer sat on the feed sack couch, the package on his lap.

But there was no turning back now. Katie glanced at Zeb, eyes wary. She'd seen it, too. He nodded and tugged her toward the soda box. Snatching two Cokes, he thrust a dime in Hazel's hand. "Thanks, Hazel. We'll take these to go."

Fred snarled. "Don't run off with them bottles."

Once outside, Katie pulled Zeb to the end of the porch. "I've got an idea. Are you game?"

Zeb's curiosity overrode his sound judgment. "Show me."

She led him back around the house to Davey's

window, and proceeded to climb inside. "Follow me."

Zeb's mouth hung open. Trespassing? *Oh, Katie.* But he followed her lead.

Since the entire back and part of one side of the structure served as living quarters for Davey and his grandparents, this bedroom, as well as the kitchen, shared common walls with the store.

Putting a finger to her lips, she indicated a small settee. She pressed her lips against his ear. "If you sit there and look through that crack, you can see and hear everything that goes on in the store."

Without a word, he lowered himself onto the small piece of furniture and did as she said. The gal was right.

She sat beside him. "Go ahead. I'll serve as lookout."

Zeb grimaced. Lookout. Right. What were they supposed to do if someone decided to come in here?

The conversation in the next room grabbed his attention. Fred stood facing Boomer, hand extended. "Where'dja get that thing? That's mine. Give it to me."

Boomer stashed it behind his back. "Not so fast. Where'd you get the fifty dollars that's in here?"

"You opened it. You broke the law. That's a federal crime. You tampered with the U.S. mail." Fred sputtered and shook his fist at Boomer.

Zeb swallowed against the cottony sensation that threatened to clog his throat. He raked a sweaty palm across his pant leg. Even Fred knew it was a crime to tamper with the mail.

Hazel crossed the room and pushed Fred toward a

chair. He plopped onto it, his eyes full of... what? Fear?

The woman leaned forward, her face an inch from his. "We know where you got that money, don't we, Fred? We know about the empty cigar box in the back bedroom. You know, the one that used to hold the money I'd been saving for Davey's college. That is, if he'd had the chance to grow up and use it." Her voice broke and she sank into the chair next to her husband.

Boomer stood, a cocky twist to his head. True to form. "Truth is, I didn't touch your mailbox. I saw Tip Bailor with his hand in it, and I took the liberty of stopping him before he stole your mail, and guess what? I don't think Charlie Eugene is even in Cape. And you know what else? I don't think he could help you, even if you found him. Because I think you're beyond help."

He strutted across the room until he was directly in front of Hazel's chair. "Here, I didn't even bother to open this other envelope that's stuck to the bottom. I'm not in the habit of prying into other people's business."

Thrusting the package into Hazel's hands, he tipped his head in mock respect. "Good evening." And he pivoted and strode out the door.

Zeb, thankful for his newly acquired vantage point, watched Hazel tear open the small brown envelope. Fred sat with his head down.

In no time the woman let out a gasp that made Fred and Zeb jump with a start. "Oh, dear Jesus." She held the note out to her husband. "Read it aloud. See for yourself."

Fred, hands trembling, took the paper and read.

FORGET IT, FOLKS. DAVEY WON'T BE BACK NO MORE. STOP THE SEARCH AND NOBODY WON'T GET HURT. LYLE PIPER.

Fred threw the note to the floor and took Hazel in his arms.

Weakness engulfed Zeb's body, and his headache threatened to return full force. He kept his voice low. "Fred's hugging Hazel."

But Katie was crouched near the window sill, her eyes focused outside. "Boomer went in your back door. Let's get out of here while we still can."

Rubbery legs carried him across the room. He grabbed the empty Coke bottles, the only evidence of their presence in the room and dropped to the ground behind Katie. In the gathering darkness, they made a dash for the highway and hastened into the refuge of the shadowy lane.

Zeb's heart pounded. "He hugged her. I think he needs to be put on the next train to Hollywood."

"Do you think there's any chance Tip Bailor and Lyle Piper could be in cahoots. Do you think Piper's in the area, and Tip is serving as his underling? And, if so, do you think Piper would have taken Davey, and then hurt him?"

His heart pounded. He'd never thought of that. Tip Bailor and Lyle Piper as a team. Heaven help us. "I don't know. I just don't know."

Silence.

He dreaded uttering the next words. "But you're going to try to find out, aren't you?"

They stood in front of the Banks' home. A lamp shone from the window, its beam illuminating the porch. "Yeah, I'm gonna try."

He was afraid for her, but he knew arguing with the little gal would be like spitting into the wind and expecting to keep a dry face. He drew her close. "Be sure to take your bluebird along."

She ran a hand along the back of his hair, causing tingles to race along his neck and into his proverbial gizzard. Then, pressing her lips to his, she left a brief but powerful reminder that he couldn't live without her.

She pulled away and turned toward the house. "I'll be careful."

Chapter 20

Katie was up a tree. Literally. After dropping the boys off at school Monday morning, she had circled around and taken a little detour through the woods that skirted the Bailor property. Upon hearing voices, she'd skittered up the closest tree and hidden herself among its leafy branches. Just in time.

Fred and Tip came into view and stopped no more than three feet from her hiding place. Fred leaned against the tree trunk and ran an arm across his perspiring face. "You should not never have took 'im, Tip. I could'a toldja that wouldn't work."

Tip sniffled. "I woulda brought 'im back."

"Well, you cain't bring 'im back now. He's dead. How in the world couldja let that happen, Tip?"

Katie's body went numb. She clutched the branch, fearing she might come tumbling down in front of them. *Dead.* The word entered her brain and reverberated through every inch of her consciousness. A wave of nausea swept over her, making her glad she hadn't taken the time for breakfast.

Tip's shoulders shook, and he brushed a hand across his eyes. "I'm awful sorry."

Fred huffed. "Don't apologize to me. He wasn't mine. And quit that cryin'. I jist hate a cryin' man, and it won't fix nothin' no way. Now tell me whatcha done."

Katie wanted to wring Fred's neck. Wasn't his! Just what would you call it, if Davey wasn't his grandson?

Tip trudged to a fallen log and sank onto it. He sniffled again and wiped his nose on his shirt sleeve. "I knew Bone was after 'im. When I got over here with'im I seen Bone a-comin.' So anyways, I just pushed 'im in the root cellar before old Bone got here."

Fred scratched his head. "Didn't e'holler?"

"Nope. I guess it knocked 'im out. When I come back to git 'im later, I found 'im a-layin' dead over there." He indicated a spot some distance away. "Looked like he'd lost a fight with a bobcat, or somethin' like that. Anyways, he was all tore up. I know that."

Katie's stomach lurched, and the horizon dipped and twirled. She shut her eyes and clung to the tree.

Fred sucked loudly on a tooth. "Didn'tcha shut the cellar door?"

Katie opened her eyes in time to see Tip shrug and flash a sheepish grin. "Guess not."

The older man advanced on the younger and slapped him across the face. "You're crazy. What'dja do with 'im?"

Tip rubbed his injured cheek. "What could I do? I buried 'im."

Fred grabbed Tip by the shirt collar. "Where?"

Tip started to cry again. "I wrapped 'im in a old red flannel shirt that used to be Flat's. Then I drug 'im up in the woods and I buried 'im by Tully's cave. Nobody ever goes up there."

Fred whirled away and took a few steps, then stopped and retraced them. Jabbing a finger against Tip's chest, he spat out the words. "Well, let's just hope nobody goes up there. You need to go to Farmington and stay. You've lost it, boy. I hope you buried 'im deep enough. If you didn't, he'll stink. I'm goin' home." With that, he turned his back and shuffled across the field.

Tip hung his head and spoke to no one. "I didn't mean it. I didn't mean to let 'im be dead. I woulda brung 'im back." He took off through the woods, shaking his head and muttering to himself.

When both men were out of sight, Katie shinnied down the tree and let herself collapse on the ground beneath it. Sitting cross-legged in the dirt, she wrestled with her own thoughts. Should she try to find the grave? But for what? She couldn't save Davey now—not if he was... if he was... She couldn't bring herself to even think it. She had to get help.

Picking her way through briers and brambles, she advanced through the woods until Aunt Nellie's house came into view. Emerging from among the trees, she ran up the steps and pounded on the front door. "Deputy Fox. Deputy Fox, are you in there?"

The house was eerily quiet, and a sense of foreboding dug its fingers into a spot behind Katie's eyes, blurring her vision. She sat on the porch swing to clear her head. Of course, Deputy Fox wasn't here. The patrol car was gone. He and Rebel must be out following trails of their own. But she had to find them.

The sun was high in the sky. Was it noon already? Her stomach rumbled, but not from hunger. She laid her palms against her midsection and pressed. She took a deep breath and held it. Then she let it out in a rush and swallowed the pool of saliva that had gathered under her tongue.

She had to do this. Pushing to a standing position, she leaned with one hand on the porch rail. Sliding the other hand in her pocket, she ran her fingers across the smooth enamel of her bluebird's wings. The message of Isaiah 40:31 came to her mind.

God said all who placed their hope in Him would renew their strength as though they soared on mighty eagles' wings. He said they would run and never grow tired, and they would walk without fainting.

She squared her shoulders and raised her eyes toward the sky. *Thank You, Lord.*

Her strength renewed, she cleared the steps and sprinted across the yard.

Racing down the lane across from Aunt Nellie's house, she followed the creek bank to the Hollisters' property. Sure enough, Fred sat on the front porch, his chair tilted back against the wooden slats of the building's front wall, his arms folded across his belly.

The familiar patrol car sat parked by the gas

pump.

Crud.

She couldn't talk to Deputy Fox if Fred was within hearing range.

Making a wide jaunt to the west, she crossed the highway and cut across the field to the Banks' home. The house in sight, and her mind in a tither, she carelessly crossed in front of the open barn door. A hand reached out and touched her arm.

Manfred Olsen.

The man emerged into the daylight. "Katie, please. I need to talk to you."

Zeb's words screamed in her mind. *What does any man want?* What indeed? Adrenalin pumping, she bolted for the house.

"Well, my goodness." Ella shifted Molly in her arms and rocked the porch swing. "Where's the emergency?"

Katie stopped short. Squatting on the ball of one foot, Marcus leaned against the wall near the front door. Aunt Nellie sat in a chair at the other end of the porch, her apron full of the green beans she was breaking and dropping into a pan.

Marcus shifted to the other foot. His voice was kind, but it reeked of curiosity. "Where have you been? Must have been somewhere important. Do you know you've missed your noon meal?"

Katie ignored the question and eased onto the swing next to her aunt. "That's okay. I'm not very hungry."

Ella reached over and laid a hand on Katie's

forehead. "Are you feeling alright? You know, you do look a little pale."

Katie leaned back against the swing, straightening her legs and extending them in midair before her. Stretching and locking her fingers behind her head, she tried to appear calm. "Oh, I'm fine. I've been running."

"Why?" Marcus cocked his head, a skeptical tinge to his voice.

"Well, I knew I was running a little late, and wanted to get home and get a bite to eat before picking up the boys from school."

Drat it all.

She'd just contradicted herself. She had said she wasn't hungry, but she wanted to get home to get a bite to eat. Wanted it bad enough to run. How embarrassing. Heat crawled up her neck and engulfed her face and ears.

Marcus and Ella exchanged puzzled looks. And Katie wilted.

Marcus pulled out a pocket watch. "It's only 1:30. There's plenty of time to eat, or not, or do whatever it is you're in such a hurry to do before time for school to let out. I'm gonna go find Olsen to help me fix that loose board on the barn."

When Marcus was gone, Katie's mind rushed to Davey, Tip, Fred... Should she tell Ella and Marcus what she'd overheard? No, this was a matter for the law. How would it help for them to know? And there was no hurry. Not anymore. Not as far as Davey was concerned. Her nausea returned. "Maybe I don't feel so good after all."

DREAMS AND SECRETS

Aunt Nellie, her apron still half full of unbroken green beans, was at her side in seconds. "Let's go in and get you a bite to eat. I've got somethin' that'll fix you right up."

Katie, her stomach now rolling, pushed to her feet and followed the woman inside. She sank onto a kitchen chair and rested her elbows on the table. Ella, eyes full of concern, placed Molly on a pallet near the day bed, then slid onto a chair across from Katie.

Aunt Nellie emptied her beans into a galvanized pan and put a teakettle on the stove. "We'll have you some herbal tea in no time. That'll fix anything that ails you."

Dear woman. If she only knew.

When mugs of hot tea and a small plate of saltine crackers were on the table in front of Ella and Katie, Aunt Nellie picked up her pan. "I need to finish breakin' these beans. I'll be on the porch if you need me."

The door clicked shut, and Katie eyed the tea. Taking a little sip, she let the soothing liquid trickle down her throat. The nausea began to subside, but the ache remained in her heart.

Ella set down her mug. "Katie, are you sick?"

Katie nibbled on a cracker, then ventured another sip of tea. "No, I'm fine. Really. Just a little edgy about all the goin's-on these last few days."

Ella's eyes narrowed. "Speaking of that, have you been hearing any news about the search for Davey? I've not been anywhere but to church since Molly was born, and I haven't had the chance to talk to very many

205

people."

Katie's mouth went dry, and she struggled to swallow. What should she tell her aunt? She didn't want to lie, and she had no solid facts. Yet.

"I haven't talked to Deputy Fox for a while. I think he may be on to something, but he's not giving out any information."

Well, he wasn't.

Her answer seemed to satisfy Ella. The woman glanced toward Molly sleeping peacefully, the picture of contentment. "It's such a shame. I know how Hazel and Fred must feel. Poor, poor Hazel. Poor, poor Fred."

Katie clamped her jaws shut. Ella had no idea. But Katie had no desire to be the bearer of bad news or carry tales.

A combination of sympathy for Hazel and rage against Fred filled her heart. The rage made her uncomfortable. She hated it.

She needed to go. Clear her head. Calm her emotions. She took one last swallow of tea and eased her chair back, taking care to not wake Molly. "I'm gonna head on over to the school."

Ella propped her elbows on the table and leaned forward. "Be careful. And tell Zeb I said hi."

A warmth surged through Katie, and she grinned. "Zeb the Great?"

The corners of Ella's mouth turned up in a half-amused, half-sad smile. "Yeah, that's the one. Tell him hello for me."

Katie's heart clinched as visions of his beloved face waltzed across her mind. "Will do."

At the end of the lane, her chest tightened. The patrol car was gone, and Fred lounged on the porch, chair tilted back, arms hanging limp at his sides.

Shoot.

She crossed the highway and hurried past the store, between Davey's still open window and Rebel's bush.

"Want a biscuit?" Boomer leaned against the fence, holding yesterday's burlap bag and balancing Tip's rifle against his leg. "Looky what I found behind the store." He raised the gun, and his haughty sneer sent cold chills across her shoulders and down her spine.

"No thanks." She rushed on, but a thought niggled at her mind and set up camp there. Boomer. Why hadn't she thought of it before? Did he have a hand in Fred's and Tip's escapade? Was he involved in Davey's murder? Was he *responsible* for it? Or was he just a smart aleck who considered himself to be God's gift to everybody?

Then another thought struck her, and her blood ran cold. Could Boomer have been the one who attacked her outside Davey's window the other day, and ripped off her pocket and stole the candy? But if so, why?

An urgency seized control of her mind. She had to talk to Zeb. Now.

Without a backward glance, she raced down the lane and sank to the ground under the tree at the edge of the playground, a river of perspiration rolling off her face and her breath coming in short gasps.

Other adults, seemingly oblivious to Katie's arrival, stood in groups, fiddling with pocket watches and keeping eyes on the door.

Fine. She had more important things to engage her brain than thinking of ways to be sociable.

The moment the door opened, students raced to join their respective escorts and head toward home.

Duke and Luke made a beeline for Katie. Tumbling onto the ground beside her, Duke flung his arms around her neck, then let go and scooted away. "You're all sweaty. Eeeew."

Luke hopped to his feet and took several steps backward. "Eeeew."

Katie swiped a hand across her brow and, attempting to glean energy from an empty supply, sprang to her feet. "I'll show you 'eeeew.'" Attempting to appear nonchalant and avoid a mental meltdown, she gave chase and grabbed at the two, making them squeal in delight.

Zeb snatched her gallus with a thumb. "Stop it. Something's wrong. What's happened?"

The warmth in his eyes, the compassion in his voice, tore at her insides. Her composure, already stretched to the breaking point, threatened to betray her. Sucking her lips between her teeth she bit down. Hard.

The twins and Mike had organized a game of tag and were chasing each other up the lane, zigzagging and laughing loudly. Katie started after them.

Zeb pulled her back. "They'll be fine. Hazel'll be waiting at the store with Cokes for them, and besides, nobody's gonna try to steal three rowdy boys all at once in broad daylight. Relax." He brushed a hand lightly against her cheek. "Now tell me what's wrong."

She wrestled with an overwhelming urge to wrap her arms around him, bury her face against his chest, and bawl her eyes out. But she refused to grant herself that luxury—or succumb to that weakness. "We have to talk. In private. Soon."

He locked his fingers with hers. "Okay. Sure. Let me walk you and the boys home, and we'll take it from there."

~

The little gal's fingers latched onto Zeb's in a death grip. He ventured a glance to his right at this silent beauty taking slow deliberate steps, eyes straight ahead.

What was going on here? "A penny for your thoughts?"

She squeezed her eyes shut and lowered her head, shaking it back and forth, but no words came.

A vise of uneasiness tightened on Zeb's brain until it seemed his head might explode. He wasn't about to find out much until they were alone—really alone.

Once on the lane leading home, the twins, lunch pails swinging precariously from their hands, engaged in a wild game of leapfrog.

"Yeee-haaa!" Duke sailed across Luke's back and rammed into Katie. He fell backward and sat down hard on the dirt road. Getting up, he cast a sidelong glance at her. "Oops."

She tousled his hair. "Oops, yourself."

While the kid had her talking, Zeb ventured another question. "So—this whole thing has something to do with your investigation, doesn't it?"

Alerted, the twins planted themselves in front of him and Katie and stopped. Duke tugged at Zeb's sleeve. "What's a invest... investi..."

Luke slapped himself on the forehead and gave a little sigh. "Investigation."

Duke grinned. "Yeah. What's that?"

Zeb turned to Katie for help.

She raised her eyebrows. "You started it."

She had him there. He knelt in front of the boys. "It's where you try to find out things."

Duke aimed a quizzical look at his brother, then focused on Zeb. "What kind of things?"

Zeb stuck out an index finger and tapped it on the tip of Duke's nose. "Things you don't know."

A grin spread across the child's face, and he eyed his brother. Luke's mischievous look matched his twin's. They stepped to the side of the lane and talked in low tones, looking up into the trees and pointing. Then, swinging their lunch pails, they sauntered on their way.

Suddenly Luke's arm went into a twirl and he let go of his lunch pail in mid-swing. It sailed upward and lodged high above in the crook of a tree.

"Luke!" Katie rushed to Duke and grabbed the other pail out of his hand before he had the chance to inflict the same fate upon it. "What's the matter with you?"

Duke answered for his brother. "It was a invest...

investi…"

Luke placed his hands on his hips and shook his head. "Investigation."

Katie rolled her eyes and curled her lip at Zeb, while Duke, wide-eyed, continued. "We didn't know how high we could throw a lunch pail, so we done a invest… investi… Well, you know." He raised his eyes, then gave Luke a two-thumbs up. "Went pretty high, didn't it?"

Zeb wanted to laugh, or cry, or—something. This was his fault. "I'll get it." He started for the tree.

Katie pulled him back. "It's too far up. That branch won't support your weight. I'll get it."

Before he could stop her, the agile gal had shinnied up that tree and stretched out along the branch reaching for the wayward lunch pail. Snatching it with one hand, she dangled it in the air. "Catch."

Zeb held up his hands just as the pail descended toward him with lightning speed. It shot between his hands and clipped his ear. *Ouch. Way to go, Swifty.*

Katie climbed down, using the tree branches like rungs of a step ladder. Swinging her legs over the last branch, she slid to the ground. RIP!

She clapped her hands over the seat of her pants. "Blasted snag. Just ruined a good pair of overalls."

While Katie was inside the house changing clothes, Zeb squatted on the front porch. A rustle in the dry grass made him jerk his head to the left. Manfred Olsen stood at the end of the porch staring at him.

This is just great. Now he's taken to staring at

everybody. Why won't he say something? Zeb's blood boiled.

"Sir?"

Zeb returned the stare. "What." The question came out as a rude statement. He hoped he could get rid of the man before Katie returned.

"Sir, Katie won't talk to me. Will you tell her not to be afraid of me?"

What kind of a request was that? Katie had every reason to be afraid of the crazy hobo. Zeb didn't answer.

"I mean no harm. I just want to talk to her—and show her something."

"I'll just bet you do." Zeb was losing patience. This guy had to be out of his gourd.

Olsen touched Zeb's sleeve. "Please. It means a lot to me."

Zeb pulled away. "I think you'd better go."

The older man's chin quivered. "You don't understand. And nobody'll let me explain. Well, thanks anyway. No hard feelings." He reached up and squeezed Zeb's shoulder, then disappeared around the corner of the house.

The screen door creaked, and Katie approached, sporting a pale yellow dress. Zeb did a double take. "Hey, I like."

Katie pushed her hair back. The bluebird pin adorned the collar. "My other pair of overalls was dirty. This is all I could find."

He popped to his feet, and taking her by the hand, led her down the lane and away from the house. The soft rustle of cotton fabric, and the lady wearing it, made it hard for him to concentrate on the issue at hand. Reaching the familiar old gate, he lifted her onto it and perched beside her. "Okay, let's talk."

She leaned against him, making his heart flutter. "Oh, Zeb. I know where Davey is. But it's too late. He's dead."

A niggle of panic rose inside Zeb. His jaw clenched, and he grasped the weathered board until his knuckles turned white. He couldn't let her see his fear, his terror. He swallowed and struggled to speak.

"How do you know?" The sound of his own voice seemed unfamiliar and far away.

"I hid in a tree and heard Tip tell Fred about it. Tip buried him on the Bailor property near Tully's cave. He said he kidnapped Davey, pushed him in the cellar, and then later came back and found him dead. Said a wild animal got him. What'll we do?" Her voice, barely above a whisper, sent shards of increasing terror shooting through Zeb's veins.

This was too big for the two of them. Searching for a missing child and his kidnapper was one thing. That wild animal story was probably nothing but a cover-up. If Davey was really dead, they more than likely had a killer in their midst. And dealing with a murderer was a completely different ball game with a new set of rules.

He slid from his perch, placed his hands around Katie's waist and set her on the ground in front of him. "We have to notify Deputy Fox."

She nodded. "He wasn't at the store, was he? Do you think maybe he's home?"

Zeb knew *home* for the time being meant Aunt Nellie's house. "Either that, or he's gone back to town. I heard him tell Hazel the other day that he needed to check in with Sheriff Barton. But we could go see."

Zeb wanted to flee to his prayer nook, take Katie with him, and stay forever. And his most urgent desire was for Davey to be alive. But things didn't change to his liking just because of what he wanted. Boomer was the prime example of that fact. The sun glinted off Katie's bluebird pin, and Zeb wished he could fly away on its wings.

Two police cars sat beside Aunt Nellie's house. Zeb led Katie up the front porch steps and knocked on the door.

A familiar voice sounded from inside. "It's open."

Zeb held the door and stepped back to let Katie enter before him. His old friend, Sheriff Clay Barton, sat at the table across from Deputy Fox, maps and pictures spread between them.

Barton stood and extended a hand. "Hey. Good to see ya."

Zeb grasped the hand of his old friend. "Guys, we've got a problem."

"Have a seat." Fox motioned toward Aunt Nellie's worn couch in front of the window.

Katie plopped down among the soft cushions, and Zeb sat beside her, leaning back and letting his body go lax. The two men in uniform, guns hanging at their sides—assurance that he and Katie wouldn't have to go it alone—brought a welcome respite from the tension that had pushed his nerves near the breaking point.

He nudged Katie with the back of his hand. "Go ahead. Tell them what you know."

Katie minced no words. "Davey's dead."

Both officers sat up straight, eyes fixed on the young woman. Deputy Fox spoke first. "How do you know this?"

Katie explained the happenings of the morning, including her suspicions about Tip, Fred, and Bone. "I think Tip kidnapped him, Fred was somehow involved, and Bone wanted to, but they beat him to it. And I'm still wondering if Tip did the killing, or if..."

Her voice broke. "Excuse me." She pushed to her feet and stepped out onto the front porch.

Zeb started to follow her, but thought better of it. Sometimes a person needed a few minutes alone and, strong as she was, she'd just experienced something that had the potential to bring the toughest old lumberjack to his knees.

Sheriff Barton stood. Grabbing a rifle that had been propped against the door, he turned to Deputy Fox. "Get a shovel and let's go."

Fox made a dash for the back door and Barton followed. The sheriff, his mouth forming a grim line, locked eyes with his old friend. "Zeb, bring Katie and meet us in the back yard, and we'll get these guys."

Zeb pushed open the front door. Katie stood leaning on the porch rail, head down. He laid a hand on her arm. "You alright?"

She answered without looking up. "Yeah, I'm okay. Just needed some air."

"We're goin' after 'em. You up to the chase?"

She placed a hand over his and squeezed. "Wouldn't miss it."

In the back yard, Jesse Fox reached over to pat Katie on the shoulder. "You've done some good spy work, ma'am. Now you just lead the way, and we'll take it from here."

She nodded. "Thank you."

Katie took the lead, followed by Sheriff Barton toting his rifle, Deputy Fox wielding a shovel, Rebel on leash but not on command, and Zeb.

Picking through brambles and across fallen logs, Zeb's tension started to build again.

A crow cawed overhead. It sounded like a foghorn to Zeb. The crack of every twig made him jump, expecting somebody—or something—to pop out of the woods and attack their little party. He reached up with trembling fingers to brush the perspiration from his face. He was glad he was bringing up the rear.

The group came to a sudden stop. Zeb almost stepped on Rebel. Katie leaned toward Sheriff Barton and spoke in a low voice. "There it is." She indicated a little mound of fresh dirt, three feet away from the cave's dark opening.

Fox handed Rebel's leash to Katie. "Keep him back."

She led the little dog to a shady spot and sank to the ground beside him. Zeb knelt near them.

Barton and Fox approached the mound and squatted beside it, examining the area and talking in low tones. Barton nodded and rose to his feet. Holding the rifle, he stepped back while Fox stood over the grave. Putting the tip of the shovel near the edge of the mound, he placed his foot on it and pressed down.

Chapter 21

Zeb ventured a look at Katie. Her eyes were fixed on the two men, her hands clasped tightly in her lap.

"Grrr." A low rumble erupted from Rebel's throat, and his hair bristled. Zeb placed a hand on the little dog's scruff, but the beagle remained on alert.

A twig snapped, and Tip Bailor pushed through a tangle of brambles and started toward the cave. Fox let the shovel clatter to the ground and laid his hand on the pistol in his holster. Tip's mouth flew open and his eyes widened. He spun around, ready to bolt.

Barton raised the rifle and aimed it at Tip. "Hold it right there."

Tip fell to his knees, hands in the air, and wailed. "Don't shoot me. I'll 'fess up. I'll tell."

Deputy Fox stared at the man, now lying prostrate on the ground, and wailing at the top of his lungs. The deputy shot a dumbfounded look Zeb's way. "That's the worst I've ever seen him."

Zeb shrugged. "I know. That's just how he is."

Fox shook his head. Taking his hand away from his pistol, he walked over and peered down at Tip. Barton kept his rifle trained on the sobbing man.

Tip grabbed Fox's pant leg and whimpered, but Fox stepped back. Tip rolled over on his back, wallowing in the dirt and clawing at his eyes. "I done it. No. The bobcat done it. But it's my fault. So I killed 'im. But I didn't mean it. Am I goin' to jail?"

Fox glared at Tip. "Probably." In disgust, he picked up the shovel and walked away from the out-of-control man.

Barton sat on a stump, rifle aimed and ready.

The swish of the shovel as dirt was scooped away blotted everything else from Zeb's mind. He saw only Davey's face, heard his *pway,* thought of the child's love of "Amazing Grace." Where was God's grace now? Even if Tip was put away for life, where was the real justice? That wouldn't bring Davey back. Zeb locked his fingers together and pressed them against his mouth, heart pounding.

Fox slowed his operation. A fragment of red flannel extended out of the little pile of earth. Zeb ventured another look at Katie. She was sitting with her arm around Rebel, her face buried in his fur.

Deputy Fox scraped back the dirt, a little at a time, as more and more red flannel appeared. Laying down the shovel, he reached into his hip pocket and drew out a pair of gloves. Slipping them on, he knelt beside the shallow grave and carefully tugged on the flannel.

A pungent smell reached Zeb's nose—the unmistakable smell of death. His stomach lurched, and he wanted to gag. He covered his mouth and nose with his hands.

Fox raised his head. "Oh, my stars. Look here, Sheriff."

Barton, forgetting the man on the ground, walked to the grave and bent over it. "It's a goat." His chuckle turned into a laugh.

Relief flooded Zeb's body.

Katie sprang to her feet. "You mean it's not Davey?"

Fox sauntered over to her. "Obviously not."

Tip got to his hands and knees, then pushed to a standing position. His eyes blazed in fury. "Davey! You thought I killed Davey? I coulda toldja it was a goat. I coulda toldja. I never killed no human in my life. My name ain't Tank."

Fox picked up the shovel and thrust it into Tip's hands. "Here. Take this and go bury him right this time. We'll deal with you later."

Sheriff Barton scratched his head. "Who raises goats around here?"

Tip pushed the shoved into the dry earth. "Old Man Hawkins. I done went and took it from 'im."

"Why?" The sheriff intended to conduct an interrogation on site.

Tip leaned on the shovel. "'Cause he wouldn't let us hunt squirrels around his house no more."

Sunday afternoon's incident replayed in Zeb's mind. He remembered Tip's same words.

Tip dropped another shovelful of dirt on the body of the poor unfortunate goat. He laid the shovel down and stood facing the sheriff. "Fred got hungry for squirrels. He said he'd pay me for 'em if I'd shoot 'em and clean 'em. So I wanted to get some extry ones, and they was lots of 'em on Old Man Hawkins' land. But he run me off, and then I had to go to the ridge. And they ain't hardly none there. I wanted to get even with 'im. So I tuck the goat."

Sheriff Barton leaned against a tree. "That's ridiculous."

Tip grinned. "Well I got to it before Bone did. But I shore never meant to kill it. I was a'gonna give it back when the fun was over."

Fun? At a poor animal's expense? Zeb wanted to sock the guy in the face.

Deputy Fox squatted beside Rebel. "Why did Bone want it?"

Tip propped the shovel against a stump. "'Cause it wudden his. He steals."

Katie got up, her head tilted. "Did Fred tell you to take that goat?"

The guy grinned and scuffed a toe in the dirt. "Naw. Fred said I was crazy. Said he coulda told me it wouldn't work."

Zeb broke away from the group, made his way to the cave's opening, and stood before the little grave. He took a deep breath—and wished he hadn't. The rancid odor penetrated his nostrils and sent invisible fingers of fire careening along the inside of his throat. He stared down at the partially buried remains of the unfortunate goat.

Poor little guy.

His vet's heart longed to see critters saved, not killed. Silent tears played at the corners of his eyes. He blinked. One of God's creatures. God knew and cared when anything, or anyone, suffered, even something as small and insignificant as a sparrow—or a goat. Why couldn't Boomer see that, and not contribute to the suffering?

Come to think of it, he wouldn't be surprised if Boomer had a hand in Davey's disappearance after all. He was that mean.

Zeb finished Tip's job. When he'd dug a new and deeper hole, he gently lowered the small animal's body into it, covered it with dirt, and smoothed the surface.

Barton's voice carried across the small gathering. "Go on home, Tip. But you've not seen the last of us. You'll have to make restitution for that goat."

Tip responded in a whiny voice. "Make whut?"

"Forget it. Go home."

"Okay." Tip spun and ran off through the brambles.

Zeb moved to Katie's side, hoping she wouldn't notice his tears of sympathy for the goat. She gently cuffed him on the arm. He needed that. Then she looped Rebel's leash around one hand and reached down to pet the dog. "I guess that takes us back to square one."

Deputy Fox claimed the leash from Katie's hand. "Not exactly."

~

Katie's mouth went dry and goose bumps prickled

her neck and shoulders. Giving Rebel a pat and a promise, she rose to her feet and faced Jesse Fox. "What do you mean?"

Fox swiped a forefinger across his nose. "Sheriff Barton was here today for a reason. We've received word that Lyle Piper has been seen in the St. Louis area, and I'm going up there to check out the story. I may be gone for several days."

Barton joined the group and pointed a reassuring finger at Zeb. "I'll be around if anything transpires and you happen to need me."

Katie mentally scanned her suspect list. Tip was a bit lacking in the gray matter department, but would do about anything for money. Was he still a possibility? And it was a given that Bone was a thief and a drunk. But would he go so far as to target a child?

She turned to Deputy Fox, "How can we..."

The man cut her off. "I'm glad you asked that."

He swept his eyes from Katie to Zeb and back to Katie. "Here's what we want you to do while I'm gone. We need you to keep an eye on Fred." Then he shifted his focus back to Zeb. "And Boomer."

Katie's breath caught. So they *did* suspect the old weasel. Was Zeb's family in any real danger? Zeb could take care of himself—and them. Couldn't he?

The schoolmaster nodded, his face somber. "I can do that. You can't beat an on-the-site vantage point. If anything out of the ordinary goes on, I'll find it."

Fox clapped him on the shoulder. "I was hoping you'd see it that way. Now don't either of you do anything on your own. If you notice anything suspicious, contact Sheriff Barton."

Katie smoothed her skirt, then reached up to straighten her collar, making sure the bluebird pin was still there. "What about Tip? And Bone?"

The deputy's eyes bore into hers, his expression hard to decipher. "It wouldn't hurt to keep an eye out. If you get the chance."

The focus had shifted. Bone and Tip, with all their craziness, weren't raising any red flags, at least as far as the officers were concerned. But something was up. She'd pay special attention to the goings-on at Hollisters' store.

She extended a hand to Deputy Fox. "Thanks for all your trouble. You too, Sheriff Barton."

Fox took her hand in both of his. "It's our job. I'm just thankful it wasn't the little boy. I'll be heading out in the morning. You two be careful."

Katie attempted a smile, her heart yearning for her mother to be happy and for a chance to get to know this Jesse Fox a whole lot better. "You, too."

The officers headed back the way they'd come, Rebel bouncing along between them. Katie read the sadness on Zeb's face. "I'm sorry about the little goat."

He slid an arm around her waist, his voice soft, satisfying. "Yeah, me too. Let's go home."

Side by side, they picked their way through the woods, the grip of Zeb's large hand firm around her smaller one. When they reached the gate, *their gate,* he paused. "Got a few minutes?"

The familiar, peaceful sensation engulfed her. That sensation she experienced every time the guy was near her, alone, enchanting her with the calmness of his deep, soothing baritone and those lucid brown eyes.

Are you kidding? For you, I've got a lifetime.

She tossed her head. "Sure. Why not?"

His gentle hands around her waist lifted her to the top of the gate— to heaven. He hopped up and perched beside her. Leaning forward, he clasped his fingers together and rested his elbows on his knees. "They suspect Boomer, don't they?"

How should she respond? She placed a hand on his arm. "I don't know. Probably just covering all angles."

He lowered his head and pressed his hands to his temples. "They suspect him. They *suspect* him. What am I gonna do?"

At a loss for words, she put her arms around him and held him tight. Returning the embrace, he pressed his face against her cheek. "Don't breathe a word of this to anyone. If he's guilty of…" He paused and took a long, shaky breath. "If he's done anything, we'll just have to deal with it. Are you with me?"

She pulled back and cupped his face in her hands. It broke her heart to see the pain in those gentle eyes, the pain she wanted so badly to relieve, and had no idea how. "I'm with you every step of the way."

"Thank you." A sturdy hand crept around the back of her neck and gently cradled her head. Placing his lips over hers, he lingered, pulling her close. Her breath came in a long sigh, and she was in paradise.

The kiss was over too soon. Always too soon. Zeb

slid to the ground and lifted Katie to stand in front of him. His voice was husky. "No matter what, we're in this together. We're a team. Okay?"

"Okay."

He persisted. "No, I mean it. No matter what happens, you'll stick with me? No matter what?"

The man was pleading, begging. He was tearing out her heart. "I'm not going anywhere. We can get through this—together."

When he left her at her front door, Katie paused before going inside. Sitting in the porch swing, she let her thoughts take control. She needed to keep an eye on Fred. And what better way to do that than to spend some time with Hazel? Sure, that's what she'd do. Now to decide how to pull it off without appearing obvious.

"Want some beans and cornbread?" Duke swung open the screen door and danced a little jig.

So much for her ponderings for now. She'd have to devise a plan later.

"Sure, sounds yummy." She followed the child inside and took her place at the supper table.

By the time the supper dishes were done, and the kids were in their pajamas, Katie's eyes were drooping. It felt good to slip into her nightgown and sink into her familiar featherbed, allowing the sheets' fresh outdoor fragrance to lull her into a peaceful sleep.

THUMP! Something hit the side of the house. Katie jolted awake. Tuesday morning already? A movement at the window caught her eye. A small upside-down head appeared, dangling outside the upper part of her bedroom window.

"Luke! What are you doing?" She sprang out of bed.

The child waved and giggled.

Not bothering to put on her shoes, Katie flew out the front door and around the house. Luke hung suspended by a rope tied around his waist and wrapped around the chimney. Duke's smiling face peered down at her from the edge of the roof. "Hi, Katie."

Her heart skipped a beat. How did he get up there? She grabbed Luke and freed him from his would-be shackle. Setting him on his feet, she glared up at Duke. "Don't move."

"I can't get down if I don't move. Ladder's on the other side."

Maintaining her position on the ground directly underneath the child, she turned to his brother. "Luke, run and get your dad."

"I'll get the ladder." Manfred Olsen stood behind her. Her fear of Olsen took a back seat to her concern for the boys' safety.

Without another word, the man rounded the corner of the house, and in seconds, came back easily toting the ladder in one hand. He propped it against the roof's edge and spoke calmly to the child. "Come on down, Duke. I've got the ladder. Slow and easy now."

"Just a second." The child crawled across the roof's slanted surface to the chimney and unwound the rope. "Catch."

The rope slid across the shingles and landed in a

tangle at Katie's feet, barely missing Luke. She wanted to wring Duke's neck—if he didn't break it first.

The hobo, securing the ladder with both hands, spoke reassuringly to Duke. "Come on, Son."

Slowly, rung by rung, Duke descended the ladder and slid into the safety of Manfred Olsen's arms. He patted the child on the back. Duke turned and wrapped his arms around the hobo, who returned the hug, a warm smile playing at the corners of his mouth and encompassing his eyes. He stood and picked up the ladder. "I'll put this away."

In an instant, Katie saw the man in a new light. A calmness pulsed through her body, and compassion for him tugged at her heart. He cared for her little cousins, and he hadn't hurt them—or her. "Thank you."

He paused for a split second, and smiled at her. "You're welcome."

Now that both boys were on solid ground, Katie knelt between them and took each one by an arm. "What in the world were you trying to prove? You could have both been hurt, or killed."

Duke stared at her with soulful eyes. "We was just doin' a invest... investi..." He directed a pleading look at his brother.

Luke folded his arms and shook his head. "Investigation."

Katie's mind ran the gamut of what-ifs. "Go on."

Duke raked his bare toes through the dirt and hung his head. "We wanted to find out if Luke could fly if he jumped off a house. But we was kinda afraid he couldn't, so we used a rope just in case."

Thank you, Jesus, for protecting my little buddies.

She pulled them close. "Guys, you gave me the scare of my life. Why would you do that?"

Duke gave her his "don't-you-get-it?" shrug. "'Cause it was somethin' we didn't know, and we wanted to find out." He leaned his head on her shoulder. "Are ya mad?"

Luke followed suit on her other shoulder. "Mad?"

She made a mental note to have a word with Zeb about what ideas he suggested in front of the twins.

Weighing her words, she mustered up the sternest tone she could. "No, I'm not mad, but I should be. Next time you want to investigate something, ask me about it first. Okay?"

No answer.

Duke changed the subject. "Luke, show 'er what you found."

Luke reached into his overall bib pocket, pulled out a crumpled paper, and handed it to Katie. The paper turned out to be a tattered photo of a woman's face. The background indicated she'd been standing in front of a wooded area when the picture was taken.

Duke put an arm around his brother. "Look close. It's you."

Luke snapped his fingers. "You."

Katie scrutinized the picture's details. Her brain did a double take, and her head spun. The young woman, light hair framing her face, could be Katie's twin. "Where did you get this?"

Luke pointed toward the barn.

Duke's face lit up. "It's a good picture, ain't it. He

found it on the ground over by the barn door."

Olsen's face drifted through the corridors of her mind. Who was this girl? Was this the reason the hobo kept staring at her?

Inside her room, Katie shook out her yellow dress. It would do for one more day. She'd help rinse out some clothes when she returned from taking the boys to school and maybe try to repair her torn overalls.

Wait a minute. This was the perfect excuse to spend time with Hazel. She'd take the overalls with her and ask to use Hazel's sewing kit in the back room to repair them. Of course. She stuffed the ripped garment in a bag and, beckoning the boys, headed off to the school—and Zeb.

"Foul ball!"

Duke and Luke skidded toward the outfield the minute their feet touched the soft dirt of the playground. Zeb stood to the side, arms folded across his chest. Walter snatched the ball from the air and tossed it to Kevin on the pitcher's mound, then shaded his eyes and scanned the line of trees hemming the school yard.

Katie couldn't tear her eyes from the schoolmaster in tan slacks, a tucked-in blue shirt, and the ever-present cowboy boots. How could any one person be so doggone handsome?

"Looks like Walter's still on duty." She sidled up next to Zeb, aggravated at herself for the shivers that skittered up and down her arms when she was near him.

He turned weary eyes on her and cuffed her

shoulder. "Yeah, he's been the best. I wish we could zero in on our culprit, return things to normal, and bring Davey home."

"We will." She smiled and cuffed him back, wishing she could believe her own words.

He ran slender fingers up and down his forehead. "Sure. It's time to go in. See ya after school."

"Okay. See ya."

She stood in silence, watching until teacher and students had entered the schoolhouse and shut the door. Then, her parcel under her arm, she headed for Hollisters' store.

Zeb's face eased into her mind and drifted there. She'd heard of love at first sight, but this was ridiculous. She'd only known the man eleven days. *Eleven days.* It didn't make sense. She couldn't love him.

But she did.

She found Hazel behind the counter arranging the candies in their glass-fronted case. The woman glanced up and smiled. "Hi, honey. Whatcha got under your arm?"

Katie unwrapped the bundle and held up the overalls. "I was wondering if you could maybe let me use your sewing kit again."

Hazel's eyes grew wide and her mouth flopped open. "That's a big ole tear. What'd'ja do? Catch 'em on a nail?"

"No, I slid out of a tree."

Hazel shook her head and sighed. "Let me finish neatin' up this candy case, and then I'll fix 'em for ya.

But you're gonna hafta leave 'em with me. Want a cinnamon drop?"

"Thanks." Katie took the treat and popped it into her mouth.

"Welcome. That delivery man'll be here today, and I need to make room for what he brings. This is the day for special orders, too. I don't wanna miss 'im. We hafta check and double check that list."

Katie seized the opportunity. "Does Fred ever make special orders?"

The woman stepped in front of the counter and took the overalls, shaking them and *tsk-tsk*ing the tear. "Child, that husband of mine never goes near the delivery man. I think he's allergic to spendin' money for necessary things. Don't know how he thinks we'll get 'em if we don't pay for 'em."

Katie watched Hazel swing the overalls back and forth. "I'd be glad to do the repairs, if you wouldn't mind me using your kit."

Hazel's eyes flashed. "I said I'd do it for you."

Katie stepped backward at the abrupt statement. Hazel had never before snapped at her, but the woman had been under a great deal of stress lately.

Hazel folded the overalls and draped them over one arm. "I was rude. I'm sorry. It's just that…" She sank onto a chair. "Oh, you wouldn't understand. Nobody would."

Katie stepped beside her and laid a hand on her arm. "Try me."

The older woman's eyes filled with tears, and she wiped them on Katie's overalls. "It's just that… I wish

Mother were alive. I need to talk to her."

Katie's heart melted for the woman. How horrible would it be to be married to a man like Fred? A sudden overwhelming urge gripped her—an urge to travel to St. Louis to visit her own mother. "If you think it might help to talk about it, I'm a good listener."

Hazel gripped a leg of the poor overalls and twisted them between her hands. "It's too much. I can't take it anymore. Davey's gone, and I'll never see 'im again. I didn't want it to be that way. All I've got left is Fred and that stupid Charlie Eugene— somewhere out in the world 'a-causin' trouble. Shoot, shoot, shoot." She buried her face in the overalls, her shoulders shaking.

Katie struggled with what to do. Kneeling next to the woman, she searched for the right words. "It'll be alright. Let me take those on back home, and you try to take it easy. Want me to pray with you before I go?"

Hazel snatched the garment out of Katie's reach, much like a grabby child would do with a coveted toy. "No. They ain't no need to pray. I've been a-prayin,' but God ain't a-listenin' to me."

"God *always* listens."

The woman wadded the overalls into a knot on her lap. "Nope. Not this time." She shut her eyes and gave a loud sniff. "You just leave these here and check back with me this afternoon. I'll have 'em ready for you." And she rose and hurried toward the back room.

Two-thirty couldn't come soon enough for Katie. Rushing down the lane in an unbecoming manner for a young woman in a flowing yellow dress, she made it to the store in record time. Her curiosity and her concern for Hazel were neck-and-neck, vying for top position on her priority list. She bounded across the store's drive and onto the porch. Grabbing the door handle, she started to fling it open and stopped short.

Voices sounded from the kitchen. Loud voices. She backed off the porch and crept around the corner of the house, flattening herself against the outer wall. Standing as near as she dared to the open kitchen window, she strained to hear.

"I love too intensely. Care too much. And my heart breaks too easily." Hazel was sobbing.

"Hogwash."

"I was wrong, Boomer. I shouldn't a'told you to do it."

His cocky voice rose in anger. "I didn't hurt 'er. Tore 'er clothes a little, but that's all. And she didn't even recognize me."

Katie's heart lodged in her throat, and her pulse pounded. Boomer. So it *was* Boomer who attacked her outside Davey's window. But Hazel? What in the world was going on here?

Hazel's voice softened. "But it's wrong. It's all wrong. I'm a liar. A phony."

Boomer's voice held no sympathy, no compassion. "I didn't understand it then. Don't understand it now. Who cares about some old candy stick?"

"You don't get it a'tall, do you? You're just too mean and hard-hearted."

The man gave a wicked laugh. "Thank you."

"Go home, Boomer." Hazel's bitter tone made

Katie's skin crawl.

"Glad to oblige, ma'am." Heavy footsteps sounded on the hard wood floor, and the back door slammed.

Katie crouched beside the building, peering around the corner until she saw Boomer strut across his back yard. Then she made a mad dash from her hiding place and slipped from tree to tree until she reached the cover of the woods.

Adrenaline pumping, she cast one last hasty glance over her shoulder. Satisfied she wasn't being followed, she sprinted toward the school, questions flooding her mind.

Chapter 22

Zeb flung open the schoolhouse door. Warm bodies pushed past him into the afternoon sunlight.

"Bye, Mr. Harlow."

"See ya tomorrow."

"Later, gator."

Whew, what a day. The kids had been great, and Walter was a life saver. But Zeb's stress levels had skyrocketed. He pinched himself, wishing he could wake up in his own bed and find this was all a bad dream and knowing that wouldn't happen.

A flash of yellow caught his attention. Katie dashed out of the woods and approached him in short, quick steps.

"We need to talk. It's urgent." Huge blue eyes searched his, and she leaned against the building to catch her breath.

He touched her arm, and a familiar warmth surged through his body. "Sure. Let's get Mike home. We can leave the twins with Hazel and get off to ourselves for a few minutes."

She pushed away from the wall and locked her fingers around his arm in a death grip. "No!"

Whoa... Something wasn't right here. He placed his hand over hers and studied the lines of tension lacing their way across her forehead. "Why not?"

She stared toward the woods. "Uh, just let me take the boys on home, and I'll come back. What say we meet at our spot on the bluff?"

"Sure, I'll be there."

The gal wasn't making a whole lot of sense, but if it meant spending time alone with her, he wasn't about to question it.

"Let's not let the kids get too far ahead of us." Katie tugged on Zeb's hand and broke into an easy trot behind the boys.

Zeb locked fingers with her and set his pace to match hers.

Duke, a few feet ahead of them, reached the store first and hopped onto the porch.

"Dad!"

Marcus knelt, arms open wide. "C'mere, you two." He crooked an arm around each twin's neck in a mock wrestling maneuver. "Run on in the store and grab yourselves a Coke apiece, and we'll head for home."

When the boys emerged, each bearing a bottle of Coke, Fred frowned. "Don't mess around and lose them bottles. They cost money, ya know."

Marcus reached in his pocket, retrieved a dime, and flipped it onto Fred's lap. "There ya go, big spender. There's a bit of security. But we'll return these tomorrow." He winked at Katie and Zeb.

Katie sidled up to him. "Uncle Marcus, if you plan to take the boys with you, I have a few things I need to do this afternoon. I'll be along later. Okay?"

Marcus stood and gave her a grin and another wink. "Go ahead. I've got the bases covered here." Then, scruffing each boy's head, he started across the drive. "Let's go, guys."

When Marcus and the kids had crossed the highway, Zeb led Katie out of earshot of Fred. "What's up?"

Katie chewed on her bottom lip and seized Zeb's hand. Without a word, she dragged him down the lane and up the narrow path to their forest retreat. Easing herself onto the ground under the huge tree, she patted the spot next to her. He sat—a little more willingly than he'd like to admit.

"Do you remember that day when I came into the store with my pocket torn?"

He dreaded what he was about to hear. "I remember."

She leaned against him. "I was attacked. Someone attacked me from behind and took a cinnamon stick I'd found on the ground under Davey's window and ripped my pocket trying to get it. I hit my head against the window sill and almost passed out. The person ran away, but I didn't get a good look at him, so I didn't know who it was."

Zeb's mind envisioned the scenario, and anger boiled in him. "But you do now?"

"I think so." She hesitated. "Zeb, you said we're in

this together, no matter what. There's something you need to know."

Sweat popped out on Zeb's forehead, and a chilly clamminess spread across his palms. "Go on."

"I'm pretty sure it was Boomer."

His world skidded to a halt. He wanted to scream—grab a crow bar and bash in his stepdad's brains. What was the man thinking? He had no consoling words, no ready response. He swallowed the huge lump that had formed in his throat. "What makes you think so?"

The sadness in her eyes rivaled the grief in his heart. "I overheard a conversation."

He listened intently, hanging on every word, as Katie described the encounter between Boomer and Hazel. When she was finished, he sat cross-legged before her. "Do you think Boomer and Hazel did something with Davey? And if so, why?"

Katie flattened her palms and rubbed them together. "I don't know what to think at this point, but I'm pretty sure Boomer was taking orders from Hazel, and I don't think he knew—or cared—what was really going on."

Zeb leaned forward. "He just liked the chance to get in on some violence."

"That's about the size of it. And I'm beginning to wonder if Hazel's losing it, if you know what I mean. She snapped at me today. She's never done that before."

A terrible thought crossed Zeb's mind. "Do you think Hazel would do something to Davey…"

Katie interrupted. "You mean—kill him, rather than risk Lyle Piper or even Charlie Eugene ever getting their hands on him?"

Zeb's muscles tightened. "That's what I mean. Stress can do weird things to a person."

The little gal leaned her head on his chest and buried her face against him. "Hazel did it, didn't she? She killed her own grandson." Then she sat upright. "No, she had Boomer do it. That's what she did."

Bile rose in Zeb's throat, and his stomach lurched. He swallowed hard and leaned back against the tree. Heart pounding, he turned to Katie. "We have to prove it."

Katie threw her arms around his neck and held on. "We're in this together. No matter what hap..." Her voice broke and silent tears leaked from the corners of her eyes.

He embraced her, drawing her closer, searching for words where there were no words. In the few short days he'd known her, this gal had won his heart. He loved her. No question about it. But he couldn't expect her to feel the same about him. At least, not yet. Especially not now.

She drew back and swiped a hand across her eyes. "We have to be careful. Very careful. We need to get all the facts we can, then notify Sheriff Barton. Let's go."

Zeb walked beside Katie in silence, his mind whirling. If Boomer was, in fact, a murderer, then no one was safe until the law had him in custody. And, heaven help them, he exhibited the potential.

"Zeb." Mike ran down the lane to meet them as they approached the store. "The cow's out. Dad says for me to get you to come and help."

Zeb gritted his teeth. His jaw clenched. "I'm coming." He knew who would suffer if he didn't. He wished he could just shoot that cow and get the whole thing over. No. Better to let the cow live and shoot Boomer. But even then, it would be too late for Davey.

It is Mine to avenge, Son. Remember that.

The bluebird pin sparkled against the collar of Katie's yellow dress. Zeb eyed it. He needed a bluebird. He just plain Needed. A. Bluebird. "Katie, I'm sorry. I'm so sorry. I'll be over later."

She squeezed his hand, then unpinned the brooch from her collar. "Here, you need this more than I do right now. Take care of it for me."

"I couldn't."

She pressed it into his palm. "Sure, you could. And it's not like it's gone. You can give it back later."

Before he could formulate a response, she was across the highway and headed for home.

Zeb pushed the delicate pin deep into his pocket, and trudged down the path Mike had taken.

When the cow was secured once more, Zeb strode up the Banks' lane with a purpose. He had to see Katie, discuss their strategies, and return her pin. He couldn't keep it, though he'd love to lay claim to it—and her.

At the end of the tree line, Zeb happened to glance toward the barn, and he froze. Emerging through the door was Manfred Olsen, absorbed in what seemed to be a friendly conversation—with

Katie.

They've been in the barn together. Alone.

His eyes must be playing tricks on him. Not Katie. Not with *him*. Shock gave way to resentment. Then rage took over.

She peered up and their eyes met. She turned to the hobo and patted his arm, then, smiling and waving, made her way toward Zeb.

"Hey, there, I didn't expect to see you here this soon." She grinned and reached a hand out to touch him.

He drew back. "That's apparent."

Katie's face clouded, and she dropped her hand to her side.

Zeb's eyes grew hot, and he struggled to remain calm. "I saw you with that bum. I thought I told you to stay away from him."

She took a step closer. "Don't you trust me?"

His insides wove themselves into a tight knot. "I thought I did, but now I'm beginning to wonder. And I sure as shooting don't trust *him*."

"But, you don't understand. It's not what you think. Everything's okay."

He tried to control the shakiness in his voice. "I don't want to hear it. I know what I saw." Fumbling in his pocket, he withdrew the pin and thrust it into her hand. "Here, take your old bluebird. Give it to that tramp. It doesn't work anyway."

"Zeb, wait. I can explain." She stood clutching the treasured pin, her blond hair enhanced against the bright material of her dress.

"There's nothing to explain. Goodbye." Zeb spun on his heel and strode off down the lane and away from Katie, hot tears stinging his eyes and his heart in shambles.

Crossing the highway west of his house, he made a wide girth and headed for the barn. In the familiar loft, he lay on his back on the hay and let the tears pool in his eyes until they streamed in rivulets down the sides of his face. He didn't care. His heart was broken. His dad was dead. His mom was a wimp for allowing Boomer to abuse her. Boomer was a murderer. His brother was a nuisance for calling the old wart "Dad." What was the use?

Who cared for him? Zeb Harlow. He wished he was dead.

Zeb!

He sat up with a start. There was no one there. But the voice in his head rang clear as a bell. He reached for the trunk and took Zeke Harlow's Bible in his hands. It fell open to the book of Matthew, chapter eleven.

The invitation was clear. Come to Jesus, bring your burdens, and exchange them for a lighter load, an easier yoke.

Jesus, gentle and humble in heart, was offering to bear his burdens for him. Right now. But for his soul to find that rest, Zeb had to let go and give it all to Jesus.

He reread the words, and he understood.

"Lord, I'm sorry. I shouldn't have been so hasty. I release it all to you. All of it. I can't handle it. I can't do it. Take it. I place it in Your hands."

You need to let go of it first, son. I can handle it for you. Trust me.

"Lord, I'm trying. I need a bluebird."

You had one. Remember? But a bluebird isn't what you need.

He clutched the Bible to him and closed his eyes. God's presence filled the loft. A peace settled over him, and he sat in silence until the lengthening shadows told him night was fast approaching. Loath to leave his sanctuary, he took his time replacing the Bible in its hiding place and descended the ladder. He should go in to see if he could do anything to help Mom.

Blinking in the dim light of the house's interior, Zeb made out the form of his mother standing outside his bedroom door. She raised a hand and placed her finger over her lips to signify silence. He crept toward her and stopped the other side of the door. She mouthed the word "listen."

"...so you see, it's a gift. You can't earn salvation. Jesus died on the cross to pay for your sins. But you've gotta understand that you're a sinner, and that you need His help. And then tell Him you're sorry for what all you've done wrong, and ask Him to forgive you for it, and then place your trust in Him and tell him you wanna be saved. And if you mean it, then you're saved!" Mike's final sentence was nothing short of jubilant.

"Lord, I've done wrong." Fred's shaky voice caused prickles of excitement to skitter up Zeb's spine as realization dawned on him. "I ain't been worth nothin' for years. And I'm awful sorry. I'm a-askin' You ta forgive me, and I'm a-placin' my trust in You right this minute. Thank You, Lord, for savin' my old mean soul."

"Did you mean it, Fred?"

"I shore did, Mike. I shore did!"

Mike's voice was a high-pitched squeal. "Then let's go tell somebody."

The two burst through the bedroom door, and Zeb and Mom stepped back. Fred turned his head from side to side and displayed a huge smile for the two eavesdroppers. "I'm saved. I'm saved! I'm a-goin' ta heaven one a'these days."

The back door creaked, causing a hush to fall over the group as Boomer strode toward their little gathering. He headed for his wife. Flinching, she ducked her head and backed away. Zeb grabbed Boomer's arm. "Not this time, old man."

Boomer spun and threw both arms around Zeb in a bear hug. "I've come home, Son. I'm saved."

Fred cocked his head to one side. "Are you a-makin' fun a'me?"

Boomer released Zeb, and his face turned solemn. "I'm not makin' fun of nobody. I seen you go in our house and went and stood outside the window to see what you was up to. I thought you'd come to try to make time with my wife, and I was preparin' to beat the livin' daylights outta you. Then I heard Mike talkin' to you, so I thought I'd listen in."

Zeb was dumbfounded. Was this situation too good to be true?

Boomer moved to put an arm around Mom's

shoulders. "The more I heard, the more I knew I'd had enough of this life, and how wrong I'd been. So I prayed that prayer, too, and I got saved when Fred did."

Tears flowed down Mom's face, and Boomer reached to brush them away. "I'm sorry, baby. I'm so sorry. But things'll be different from now on. Just you wait and see. I'll make it up to you. I'll make it up to all of you."

Zeb's mind whirled. Wow. Oh, wow.

I told you I could handle it. It'll be alright. Now trust Me.

Zeb woke early Wednesday morning. He needed to see Katie. Talk to her. Make things right. He'd just have to catch her when she brought the boys to school and make her talk to him. Not that he could *make* her do much of anything. But he could try.

From the school yard, Zeb watched the lane. Luke's head popped out from between two bushes, followed by the rest of him, followed by Duke. Zeb straightened his shirt and mustered up his courage. He stepped forward. It was now or never.

But Katie didn't follow the boys. No one did. Were they alone? Surely not.

The twins scurried onto the makeshift ball field, and Duke turned back, raising his arm in a wave. "Bye, Mr. Olsen. See ya after school."

The grinning hobo stuck his head around a tree and waved back. "Be good." Then he took off up the lane without a word.

Zeb motioned for Duke. The child trotted over to

stand beside him. "Where's Katie?"

The lad looked down and scuffed a toe in the dirt. "Oh, she had to go somewhere. That's how come Mr. Olsen brung us to school."

Luke, seeing Duke talking to their teacher, came over and stood beside his brother.

Zeb couldn't hide his concern. "Aren't you afraid of Mr. Olsen?"

They both laughed. Duke spoke up. "Heck, no. He's nice. He's our friend."

Luke displayed a wide smile and nodded. "Friend."

The school day seemed endless. Hoping against hope for Katie to be the one to pick up the boys at the end of the day, Zeb's heart broke anew when Manfred Olsen appeared under Katie's tree.

When the school yard had emptied, Zeb made a trek to the Banks' home. Aunt Nellie sat on the porch. He scanned the field and barnyard, but no Katie. Maybe she was in the house. "Where's Katie?"

The woman shook her head. "She's gone. Left with her uncle Rance this morning. Went to St. Louis to see her mother and sister."

Zeb lowered himself to the top step. "When will she be back?"

"I don't know. She didn't say."

He remained on the step, his energy drained.

Aunt Nellie reached over and patted his arm. "I'm sorry, hon."

He pushed to a standing position. "Thanks. Guess I'll be goin' then."

He made his way to *their gate* and perched on the

top rail, head in his hands, eyes closed. He hadn't even had the chance to apologize. Tell her he was sorry for being so rude. Tell her he'd listen, if she'd just talk to him again. "Oh, Lord, what am I gonna do?"

"Well, I don't rightly know, son. But if you'll tell me what's wrong, I might be able to help."

Zeb nearly fell off his perch. His eyes flew open. Manfred Olsen stood before him. "Didn't mean to startle you."

"You didn't startle me." *Well, not much anyway.* A mixture of emotions invaded Zeb's mind. Should he talk to the man? Why not? Katie was gone. The hobo couldn't hurt her now. And Zeb could care less if the guy hurt him. His rage was gone. Fatigue—mental and physical—took its place.

"I think there's something you should know." Leaning against the gate post, Olsen reached into his pocket and extracted a crumpled piece of paper. He held it out.

Zeb took it and turned it over in his hands. Confusion clouded his mind. "Where did you get this?"

"That's my mother. Looks like your girl, don't it?"

"It looks like Katie." Memories of her face took front and center in his mind, and he struggled with the next words. "But she's not my girl."

"Look, Son. My mother is a sister to Katie's grandma, Anna Burrow Tillman. So that makes Katie and me cousins. If you don't believe me, ask Nellie. She's got a photo album with one of these in it, and Katie's grandma. Pretty strong family resemblance, ain't there?"

Zeb was speechless. He slid off the gate and stood leaning against it.

Olsen eyed him. "I saw you lookin' at us as we come out of the barn yesterday. She was in there talkin' about it with me. I'd lost it, and the boys found it and brought it back to me. But not until Nellie had had a good look at it and made the connection."

Zeb felt his face grow hot and hated himself for it. He cleared his throat. "I guess I owe you an apology. I shouldn't have been so rude to you. I thought..."

Olsen sighed. "I know what you thought. But you thought wrong."

Zeb had the urge to bolt, but he stayed. "Well, I, uh..."

"Never mind about that. No hard feelings. It's already forgotten. I realize it's easy to jump to conclusions, and you had no reason to trust me. You didn't even know me." The hobo paused, then clamped a hand on Zeb's shoulder. "She's a good girl, and I can see you care about her. Don't lose her."

The man walked away, stuffing his mother's picture back into his pocket.

Zeb crammed his hands in his own pockets, painfully aware of the absence of Katie's bluebird pin, and the absence of Katie.

Chapter 23

Katie let her head rest against the back of the passenger side seat in Rance Tillman's car. Her uncle's old Model A Ford rattled north on highway 67, each mile taking them closer to St. Louis—and farther away from Zeb. But what did she care? He didn't trust her, he wouldn't listen to her, and he'd told her goodbye. Their relationship had ended before it even had the chance to get a good start.

Trees swished by, and the rapid shift from sun to shade caused her eyes to water and gave her a headache. She touched the pin on her collar. Poor little bluebird. It was just a pin, only a token. It was given in love, but it couldn't bring happiness. It couldn't fix anything.

But I can. Let go of it, Katie. Turn it over to Me.

"A penny for your thoughts?" Uncle Rance leaned over and bumped her shoulder.

His innocent question ripped into her heart. Zeb's voice cruised through her mind, and she wanted to scream. She stroked her little enamel bluebird. "They're too deep to explain."

He accepted her response and didn't push further. "Won't it be fun to see your mom and Ruth again? Won't they be surprised when we pull up in front of their house?" Her uncle turned his face toward hers, and the kindness in his eyes made her want to bawl. She loved him so much. He was using up his time and gas money just for her.

"It sure will. I can't wai..." Her voice broke in spite of herself. She bit her lip and took a trembling breath. "I can't wait."

Uncle Rance glanced toward her and, slowing his vehicle, pulled onto the highway's shoulder. The car rattled to a stop. He peered at her with eyes narrowed. "What's the matter, little girl?"

She straightened—cleared her throat. "Nothing."

He'd have no part of that. "Come on. What is it?"

She was tough, but she was tired. Tired of being the strong one. Tired of caring too much and falling too hard.

Even so, she could handle Hazel's sharp tongue, Zeb's rejection, Boomer's attack, the terror of not knowing what happened to Davey, and still keep a stiff upper lip as the old saying proclaimed. But Uncle Rance's genuine kindness, filled with understanding and unconditional love, was her undoing. She fell apart right in front of him.

Much to her dismay and embarrassment, the tears came in a torrent, rolling down her cheeks and falling in huge, sloppy droplets on the soft material of her light blue dress. Uncle Rance pressed a handkerchief into her hands, then sat in silence, patting her shoulder from time to time.

She held the handkerchief over her face, dying inside. It seemed an eternity before she dared trust her own voice. "I'm sorry, Uncle Rance."

He smiled that warm smile, and her tears threatened to start again. "Don't be. People need people. Nobody should have to go it alone. And your Uncle Rance is right here. Now talk to me, little girl."

Weary of holding it inside, she poured out her heart to this wonderful man, her mother's younger brother. She told him about the attack outside Davey's window, and how she was sure now that it was Boomer. She told about Hazel's unkind words, and the conversation she overheard between Hazel and Boomer, and about her suspicion that Davey was already dead, and that Hazel was somehow involved.

And she told him about Zeb. Lots of things about Zeb.

The man eyed her intently, the corners of his mouth curving upward ever so slightly. "You love him, don't you?"

Her heart leaped at the thought. "I can't love him. He doesn't love me. Besides, I've only known him for a few days, and you can't fall in love that fast."

Her uncle's expression became serious. "Oh, but you can. Believe me, you can."

She detected a note of sadness in his voice. "How do you know?"

He patted her hand. "I just know. But that's a

story better left untold. You can't turn back time. But, *you* still have time. Don't give up. Everything'll be alright." Then he produced a grin, and winked at her. "Ready to get rollin' again?"

She nodded. "Thanks."

"That's what friends are for."

It was as though a heavy burden had lifted from Katie's heart. But a question still lingered in the front of her mind. "How can you say everything'll be alright? That's a powerful statement."

He gripped the steering wheel and focused on the road ahead. "I'm aware of that, but you see, we have a powerful God. And me and Him had a little talk about—things. I don't know when He'll do it. I don't know how He'll do it. But He's gonna take care of things like you wouldn't believe. You just watch and see if I'm not right."

Katie eased back in the seat and closed her eyes, and the years fell away. She was a little girl again, snuggled underneath Mama's goose down comforter. The world drifted by in slow motion, Mama singing songs to her and Ruth, a midsummer evening breeze stirring the curtains, sounds of the city at night...

"Wake up, Katie." A hand touched her arm.

She brushed it away, unwilling to leave this world she once called home.

"Wake up. We're here." Uncle Rance nudged her shoulder and gave a chuckle. "You musta trusted my drivin' a whole lot. You sure had a good nap."

An ebony sky, sprinkled with a million stars, joined the spattering of street lights and glowing windows.

This was St. Louis. This was home. Or not. Her thoughts traveled to a worn wooden gate and a guy in big old cowboy boots, and she longed for him so much it hurt. She gave herself a mental lashing. *Forget him, Katie. You're wasting your time. He doesn't want you.*

"But I want *him*."

"What?" Uncle Rance pulled open her door and grabbed her satchel from the back seat.

Had she actually uttered that aloud? Good grief. She thought fast. "Uh, I said let's go in."

He laughed out loud. "Well, come on then. Let's go surprise 'em."

Rance tapped on the door. A curtain eased aside, and a face peered through. Suddenly the face disappeared, and the door was flung open.

"Katie! Katie! Katie!" Ruth threw her arms around her sister and hung on, burying her face in Katie's hair. "I've missed you so much."

Katie returned the hug from her seventeen-year-old sister, her best friend.

Suddenly the girl drew back. "Where are my manners? Come on in." She grabbed Katie's arm and dragged her into the front room, ushering her to a daybed and plopping down beside her.

Rance stepped in and shut the door. "Where's Norma?"

"She's around here somewhere." Ruth rared back and opened her mouth wide. "Maaaama, we've got company."

Soft footsteps sounded down the hall, and her mother, face glowing, appeared in the doorway. Her slender frame in a green cotton dress, her short brown curls, and that gentle smile—Katie pressed her lips together to stop them from trembling.

Rance stepped forward and took both of Norma's hands in his. "Hey, Big Sister. Thought we'd drop by and surprise you. Did we?"

Her eyes sparkled, and she winked at Katie. "Well, you most certainly did surprise me. But as far as the dropping-by part, it looks to me like you had to do a whole lot more than drop by to get here. Of course, you're staying a few days. And I know you're both starved. Come on in the kitchen and catch us up on the latest news while I fix you a bite to eat. Would an egg sandwich tide you two over till morning?"

Visions of her mother's bacon and egg breakfasts danced in Katie's head, and she folded her arms and pressed them against her midsection. Ruth grinned and jabbed her on the shoulder. "Stomach about to growl?"

Katie tried to frown at her, but failed. "Well, it *has* been a long time since we ate."

Her sister gave her a little nudge in the direction of the kitchen. "Hey, Mama. You maybe oughta put a couple slices of bacon on those sandwiches, too."

Ruth set glasses on the table in front of Rance and Katie. "What'll it be—milk or milk?" She laughed. "Or, of course, you can have water."

Katie glanced at her uncle. "Water?"

He nodded. "That'll be fine."

Ruth filled the glasses and added some for herself and Norma as well. "How's Uncle Everett?"

"He's fine and can still cook a mighty mean breakfast. Just like your mama."

While Norma and Ruth quizzed Rance about the rest of the family, and the smell of frying bacon tantalized Katie's nostrils, she let her mind drift over the miles, all the way back to Bluebird Valley. The kitchen became a blur as thoughts of Zeb, then Jesse Fox, took shape. Deputy Fox would be perfect for Mama. She needed to convince him of that—the easy part. Then she'd have to convince Mama.

"Do you?" She jolted from her reverie. Ruth stared at her from across the table.

"Do I what?"

"Do you want a slice of tomato on your sandwich?" Her sister's blue eyes pierced her own, communicating the old familiar message. *We need to talk later.*

Katie's nod held a double meaning. Ruth lifted Katie's bread and forked a juicy tomato slice on top of the bacon.

Once they had eaten their fill and Katie and Ruth had washed the dishes, Mama put her hands on the table and leaned toward her brother. "I'm afraid I'll need to go to bed soon. Morning comes awfully early, and they want me at the candy factory by six-thirty. Katie, you can share Ruth's bed, and Rance, do you mind sleeping on the daybed?"

Rance pushed to his feet and raised his arms behind his head with a huge stretch and a grunt. "Course not. It's made for sleepin.' That's why it's called a bed. And speakin' of bed—I'm about ready to turn in, too."

Katie stretched out on her back on one side of Ruth's double bed and let her head sink into the coolness of the thick feather pillow. Moonlight filtered through the window, and faint city sounds rocked the cradle of her mind. Where had her childhood gone? How had everything managed to get so complicated?

Ruth plopped onto her side of the bed and propped her head against a bent right arm. "Okay, Sis. Let's have it."

Katie was not to be manipulated so easily. Not even by her beloved sister. "You first."

"Oh, so it's gonna be that way, huh?" Her little sister reached over and poked her in the ear. "Oops."

Katie grabbed her hand. "Ow! Don't be poking people when you can't see what you're doing."

Ruth jerked her hand back and giggled. "So does that mean it's okay to poke people when I can see what I'm doing?"

Katie gave a sigh of resignation. *Some things never change.* "I'm serious. How have things been going for you?"

The bed shifted as Ruth stretched out beside her. "Don't say anything, but money's been pretty tight around here. Mama works at that candy factory, but it's not enough to make ends meet. She's actually been talking about us moving back to the country where she grew up—where things are cheaper, and life's simpler."

A tingle of excitement squeezed its way into Katie's stomach and made her want to shout. She took a deep breath and answered in an even tone. "Go on."

"Since I graduated from high school, I've been doing some babysitting to earn money to help Mama. I want to be a teacher someday, so working with kids is right up my alley and I don't mind it at all, and these two are little sweethearts."

The mention of a teacher brought memories of Zeb flooding through her mind and her heart ached anew. Tears pooled in her eyes and a lump formed in her throat. She hesitated.

"You asleep?"

Katie swallowed, thankful her sister couldn't see her face. "No, just thinking. Tell me about the two little kids you babysit."

Ruth needed no more encouragement. "It's a little girl and a little boy. The girl's name is Mabel Rettinger and she's four, but they only bring her when both parents are busy the same day. She won't be here tomorrow. The little boy's name is Ray Wymore, and he's almost three. He comes every day but the weekend. His mom brings him of a morning on her way to work around seven, and picks him up around five every afternoon. I don't think there's a dad in the home. So you'll get to meet Ray tomorrow. Now tell me about you."

Katie wasn't ready to talk about it yet. Wasn't even sure she could. The hurt was too deep—too new. Tears came too easily. She didn't want a repeat of the episode in the car earlier that day, especially not in front of her little sister, but she owed her sister an explanation. She opened her mouth to try and respond.

Soft, steady breathing reached her ears. Ruth was asleep. *Thank You, Jesus.*

Katie snuggled into the comfort of the feather bed, and let the darkness and sounds of the city at night lull her to sleep as well.

The unmistakable aroma of frying bacon nudged Katie awake, or was it Ruth gently shaking her shoulder? "Get up, Sis. I've got something for you."

Katie opened her eyes to slits. Ruth stood beside the bed holding a maroon dress with little seahorse patterns dancing all over it. Her bluebird pin was already fastened to the collar.

Katie sat up and ran a hand along the soft fabric. "It's gorgeous."

Ruth draped the dress across the foot of the bed. "It's yours. I have four, and I want to share this one with you."

Katie realized her sister's sacrifice, and was sure it was the best of her four. "I can't take this. You'll need it."

Ruth sank onto the bed. "You wore one yesterday and brought one extra. I snooped. Now we have three apiece." She punched Katie's arm. "Put it on. Then come in and model it at breakfast."

Ignoring any further protest, Ruth slipped out of the room, closing the door behind her. Katie donned the dress and realized she and her sister were still the same size.

By six o'clock, Rance and Norma had climbed into Rance's car and headed for the candy factory. Ruth gathered the dishes and put them in the dishpan. "I'm really glad Uncle Rance took Mama to work. Sure beats her having to walk every morning."

A sadness gripped Katie at the thought of her mother walking the St. Louis streets alone in the early morning hours—and the late afternoons.

Ruth grabbed a dish towel and flicked it in the air, making a loud pop. "I'll do the dishes if you'll go make the bed."

"Sure." Katie twirled, half alert, and made her way to Ruth's bedroom. When the bed was made, she flopped onto a chair and stared out the window. Not really focusing on any one thing, she became vaguely aware of a little bird perched on the iron fence outside. A bluebird. Maybe God was telling her everything was going to be alright after all. But how could it? Zeb was mad at her, Davey was gone, and her mother was alone because of her.

Someone knocked at the front door. She heard it open, then click shut.

"Katie? Ray's here. Come meet him."

It'd be fun to meet the little boy. She could help Ruth babysit him—maybe take her mind off things for a few hours. She pushed to her feet and started for the front room.

In the doorway, she came to an abrupt halt and her breath caught. The child squealed and flew past Ruth and into Katie's arms.

Davey.

Chapter 24

"Rise and shine, boys." Boomer, a huge grin on his face, stood in the bedroom doorway sporting an apron and carrying a dish towel. "I've got biscuits in the oven, gravy on the stove, and coffee all 'round. It'll be ready by the time you get in there."

Zeb sat up and swung his legs over the side of the bed. Thursday morning. Early Thursday morning.

Mike raised up on one elbow and blinked. "Can he cook?"

Zeb entertained the same thought. "I sure hope so. Can't say that I've ever known him to try." He paused. "By the way, do you drink coffee?"

His brother chuckled. "Never have. But it looks like I'm about to start."

Zeb pulled on his jeans and boots, then grabbed a shirt from the back of the only chair in the room. Drawing back the curtain, he peered out the window in the direction of Hollisters' store.

Fred sat on the porch step, Davey's little terrier

snuggled on his lap. An undertone of sadness for his little buddy tugged at Zeb's heart. *Pway* echoed in his mind as he slipped the harmonica into his pocket and followed Mike into the kitchen.

"Get in here, boys, and grab a seat." Boomer indicated the table set for four, loaded with everything he'd promised. Zeb savored the tantalizing aromas as he took a seat on a wooden chair. If those smells were any indication of how this meal would taste, Zeb was all for it.

Pulling out a chair for Mom, Boomer bent and planted a kiss on top of her head. Then, taking his place beside her, he eyed Zeb. "Son, would you say the blessing over this here food? I ain't learned how to do that yet."

Zeb bowed his head, hesitating a moment to steady his voice. Never in his wildest dreams could he have imagined he'd actually live to see this day.

I told you I could take care of it, Zeb. Now trust Me.

When the amens were said, Boomer reached for Mom's plate. "Ladies first." Loading it with two biscuits and dousing them with an ample supply of sausage gravy, he gently placed it before her. "Okay, guys, dig in."

One bite told Zeb the man need not take a back seat to anyone when it came to skill in the kitchen. Doggone him. He could have been doing this all along.

Zeb...

Mom offered a shy smile that melted Zeb's heart. "Boomer, this is delicious."

The man beamed, and lowering his eyes, gave her hand a squeeze. "Thanks."

Breakfast ended, and Boomer pushed back his chair and made a sweeping motion with his hand. "Now shoo, everybody. You guys need to head on out to school. And, Darlin,' you go on out in the front room and relax."

Zeb had to force himself to close his gaped mouth and stop staring at this new Boomer. He pinched himself. No, he wasn't dreaming.

The man gripped Zeb's shoulder. "Go on now. I've got a lot of makin' up to do, and I mean to start doin' it today." He picked up a plate and, whistling a tune, scraped the bits of leftover gravy and biscuit into a small bowl. "That little pup next door might like this."

Zeb's veterinarian heart did a flip-flop. "I'll take it over there."

"Naw, I think I'd like to give it to him myself." Boomer grabbed another plate and repeated the procedure.

Belly full and his heart as happy as possible, considering that Katie was gone and Davey was still missing, Zeb strode across the parking lot toward Hollisters' store. Mike trotted ahead of him, plopping down beside Fred, and scratched the little dog behind the ears.

Hazel pushed open the screen and stuck out her head. "You two hungry?"

Zeb patted his stomach. "No."

She thrust a little bag into his hands. "How about a couple comma-doodles for lunch then?"

Comma-doodles. Katie. Why did everything under the sun have to remind him of Katie? "Thanks. We'll enjoy these."

She raked a hand across her forehead, pushing a few loose strands of hair into place. "You're welcome." The corners of her mouth turned up in a grin. "But be sure to eat 'em outside."

He grabbed her hand and squeezed it. "We'll remember."

The day passed at a snail's pace and Walter as usual was a godsend. An hour before dismissal time, smack-dab in the middle of seventh grade recitation class, one of the younger girls raised a hand. "Mr. Harlow, I need to be excused."

Zeb nodded to Walter. He and Zeb had devised a system in which the girls would be escorted in twos, so Walter selected the child's seatmate to accompany them and followed the two out the door.

In minutes the door opened, and a little face peered into the room. "Mr. Harlow, we found something."

At her tone, a sense of unease pervaded Zeb's mind, and he shook his head to remove it. Where was Walter? "What did you find?"

"Well, uh, it's a sack." The child stepped inside, followed by her young seatmate.

Zeb's senses went on high alert. "Where is it?"

"Outside. Walter gots it."

Something wasn't right. "Go ahead and sit down, girls."

As they obeyed, Zeb stepped outside the door.

Walter stood clutching a small burlap bag bulging with—something. He stepped toward Zeb, his face somber.

Zeb's heartbeat pounded in his neck. "Whatcha got there, son?"

Hands trembling, the young man extended the bag to Zeb. "The girls found this just inside the door of the girls' outhouse. I don't think it was there earlier. At least, nobody mentioned it till now. I...uh...looked inside it, but I think you'd better see for yourself."

Nerves tingling, Zeb took the bag and pulled the top open. Inside was a jumble of envelopes and crumpled pieces of paper. He extracted one and smoothed it against the leg of his jeans.

Walter shifted from one foot to the other. "Read it, Mr. Harlow."

Zeb opened his mouth, but his voice became a whisper as he read. FORGET ABOUT DAVEY. HE AIN'T COMEN BAK. LYLE PIPER.

Zeb glanced up at Walter. The teen nodded, the corners of his mouth turned down in a grim line. "Read another one."

Note after note revealed basically the same message, all bearing the name Lyle Piper. Zeb stuffed the contents back inside the bag and folded down the top.

Walter bit his lower lip. "How do you think they got there? What do you think this all means?"

Zeb *knew* what it meant. Someone had been planting those notes in the Hollisters' mailbox to throw everyone off the trail. But who? And why had they stashed the bag in the outhouse, where it was sure to be discovered?

His heart went out to the frightened teen—his good right hand. "I'm not sure, Walter. But I'll need to let the sheriff know about this. Come on. Let's go in and finish the day, then I'll contact him." He patted the young man on the back. "Good job. You did the right thing by bringing these to me."

Hastening to stash the bag deep inside a desk drawer before any of the students' parents arrived for the afternoon trek home, Zeb encountered curious glances from several of his charges. He put on a stern face and met their stares eye-to-eye, and nobody was brave enough to venture any questions.

By the time the students were dismissed and the school yard cleared, Zeb was a bundle of nerves. Turning, he started toward his desk to retrieve the evidence and do what he knew had to be done.

Walter stood by the big desk. "Is there anything I can do to help?" The concern in his manner showed maturity far beyond his years.

Zeb breathed a silent prayer for God to protect this young man, to give him the chance he deserved in life.

He'll be fine, Zeb. I'll protect him, as I will you.

Zeb sank onto his chair. "Not a thing. You've done what was needed again and again. I couldn't have made it without you. You just go on home and try to not worry, and we'll get to the bottom of this."

Walter extended a hand. "Thank you, Mr. Harlow."

A hearty handshake was Walter's goodbye for the day. He turned, head held high, and strode out the schoolhouse door.

Burlap bag in hand, Zeb locked the door and made his way up the lane. Trudging along, head down, he dangled the bag at his side, trying—and failing—to stifle the surge of self-pity that welled up inside him. He needed a bluebird. He needed Katie.

Sunlight reflecting off something caught his attention, causing him to raise his eyes. The sheriff's car stood by Hollisters' gas pump. Sheriff Barton was here? Questions spinning through his mind, he quickened his steps and hopped onto the porch.

A car door slammed. "Hey, Zeb, wait up." Sheriff Barton strode across the gravel drive to join him. "I just got here. Haven't been inside yet. Come on, I've got news."

He followed the sheriff inside, fearing his legs would fail to support him, and sank onto the pile of feed sacks, plopping the little bag beside him. Eyes rounded, Fred pushed to a standing position from the cane-bottom chair near the kitchen door. Hazel came from around the counter and stood before the sheriff.

Barton minced no words. "We just got a call that Davey's been located. I came to let you know soon as I heard."

Hazel clutched the man's arm. "Is he... is he... dead?"

The sheriff, smiling, placed his hand over hers. "He's just fine. They told me I could come pick him up and bring him home to you."

Zeb wanted to cry, shout, laugh, and praise the Lord.

Hazel ran to Fred and threw her arms around him. "He's safe. He's safe."

Fred patted her back and guided her to a chair, taking the one beside her. He indicated another chair near the window. "Sit down, Sheriff, and give us the details."

Sheriff Barton grabbed the chair, spun it around, and swung a leg over it, leaning his arms on its back. "Well, the only thing they told me was that he was found and identified this morning, the law was alerted, and the kidnapper is in custody and being questioned."

Hazel wiped her eyes and blew her nose loudly on her apron. "Where is he?"

"St. Louis. I'm to go to the police station up there, and they'll take me to Davey."

Zeb stiffened. St. Louis. That's where Katie had gone. Why did everything have to remind him of her?

Hazel persisted. "But exactly where is he right now?"

Fred shook his head and glanced toward his high-strung wife. Sheriff Barton gave a slight wink. "They didn't say exactly where he is, but that he's in a safe place. And that I can pick him up in the morning and bring him home. I'll spend the night up there and head back here with him in the morning." He snapped his fingers. "So you get things all ready 'cause I'll have your grandson back in your arms by tomorrow night."

Hazel sniffed loudly and wiped her nose on her poor apron. "But he don't know you. He'll be a'skeered."

Barton scratched his head. "Hmmm. That's true." He unwound his legs from the chair, stood, and took a seat on a feed sack near Zeb. "How's about Zeb ride shotgun with me? Davey knows him. What say, Zeb?"

"But tomorrow's Friday. I'll have a schoolhouse full of kids to teach."

Fred hobbled over to look out the door. "I've got an idea. How about Ella? She taught here a while back, and she's great with kids."

The lightness in Zeb's chest made him feel as if he could drift to the ceiling and hang suspended there. Of course. Miss Ella. "That would be great. I'll go ask her right now, and if she agrees, I'll be back here and ready to ride in two shakes of a lamb's tail." He jumped to his feet, grabbing the burlap bag.

Fred eyed the little bag. "What's that?"

Zeb stopped, all eyes on him. "Oh, a little bag of stuff. It belongs to the sheriff." He thrust it into Sheriff Barton's hands.

The man gave him a curious stare, but accepted the bag. "Yeah, thanks, Zeb. I'll go put this in the car and get ready to go."

Hazel grabbed Fred and planted a loud, sloppy kiss on his cheek. "Oh honey, we're gonna get our baby back."

Fred pulled away, his face reddening. "Hazel!"

The woman slid a hand across the top of his head, then bustled off toward the kitchen. "So much to do by tomorrow. Gotta get things ready. What a relief. Oh, hallelujah! Our baby's comin' home."

Fred hung his head. "I'm sorry, guys. She gets worked up."

Outside, the sheriff plopped the bag onto the car seat and slid in beside it, shooting another curious look Zeb's way. "I'll be lookin' to hear from you in a few minutes. Hope it works out that you can go."

Zeb trotted to the Banks' home in record time. Before the yard came into view, shouts told him the twins were involved in a game of catch, probably involving their trusty gourd. When he reached the gate, Duke spied him and missed the gourd. "Hey, Mr. Harlow." He raced to his teacher's side.

Luke followed suit, prancing across the grass and locking an arm around Zeb's leg. "Harlow."

Aunt Nellie sat in a chair near the end of the porch and stirred something in a large bowl. Ella, cradling Molly in her arms, gently rocked the porch swing.

Zeb's eyes burned, envisioning the moment when, in that very swing, the warmth of Katie's body had thrilled him, and he'd stolen a kiss. It seemed a lifetime ago. He tried to swallow the fuzz that invaded his throat. "I've got news. Davey's been found."

Silence.

Finally Aunt Nellie pushed to her feet, clutching the now unimportant bowl. "Is he..."

Zeb propped himself against the porch post, the twins leaning on either side of him, staring up at him. He placed an arm around each of their shoulders. "He's fine."

Duke stepped away and sank to the top step. "We knew he was. 'Cause we seen the cross, and we got the candy." He laced his fingers together and stretched his arms out in front of him. "And we eat it every time."

Luke sidled next to his brother, shaking his head, and waved a finger in front of his face.

Duke paused, then his mouth curved into a grin. "I forgot. It's a secret."

Luke nodded. "Secret."

Zeb's brain screamed at him to question the boys, but he silenced it.

Aunt Nellie smoothed her apron. "Where is he?"

"St. Louis."

Ella straightened. "St. Louis?"

Zeb's heart ached. "That's what Sheriff Barton said. They want him to go up there tonight and pick Davey up first thing in the morning and bring him home. He asked me to ride along because the little guy already knows me. But the only thing is—there's school tomorrow. So, Miss Ella, I was wondering..."

His beloved teacher hugged Molly to her and pushed out of the swing. Coming to stand before him, their eyes met, and it was as though their minds were of one accord like in the old days. His mind traveled backward, and he was an eighth grader again.

Ella's eyes sparkled. "I'd be delighted to sit behind the desk of Zeb the Great for a day or so. You go on to St. Louis and get Davey." Then, glancing around, she leaned toward him, and giving a slight wink, she mouthed the words, "And find Katie."

The old, familiar tingling made its way into his chest, and his arms yearned to embrace his Katie girl again. He grabbed Ella's hand and squeezed it. Hard.

Her eyes widened, and he released his grip. "I'm sorry."

She chuckled, massaging her fingers. "Don't be. Just go do what I said."

"Thanks. I will." Zeb's feet had wings as he raced toward the highway. After a quick run by the house to let Mom know where he was going, he made a beeline for the sheriff's car and settled himself on the passenger seat.

Hazel thrust a paper bag through the car's open window. "Here, this is full'a sandwiches. You'll get hungry. But they're not comma-doodles. They're on bread. Don't want you gettin' crumbs all over this here fancy car." Easing a couple bottles of Coke into Zeb's hands, she stepped back and waved her goodbye.

Sheriff Barton pulled onto the road and headed west. "Comma-doodles?"

Zeb leaned back in the seat, ready to enjoy the ride, and hopeful about the destination. "That's sandwiches made with crackers instead of bread."

The sheriff gave him a quick glance. "Sounds good, but messy."

"Yeah."

The miles drifted by, and the men rode in silence. Presently, Barton cleared his throat. "By the way, where'd'ja get that bag of Lyle Piper notes?"

Zeb shifted his position. "You looked at them?"

The sheriff kept his eyes straight ahead. "Yep."

"A couple kids found 'em in the girls' outhouse at school. Don't think they were there this morning. Somebody musta put them there while we were all in the building."

Sheriff Barton scratched his head. "Any idea who?'

Zeb looked down at the little bag, now on the floorboard. "Not really. It was a shock to me. You have any thoughts on it?"

The sheriff remained silent for what seemed like forever. Finally he twisted his mouth and sighed. "Nope."

Just outside Farmington, Sheriff Barton pulled onto a side road. "I'm hungry. You ready for those sandwiches and Cokes Hazel sent?"

"Sure." Zeb's stomach whispered a silent "thank you."

When they finished the meal, they resumed their trek north on highway 67. A tinge of nerves, mingled with excitement, danced through Zeb's insides. "Do you know who the kidnapper is?"

The sheriff kept his eyes on the road. "No, only that they have her in custody."

Zeb's mind did a double-take. "Her?"

Barton tilted his head toward Zeb. "Yeah, it seems that some gal from over in East St. Louis had him with her. Posed as his mom and changed his name—not legally, of course. Brought him over that Municipal Bridge to St. Louis every day when she went to work and left him with a teen girl. A babysitter. Then she'd pick him up every afternoon and, BAM, back across the state line with him."

Zeb hung on his every word. "Grabbed him and took him out of state?"

The sheriff nodded. "So she's racked up a

kidnapping charge, and taking him out of state makes it a federal offense. So I think they'll probably throw the book at her. Yep, looks like she'll do some time for this little caper."

"But why would anyone do a thing like that?"

"Don't know. But it happens. They're interrogatin' 'er. Tryin' to find out if she's got any connection to that Lyle Piper character, or whether she's in cahoots with the boy's dad."

St. Louis loomed in the distance until specks turned into buildings and they entered the city. It was late, but the police station was by no means deserted. Zeb followed Sheriff Barton inside.

In seconds a furry little body slammed into Zeb's leg, and Rebel jumped against him in greeting. Zeb knelt to pet the little beagle. "Hi, buddy. Been missin' you." The dog nuzzled his hand.

Deputy Fox stepped forward, followed by a man in a uniform. Fox indicated the two newcomers. "This is my boss, Sheriff Clay Barton, and the Bluebird Valley schoolmaster, Zeb Harlow. Men, meet Deputy Tom Stover of the St. Louis Police Department."

They exchanged acknowledgements and handshakes, and Barton and Fox sat in chairs at a table with Deputy Stover. Zeb took a seat on a nearby bench, and Rebel hopped up beside him, snuggling against his long-lost friend.

Deputy Stover spoke. "We've got her in a cell back there. When we put the handcuffs on her, she screamed like we were killin' 'er. One of 'em pressed against a place on 'er wrist, and I guess it's tender.

She's got quite a scar there. Runs clear up her right arm and her watch band intersects it. The whole thing looks kinda like the shape of a cross." The man paused. "Anyway, she's locked up back there and been bawlin' her eyes out for several hours. Says she did the whole thing out of love. Said she just wanted to keep the child safe."

Zeb stroked the little dog's scruff, his vet's heart full.

Suddenly a light flickered in his brain. The deputy's words played tag in his mind. A scar. A cross. Safety. Could it be?

Deputy Fox leaned his elbows on the table. "Yeah, old Lillian put on quite a show. Sure had me fooled back there at the store when she came to visit Davey. I was convinced she cared a lot about the boy. Still am. But I never had any idea she'd be capable of a stunt like this."

Deputy Stover turned to Sheriff Barton. "We plan to do extensive questioning tomorrow, after she's had a chance to calm down a bit. Want to sit in and hear it?"

Barton glanced at Zeb. "Sure, but what about Davey? Zeb and I are supposed to get him in the morning and take him home."

Deputy Fox intervened. "I've got my car. What say Rebel and I take Zeb with us and go get the boy in the morning? He'll like Rebel, and I understand he and Zeb are already buddies. That'll give you a chance to stay as long as needed."

That decision made, Zeb joined Barton and Fox in

a back room of the St. Louis PD, where they slept on cots for the remainder of the night. Rebel curled up at the foot of Deputy Fox's cot, and his soft snores lulled Zeb into a somewhat peaceful sleep.

He woke to the sound of voices in the next room and rubbed the sleep from his eyes. After a complimentary breakfast of coffee and doughnuts Zeb, Deputy Fox, and Rebel arranged themselves in the police cruiser and Fox steered it onto the road.

Zeb rubbed damp palms along his pant legs, then picked at the seams with shaky fingers. Rebel laid his head against Zeb's side, and he put his arm around the little dog and drew him close. The beagle's furry warmth helped calm his...what?...fear of the unknown? Was Davey really where they said he'd be? Was he really safe? He drew in a breath, then let it out slowly—and more audibly than he intended.

Fox glanced his way. "It'll be okay, School Teacher. We're almost there."

Chapter 25

"Huff. Puff." Davey clapped his hands and wiggled on Rance's lap, causing the wooden rocking chair to wobble back and forth.

"Uncle Rance, you do the best ever imitation of the Big, Bad Wolf. You make that Three Little Pigs story come to life. And Davey's doing a pretty good job of imitating you. I believe you've got you a little friend there." Katie was thankful her uncle was here, and that Mama hadn't gone to work this morning. Sure, they'd said the kidnapper was in custody, but she couldn't help feeling a little uneasy at the thought of her and Ruth alone and in charge.

So much had happened in the last twenty-four hours since Davey had arrived and raced into Katie's arms. Uncle Rance had returned to the house yesterday morning and summoned the police, who had questioned Ruth and taken down the contact information "Ray's mother" had given her in case of emergency. And Ruth had stood in horrified silence when Katie told her that Ray Wymore was a missing child whose real name was Davey Ray Hollister.

A deputy had been stationed at the house until they got word that the kidnapper had been apprehended. Then he'd told the Gallaghers to keep the child with them until the Wade County sheriff could be notified and arrangements made to pick him up and return him to his grandparents. Uncle Rance had offered to take him home, but the deputy had given a long spiel about regulations.

So Davey had slept on the daybed last night under Uncle Rance's watchful eye.

The soft comforter Mama had spread across it this morning afforded Katie a semblance of security as she dangled her legs off its edge. Weary, she scooted back and leaned against the pillows, letting the back of her head rest against the wall. Allowing her eyes to droop shut for a moment, she relaxed—somewhat. Davey was safe, but too many questions remained unanswered. Where was Charlie Eugene? Did he have a hand in all this? Had they located Lyle Piper? Was he in custody?

A car door slammed. Katie's eyes flew open and a tightness gripped her stomach. A knock at the door made her muscles tense.

Uncle Rance stood, gently placed Davey in the now-empty rocker and moved to open the door. A familiar, furry body bounded into the room and headed straight for Katie.

Rebel.

Mama smiled. "Hi, little one." She bent to let the

beagle sniff her hand.

Rance held the door open wide. "Come on in, fellas." Stepping back, he ushered their visitors inside.

Deputy Fox entered the room, smiling like a travelin' rat, and extended a hand to Rance. A big pair of cowboy boots followed. She ran her tongue across her lips and pressed her palms together to stop their trembling.

Zeb's eyes met hers, and hope welled inside her. But, with an almost imperceptible nod, he quickly looked away. Her heart sank. He was still mad. Her pulse pounded in her throat and tears threatened. Pressing her fingers to her lips, she stared at the floor.

Rance's kind voice filled the room. "Norma, Ruth, I don't think you've met these guys. This is Deputy Jesse Fox from Wade County, and Zeb Harlow, our local schoolmaster."

Katie glanced up in time to see the deputy take Mama's hand and extend a warm greeting. "Glad to meet you, Norma."

"Pway?" Davey had slid from the chair and was tugging at Zeb's pant leg.

The dear man bent and lifted the child off the floor. "Amazing Grace?"

The little boy wrapped his arms around Zeb's neck and nodded. Zeb lowered himself into the rocker with Davey on his lap and pulled his harmonica from his shirt pocket. Strains of the beloved melody floated through the air, and the room fell silent. Katie's mind drifted. Should she make another effort to talk to him, to try to explain? Probably not. He'd plainly conveyed to her that he was done listening.

Davey snuggled against Zeb, swaying to the music. When the last note faded, the child squirmed to the floor and put his hands on Zeb's knees, staring into the man's face. "T'anks, pal."

Zeb's delight at Davey's new phrase was evident. His eyes full of warmth and compassion, he bent forward and tousled the child's hair. "You're welcome, little guy."

Katie watched, reliving the moments when she'd felt that tender touch. Another time, another place, it seemed a lifetime since she'd melted into the comfort of those arms around her.

The little boy pushed away and raced toward the kitchen. Snatching a small paper bag from the counter, he returned and waved it in front of Zeb's face. "Want one?"

Zeb cast a puzzled glance at Ruth.

"Go ahead and take one. He brings a bag of those cinnamon sticks with him every morning, and he loves to share them." Ruth knelt beside Davey and patted his back. "That's right, Ray, er... uh...Davey. Always share with other people."

Zeb reached in and extracted one of the candies. "Thanks."

The little boy flashed a wide grin. Zeb, unsmiling, shot Katie a raised brow.

A car door slammed. Deputy Fox went to the window and pulled back the curtain. "It's Deputy Stover. I'll be right back."

Davey approached Rebel and ran his hands along

the dog's soft coat. Rebel's nose quivered in recognition, and he nuzzled the child. Davey giggled and fell to the floor, pulling the little dog with him in a lively wrestling match. Rance grinned and winked at Katie. "Looks like this kid has no trouble makin' friends."

Katie's thoughts exactly.

Mama stood by the door, observing the conversation outside. "That other deputy's leavin'. Here comes Deputy Fox."

Katie wanted to shout. "No, Mama. That's Jesse. Call him Jesse."

Mama pulled open the door and stepped aside. Jesse Fox, his face solemn, took Mama's arm and motioned for Ruth to join them. "Ladies, I need to talk to you two."

Katie's energy drained from her like water from a sieve. Something was wrong.

Fox squatted to the woman's eye level. "There's been a new development. Davey can't leave today. The suspect has pled guilty, but she's named an accomplice."

The color drained from Zeb's face, and Katie longed to go to him, comfort him. The deputy drew in a deep breath and let it out in a whoosh before continuing. He rubbed the line that had appeared between his furrowed brows, then massaged his temples and spoke in a husky voice. "Hazel Hollister."

This time Zeb's wide eyes locked on Katie's. She read shock and relief.

"Here's what they want us to do." Jesse Fox's

attention centered on Mama. "Sheriff Barton is already on his way back to Wade County to interrogate Hazel, and they want me to keep Davey here until they give the all clear to proceed. It could be tomorrow. It could be days."

"We'll do anything we can to help." That was Mama. She'd help wherever she could, willing to ignore her own comfort and convenience. "You're welcome to anything we've got. I'm just thankful the baby's safe." She placed a reassuring hand on Jesse Fox's shoulder.

He patted her hand, a grateful smile tugging at the corners of his mouth. "Thank you, Mrs. Gallagher. Sorry to be such a burden."

Call her Norma. Her name's Norma.

Mama stroked her chin. "Let's see now. I'll need to get some more groceries, and we'll need to decide on sleeping arrangements. Deputy Fox, you and Zeb can have my room, and I'll sleep in with the girls. Rance, you and Davey can keep the front room like last night." Easing onto a soft chair near the window, she eyed Davey and Rebel, now lying side-by-side on the linoleum. "And the pup can sleep anywhere he chooses."

Rance cleared his throat. "Big Sister, that sounds a little crowded to me. What say I send Zeb and Katie on back home today in my car? Then, when Davey's cleared to go, I can ride shotgun with Deputy Fox. Would that work?" Rance tilted his head and gave Katie a subtle wink. Heat prickled up her neck.

The deputy propped a hand on the floor and faced

Zeb. "Sounds like a winner to me. How's about it? Will that do?"

Shades of pink invaded Zeb's tan complexion, and his Adam's apple bobbed up and down. "Uh… yeah… sure, if Katie's okay with that."

Katie's heart leaped in her chest. Her sister peered at her, head tilted, eyebrows raised, then a smug grin erupted on her face. The girl was too perceptive. Knew her way too well.

Katie straightened, mustering up all the composure she could manage, and nodded toward Deputy Fox. "Yes, I think that'll work alright."

Ruth rushed over and grabbed Katie's hand, practically dragging her toward the bedroom. "Let's get your things packed and get you ready to roll."

Katie, her mind whirling, let her sister take the lead.

Clicking the bedroom door shut, Ruth grabbed Katie's bag and plopped it onto the bed. "Quick, take off that dress and slip back into the maroon one. You looked beautiful in that. And put your bluebird pin back on it. That Zeb's a cute one. I think he likes you. Do you like him?"

Katie, her chin quivering, did as her sister instructed. "Ruth, I think I love him."

Ruth sat on the edge of the bed and patted the spot next to her. "C'mere, Big Sis." She squirmed around till they were face to face, then took both Katie's hands in her own. "I think you love him, too. I can see it in your eyes."

Katie bit her top lip and blinked back tears. "Say a

prayer for me, Little Sis."

"I always do." Ruth opened her arms and embraced her older sibling.

Katie, heart pounding, clung to her like a child afraid to leave her mother on the first day of school.

Let it go, Katie. I've got this. Trust Me.

Giving her sister one last squeeze, she released her death grip and drew back.

Ruth cocked her head to one side. "It'll be okay. Everything's okay." Then, grinning like the Cheshire cat, she lightly poked her sister in the ear. "And I'll come to your wedding. Count on it."

In minutes, Katie and her bag were once again in Rance's car. Only this time the road led south, and Zeb was behind the wheel.

Katie peered out the window at the small group assembled in the front yard. Davey, balanced on Rance's hip, waved an enthusiastic goodbye. Mama and Ruth, their arms around each other, waved in unison, while Rebel tugged at the leash wrapped around Jesse Fox's wrist. Katie's heartstrings stretched to the breaking point as Zeb turned right at the corner, and they were lost from her sight.

Straightening in the seat, she faced forward but averted her eyes to the left. Zeb, his jaw clenched, gripped the steering wheel with both hands and focused on the road before them. Did she dare try to explain? Would he even listen? Probably not.

She clasped and unclasped her hands in her lap, bracing herself for the long ride home.

Chapter 26

The dangerous St. Louis traffic put Zeb on edge, as did the girl beside him. From the corner of his eye, he caught her fidgeting, clearly ill at ease. She didn't want to be here, but he didn't blame her. How could she forgive him, after the way he'd treated her? And why should she?

He braked at an intersection—a little too long. *OOOO-ga.* The horn blast behind them jarred him into reality, and he stomped the gas pedal, propelling Rance's car forward with a violent jolt. Katie sat like a statue beside him.

While the city sounds surrounded him and unnerved him, they were no match for the deafening silence inside the car.

Little by little, traffic dwindled, and they cruised unhindered down the open road. A sign proclaimed U.S. 67 South, as though it were proud of its accomplishment. He sneered inwardly. *So what?*

Despite the ease of the road, the agony within Zeb

threatened to break through with full force. His knuckles, white with tension, gripped the steering wheel until they ached, and his head swam, blurring the road in front of him. This was ridiculous.

Blinking, he refocused and knew what he had to do. "Uh, Katie?"

Silence.

Pulling to the road's shoulder, he ground the car to a stop and shifted in the seat, facing her. She sat, head down, hands still clasped in her lap.

He tried again. "Katie, I'm sorry. I was wrong. I snapped at you. I hurt you. And when I came to ask your forgiveness, you were already gone."

She raised her face, the pain in her eyes sending daggers through his heart. "I can explain." She paused, lowering her head. "If you'll let me."

He placed a hand over hers. She didn't pull away. "There's nothing to explain. Olsen talked to me, showed me the picture, told me the story. I should have trusted you."

Her gaze intensified, and liquid blue eyes penetrated his soul. "You mean...?"

"I mean that I jumped the gun. I assumed facts that didn't exist. It's just that when I saw you with another man, I... I..." The inside of Zeb's mouth turned to cotton. After several attempts, he swallowed with a loud gulp and blurted the words. "It was my fault, and I'm sorry. I need some peace, Katie. I need you to forgive me."

The gal's expression transformed before his eyes, as understanding passed between them. She clenched one hand into a fist and punched him in the arm, ever so gently. Threads of tension drained from his body. "You're forgiven, Zeb the Great. 'Cause, hey, we're in this together. Remember?"

Oh, he remembered all right. He definitely remembered. Leaning forward, he placed his forehead against hers. "Thank you, Katie girl. I..." The words lodged in his throat.

Soft arms came around his neck, and warm lips pressed against his.

OOOOO-ga. A car slowed, then zipped by as wolf whistles and shouts of "way to go" permeated the air.

Katie pulled back, her face reddening. "Oops."

Zeb placed his hands on her shoulders and suppressed a chuckle. She was cute when she was flustered. "They're jealous. Bet they'd all like to have someone like my girl."

My girl.

The words rolled easily off his tongue and warmed his heart. He gave her a light cuff on the jaw. "Let's head on home and see if Sheriff Barton needs our help."

"Yeah, right." Her eyes sparkled, then turned serious. She leaned back against the seat and rubbed her palms together. "I *am* anxious to hear Hazel's take on all this. What was that woman thinking?"

"No tellin'." Zeb eased the car back onto the highway, his tension replaced by an overwhelming peace as *his girl* relaxed on the seat beside him.

An easy silence filled the car as the miles drifted by. Katie had laid her head back and closed her eyes.

This was too real—too natural. Sunbeams danced on the little bluebird pin on her collar and made her golden hair shine. He had to tell her how he felt about her. Soon.

Presently, shifting on the seat beside him, she reached over and touched his arm. "Zeb?"

At her touch, a surge of warmth traveled through his body and lodged in his heart. He fought a sudden urge to stop the car and take her in his arms. He leaned toward her. "Yeah?"

"What part do you think Hazel played in all this? Or do you think Lillian was just bluffing?"

Zeb didn't respond immediately, but fixed his eyes on a road sign a few yards ahead, measuring his words. *Entering Wade County.* They were almost home. "I'm not sure, but hopefully we'll know before long. That is, if Sheriff Barton gets any cooperation out there."

Extending his arm out the window in a left-turn signal, Zeb steered the car east onto highway 34. Familiar landmarks flashed by, the smell of new mown hay—a reminder that God would soon bathe these hills and valleys in autumn's splendor. He breathed a silent prayer of thanks for everything.

You're welcome.

He knew that voice. A smile crept across his face and into his heart.

Katie shifted in the seat beside him. He reached over to place a hand on hers. "A penny for your thoughts?"

She took his hand in both of hers and pressed it to her face, then released it and laid her head on his shoulder. The miles melted away, and time hung suspended, yet raced at an alarming speed.

"Look." Katie straightened and pointed toward Bluebird Valley Church. "There's Fred's car."

Fred's car sat parked in front of the church, the driver's door standing open. Fred sat in the driver's seat, and Brother Deren stood with his foot propped on the running board.Zeb pulled into the church yard and stopped the car. "I'm gonna go see if something's wrong. Go with me?"

"Sure." The gal swung her door open and hopped out, appearing at Zeb's door before his feet hit the ground.

The men waved a greeting. Brother Deren patted Fred on the shoulder, then faced the two. "Hey, Katie and Zeb. Glad you're here."

Zeb put a hand behind Katie's back and steered her forward. "Everything okay?"

Fred slid to the ground. "Not exactly. The sheriff come to the store and started questionin' Hazel, and she plumb went nuts." He glanced toward Brother Deren. "Shore am glad I turned my life over to Jesus. Boy oh boy! I knowed I needed to get Pastor Grayson in on this, so I hightailed it over here."

Katie's body tensed. She shot Zeb a questioning look.

His heart warmed. She hadn't been told that Fred was saved, or Boomer for that matter. He grinned and nodded.

Her eyes shone.

Fred fidgeted with his overall gallus. "We need to

get back over there. Pastor Grayson, wanna ride with me?"

In answer, Brother Deren darted around Fred's car and opened the passenger door. Fred climbed behind the wheel and waved a hand at Zeb and Katie. "You two meet us at the store. The pastor's gonna go in and see if he can help the sheriff deal with Hazel, 'cause she shore won't listen to me. I'll fill you in on the details while he's in there."

With Fred leading the way, Zeb pulled onto the road and joined the two-car convoy. Katie leaned forward and stared into his face. "Fred's saved?"

Zeb kept his eyes on the road, but couldn't prevent a huge grin from stretching his face to the limit. "So's Boomer."

Katie's mouth fell open, and she sat like a statue, staring at him—yet right through him.

He patted her hand. "It's true. I'll tell ya all about it later."

Finally her body sank against the seat next to him, her lips moving, her voice barely above a whisper. "Thank you, Jesus."

By the time Zeb and Katie arrived on Hollisters' parking lot, Fred and Brother Deren sprang from their car and sprinted toward the store. Zeb and Katie followed on their heels. The first thing they saw was Boomer and the sheriff, sitting in high-back chairs. Zeb scanned the room. "Where's Brother Deren?"

The sheriff tipped his head toward the back room. "Back there on this side of that bedroom door, tryin' to talk some sense into Hazel." He spread his hands and shrugged.

Fred sank onto the feed-sack sofa and indicated for Katie and Zeb to join him. "Boys, let's fill 'em in on what's been goin' on. Maybe they can figger out a way to help." He nodded to the sheriff.

Barton ran a hand through his hair. "Soon as I walked in the room this mornin', Hazel started askin' questions about Davey. You know, sayin' where was he, and all that."

Fred nodded. "Yeah, he told 'er Davey was fine, and they'd bring 'im home later, but she flew mad and accused 'im of doin' somethin' to the boy. He said no he didn't, and that he just needed her to answer a few questions first."

Boomer ran a hand across the back of his neck. "Yeah, that was about the time I walked in. She was screamin' that the Wade County law had promised to bring her grandson home safe and sound today, so where was he."

Fred rubbed his eyes. "Then when the sheriff tried to ask 'er some questions, she clammed up, run fer the back room, and locked 'erself in it. And cain't nobody coax 'er out."

Katie stood and smoothed her skirt. "Let me try." Without a backward glance, the gal squared her shoulders and headed across the room.

Zeb's heart soared. That was his girl. *Go, Katie girl. You can do it.*

Fred rose and plodded to the soda box, took out four cold Cokes, and popped the caps. He passed one to each of the men and took one for himself. "I think we need to wet our whistles."

"Thanks, Fred," came from all directions.

Zeb let the refreshing liquid soothe his throat and pushed to his feet. Needing to stretch his legs, he walked to the door, then squatted near it. "So, Sheriff Barton, did they find Lyle Piper in St. Louis like they thought?"

The sheriff took a sip of his Coke. "Aaah. That sure hit the spot." Then turning to Zeb, he frowned. "The Lyle Piper thing didn't pan out. Turns out they were following an anonymous tip, and when they checked into it further, they found out Piper hadn't been anywhere near St. Louis, or Wade County for that matter, in the past two months."

Zeb's mind whirled. So that made it very unlikely that Piper had anything to do with those notes bearing his name.

Fred visibly stiffened. "Where was he?"

Sheriff Barton hesitated and took another gulp of his drink. Rolling the soda bottle between his palms, he lifted his eyes to meet Fred's questioning gaze. "Canada."

Zeb drew in a quick breath. "Canada! What was he doin' up there?"

The sheriff stared at the floor. "He was—still is— doing time in jail for bashing another guy's head in."

Fred's face went white. "Whose head?"

The sheriff's lips tightened into a narrow line, then he said, "I'm sorry, Fred."

The man buried his face in his hands. "It was my boy, wasn't it? It was Charlie Eugene. How long's he been dead?"

Boomer slipped behind Fred and placed a hand on his shoulder.

Barton stood and walked to the window, focusing somewhere across the parking lot. "Yes, it was Charlie Eugene. But he's not dead. He's in the hospital up there, and they had to put a steel plate in his head, but he's gonna recover."

Boomer slapped Fred on the back. "Hear that? He's gonna be alright."

Fred shook his head. "No, my friend. He'll never be alright. Not til he gives 'is heart to the Lord." He turned sad eyes on the sheriff. "How did it happen?"

"We don't know how they ended up all the way up there together, but the report says that they both got drunk, got in a fight, and Charlie Eugene got the worst end of it."

Boomer knelt beside Fred. "What did they fight about?"

The sheriff sighed. "Who knows..." Then he brightened. "But since the kidnapping happened in August, that takes both of them out of the picture as far as suspects are concerned."

Fred set his soda bottle on the floor. "Then who? What?"

"Hey, Mr. Harlow, you're back!" The screen door flew open and Duke, followed by Luke and Marcus, rushed into the store. "Did you have a fun day?"

"Well..." Zeb averted the question. "Say, how was your day?"

Luke giggled.

Duke bounced from one foot to the other. "It was a hoot to have Mom as a teacher, but she wouldn't let us get by with anything."

"Anything." Luke slapped his leg and let out a loud guffaw.

Duke bopped his twin on the shoulder. "Yeah, she wouldn't even let us go out under the schoolhouse where we hid the cinna..." He stopped abruptly, and both boys eyed each other and clamped their mouths shut.

Duke moved closer to his brother and surveyed the room. "Where's Davey?"

Sheriff Barton smiled at the boys. "He'll be here later."

Marcus plucked a couple of Cokes out of the soda machine and handed one to each boy. "Why don't you guys take these out on the porch and drink them, but stay where I can see you. I'll be out in a few minutes."

The twins, casting suspicious looks at each of the four men, shuffled out to the porch.

When the door had clicked shut, Marcus leaned back against the counter. "Where *is* Davey? I thought sure he'd be here by now. Is there something wrong?"

Barton flattened a palm against the countertop. "To be honest with you, Marcus, there *is* a slight problem."

Fred, leaning against the door frame, faced the sheriff and repeated his previously interrupted half-questions. "Then who? What?"

"It was Lillian. We're ninety-nine percent sure she's the one who put out the false tip about Piper to throw the law off her trail. During questioning, she told us she was afraid Piper or Charlie Eugene would get Davey, so that's why she took him. Said she loved him and wanted him safe, and the only way she knew to make that happen was to take him with her and hide him."

Fred weaved and grabbed the door frame for support. Boomer was beside him in an instant, taking him by the arm and guiding him to a chair.

Barton's face showed concern. "Should I go on?"

Boomer eased Fred to a sitting position and knelt beside his chair. "You okay?"

The man raked a sleeve across his brow. "I'm fine. Go on, Sheriff."

"Well, the thing is—she lives in East St. Louis, so she took him across the state line. That makes it a federal crime. So the lady's probably lookin' at some prison time for this little caper. Davey's safe now, and he will be returning home. But, yes, Lillian *is* the one who took him." The sheriff crossed the room and sank onto the feed sacks, as though he'd just endured a major ordeal.

CRE-E-EAK. The screen door opened, and Duke's face appeared. "It looks like you know where he is, so I guess the cat's out of the bag."

His brother, grinning, sidled in beside him. "Meow."

Marcus's face was stern. "Boys! You were eavesdropping."

Duke poked a toe into a crack between floorboards. "Don't know nothin' 'bout that. But we heardja."

Luke nodded, his face now solemn.

Duke leaned against his brother. "We didn't tell, so can we have another cinnamon stick?"

Marcus knelt beside the boy. "Son, it's okay to tell some things. Secrets are for Christmas presents and surprise birthday parties and things like that. But when you know something that can help somebody, it's okay to tell. In fact, you should tell. Do you understand?"

The child plopped down on his dad's knee. "Even if you promise not to?"

Marcus put an arm around him and pulled Luke into the other arm's embrace. "Yes, even if you promise not to. Nobody should even ask you to make a promise like that. Okay?"

Duke glanced at his brother before answering. Luke gave him a thumbs-up, and his twin smiled. "Okay, Dad."

Luke hooked a hand through Duke's gallus and tugged him to a far corner of the room. After a whispered conference, both boys with arms around each other's shoulders crossed the room and stood before Sheriff Barton. Duke served as spokesman. "Okay, Sheriff. We'll come clean."

Where did they get that phrase? It would have been funny, if the situation hadn't been so serious.

The sheriff tilted his head toward Zeb and wiggled his brows, only partially succeeding in hiding the twinkle in his eyes that threatened to light up his whole face. He turned to look down at the twins, his mouth forming a grim line. "Okay, boys, let's have it."

Duke rocked on his toes, taking advantage of every inch of his height. "We seen Hazel and Aunt Lillian out by Davey's window that day."

The sheriff knelt to face them. "What day?"

"That day after Davey dis... dis..." He gave his brother a plaintive glance.

Luke shrugged and gave a little sigh. "Disappeared."

Duke nodded vigorously. " Well, Hazel was pullin' stuff out of Davey's window and givin' it to Aunt Lillian. We asked, 'Where's Davey?' and she said, 'He's safe, and if you don't say nothin' 'bout this, I'll give you candy.' And she did."

"What did she do then?"

Duke stuck his hands in and out of his pockets and twisted side to side. "Then she... she..."

The sheriff patted the child's arm. "Take your time, son. Take your time."

Luke rubbed his brother's back. "Time."

Duke tried again. "Then she tuck the bag Hazel give 'er, and tuck off through them woods lickety-split with it. But she said Davey was safe long as we didn't tell. And we seen the cross, so we knew he was."

Sheriff Barton shot a raised eyebrow look at Zeb. "Where did you see the cross?"

"On her arm. And she give us candy. Luke dropped his, but Hazel made us go on away and wouldn't let him look for it."

Luke extended his lower lip and produced a sad-eyed expression.

Suddenly Boomer leaped to his feet. "So that's

why Hazel told me to get that cinnamon stick. I bet she planned to try to clean the dirt off of it and give it back to Luke."

Luke and Duke exchanged horrified looks and chorused a simultaneous comment. "Ewww."

Boomer continued. "So the boys wouldn't come back and go snooping around there later and attract attention."

The sheriff rose to his feet and stared at Boomer through narrowed eyes. "Just what do you know about all this?"

"Well, you see, Sheriff." The old arrogance in his voice was gone, and a gentleness had taken its place, a gentleness that made Zeb want to throw his arms around the man right then and there. He had wanted to find a way to get the old Boomer to go away, but he hadn't had to. God had done it for him. And He'd replaced it with something that exceeded Zeb's wildest dreams.

Boomer pulled up a chair and sat next to Fred. "I don't know a whole lot about it, but that Hazel told me to watch the store and not let anybody snoop around back there, and if anybody showed up, for me to scare 'em off. *And* to find that cinnamon stick."

Sheriff Barton's eyes widened, and he scratched his head. "Didn't that seem strange to you?"

"I suppose so. But I didn't care. Before I invited Jesus into my life, if there was any trouble to be had, I wanted to be a part of it. So when she told me to terrorize whoever showed up, I was all for it. I had no idea Hazel was in on the kidnapping."

"Maybe she wasn't—at least not in the way it appears." All eyes turned toward Brother Deren, who had entered the room so quietly that he was unobserved until he spoke. "By the way, I came in here to tell you that a moment ago, Hazel unlocked the door and let Katie in the bedroom."

Chapter 27

Hazel held the door open barely wide enough for Katie to slip through. Slumping onto the comforter, she patted the spot beside her.

Silence shrouded the room, and eerie scenarios surfaced in Katie's mind. Was it safe to be alone with this woman?

She eased onto the bed beside Hazel, and the faint creak of the springs reverberated in her head like a sledgehammer pounding an iron post. A bird twittered outside the window. Was it a bluebird? Katie hoped so. She'd welcome even the faintest sign of encouragement right about now.

It'll be okay. You're not alone. I'm right here.

"It's hopeless, Katie. My goose is cooked. It's all over." The older woman faced her, eyes vacant, tearless.

Katie groped for the right words. Breathing a silent prayer for God's guidance, she opened her mouth, and the words came. "It's never hopeless."

Desperation clouding her eyes, the woman leaned forward, her only response a mute stare.

Katie reached for her hand. It was damp and trembling. "Tell me about it."

Hazel picked at the comforter with her free hand. "I didn't know what else to do. I was a'skeerd for the baby's life."

Katie waited.

"I'm guilty. I oughta have a spot in Hollywood for that performance. All fake. All a show. And for what? It didn't even do a frazzle a'good."

Katie patted Hazel's hand and attempted to formulate a response, the empty spot in the pit of her stomach growing larger by the second.

Before she could answer, Hazel pulled her hand away and dropped to her knees on the floor. "I'm a'gonna have to confess. I'm a'gonna have to turn myself in. I ain't got no more to lose now." She drew her apron across her face and rocked back and forth on the carpet.

Katie sat aghast, not sure what to do with the distraught woman. She placed a hand on Hazel's shoulder. "Would you like for me to go get the sheriff?"

Hazel's head jerked up. "No. No, I done it to all of 'em. I'll confess it in front of all of 'em." Placing her palms on the edge of the bed, she grunted and pushed to a standing position. "Let's go."

Katie followed as Hazel flung open the bedroom door and made her way to the front of the store.

All conversation stopped when Hazel entered the

room. Zeb cast Katie a glance that said, "Everything okay?" Katie bit her lip, nodded toward Hazel and shrugged.

The poor woman headed straight for the sheriff, falling prostrate in front of him. Zeb jumped up and grasped Hazel's arm, attempting to help her stand. Wild-eyed, she pulled away. "No, I deserve to be on the floor. Leave me alone."

Zeb drew back.

The sheriff stood. "Get up, Hazel." He took her by the hand and pulled her to her feet, then guided her onto the chair Zeb had vacated.

Zeb stepped beside Katie and placed a hand against her back. His voice was a whisper. "Marcus and the boys were here, but they went home a few minutes ago."

His presence afforded her the comfort she so desperately needed. She leaned against him. "It's just as well. I don't think the boys need to be here for this. Hazel's a basket case."

Hazel folded her hands in her lap and faced Barton. "Sheriff, this is a'gonna be hard, but I ain't got no choice. If it's okay by you, I'd like to speak my piece whilst I still got the courage to do it. Then after that, I'll answer them questions you've got for me. That alright?"

Barton pulled a note pad and pencil from his pocket, then focused his attention on Hazel. "Go ahead."

The woman twisted the corner of her apron in one hand and glanced across the room at her husband.

"Oh, Fred Baby Darlin', I hope you'll forgive me for what I'm about to say."

His face turned beet red and he looked away. "Oh, for Pete's sake."

She turned back to the sheriff. "Here goes." She shut her eyes. "Lord, help me."

Barton waited, pencil poised and ready.

"I know Charlie Eugene ain't no good, and I was a'skeerd of Lyle Piper but thought we could keep Davey safe here, where they couldn't neither one of 'em get to 'im. And I trusted Lillian. She's his mama's sister, ya know."

The sheriff nodded in acknowledgement.

"So when she come to me and told me the baby was in danger if he stayed here, and that she was willing to take 'im home with 'er and hide 'im so's they couldn't find 'im, I said okay. Guess that was a mistake."

Hazel paused, directing a forlorn look toward Fred. He sat with his head down, hands gripping the feed sacks on either side of him.

Giving her apron a violent twist, she continued. "Lillian said she'd need my cooperation because without it, they'd find Davey and no telling what would happen to 'im. He might even get killed. At the very least, I'd never see 'im again, so she come up with a plan."

Fred raised despair-filled eyes. "And you went along with it?" His voice cracked, and Boomer gripped his shoulder.

Hazel raked a finger along the corner of one eye.

"I had to, Fred. I did it to save our grandson."

He shook his head in disbelief.

Sheriff Barton scratched his ear with the pencil. "What was the plan?"

Hazel, eyes fixed on Fred, spoke in a low voice. "Lillian parked a mile or so up the road and hiked through the woods in the dark of night after bedtime. I met 'er at Davey's window and handed 'im through it to 'er. He giggled and thought it was a game. She give 'im some a'that cinnamon candy and hiked back to 'er car with 'im and took 'im on to East St. Louis with 'er that very night. I cried my eyes out after they left."

The sheriff wrote for a few more seconds, then lifted the pencil. "What night was that?"

"It was the same night that Tank Bailor shot and killed 'is brother, Flat."

Her husband stood. "You mean Davey was already gone when you went to the Bailors' that night?"

Hazel's shoulders drooped. "He was already gone before I ever left the house. So, when I come home, I had to pretend that you'd been careless, and somebody had stole 'im while you was in charge. You goin' off up to the Banks' house that mornin' made it all the more convenient for people to believe my story."

Fred gaped at his wife in horror. "You framed me? On purpose? How couldja do that, woman?" The man swayed, and Boomer eased him back onto the seat.

Hazel turned away. "A day or so later, Lillian snuck back through the woods again to get some of Davey's clothes and stuff, and I met 'er and passed 'em through the window to 'er. And that was when she brought me that bag of Lyle Piper notes, and said for me to stash 'em in our mailbox ever so often to make people think he was the one what done it."

Fred, his voice quivering, breathed a barely audible question. "Who wrote them notes?"

Her eyes flashed fire. "Lillian! Okay, Fred? Lillian wrote 'em!" A sob escaped her throat, but she swallowed and choked it back.

Zeb squeezed Katie's hand, making her heart race. She squeezed back. Hazel was indeed a candidate for Hollywood—or the mental hospital at Farmington.

The sheriff made eye contact with Fred and shook his head in a *don't get her worked up* gesture. Fred nodded.

Hazel sniffed, and raked the back of a hand across her nose. "While I was back there with Lillian, the twins showed up and asked what we was a'doin' and where was Davey, and Lillian told 'em Davey was safe, but they couldn't tell they'd seen us or somethin' bad might happen to 'im. Then she made 'em promise, and said they could have cinnamon sticks long as they didn't tell."

Katie sucked in a quick breath, and Zeb wrapped an arm around her.

"I didn't know what to do." Hazel's voice was pleading. "By then I was a'skeerd of Lillian, too, but I was more a'feared for Davey, so I kept up the act, just a'hopin' everthing'd be alright and I'd get my baby back."

"What did you do with the notes?" The sheriff's

face was grim.

"I hired Tip Bailor to put one in our mailbox ever few days, and then I had to act surprised and upset ever time we got one. Tip didn't know what was a-goin' on. He just knowed he was a-gettin' money ever time he put a note in that box. To be honest, I don't know how good he can read."

Twisting her apron and stretching the fabric to the tearing point, Hazel grimaced. "But I guess he figgered out somethin' was a-goin' on, 'cause he got cold feet and stashed the bag in the outhouse at school, and come by here and told me he was done messin' with them notes, payday or not." She clicked her tongue. "That was awful dumb of 'im. Didn't he know they'd get found?"

The woman bent forward and buried her face in her hands, her body shaking.

Sheriff Barton shook his head and replaced the pencil and note pad in his pocket. Brother Deren slipped silently across the room and knelt beside Hazel's chair.

Zeb tightened his grip on Katie's hand and led her through the kitchen and out the back door. Brushing the dust off a step, he sat and pulled her down beside him. "Don't wanna get that pretty dress all messed up."

She felt an arm come around her and leaned into the embrace. "Hazel's lost it, hasn't she?"

He bent close until his head rested on hers and drew in a deep breath that carried her with it, sending a warm sensation pulsating through her body. "It looks that way, Katie girl."

She closed her eyes, as thoughts of comma-doodles and torn overalls played tag with a million other Hazel-type memories. Such a shame.

A whippoorwill's call nearby announced its role as harbinger of nightfall. "What do you think they'll do with her? I mean, do you think she'll go to jail? And what do you think'll happen to Davey now?"

"I don't know. They'll almost have to take her in. She's already confessed to being an accessory to the crime. But from the sound of things in there, she needs professional help more than she needs jail time."

They sat in silence as twilight gave way to nighttime, the quiet and darkness interrupted only by nature's night sounds and the winking of faraway stars. Katie was in heaven.

"Zeb? Zeb, are you out here?" Boomer's hushed voice penetrated her thoughts.

"I'm here."

The man's shadow moved across the yard as he came to stand before them. "Sorry to disturb you. The sheriff's takin' Fred and Hazel to St. Louis. Right now. Brother Deren's goin' along. Don't know what's gonna happen beyond that, but just thought you oughta know. I'm goin' to the house now. See you in the mornin'."

In moments the Slocums' back door clicked shut and Zeb stood, gently pulling Katie to her feet. "It's been a long day, and I know you're tired. Let me walk you home. We can get your stuff out of Rance's car tomorrow."

Sheriff Barton's vehicle was already pulling out by the time they rounded the corner of Hollisters' building. They watched the taillights disappear from sight, then crossed the highway.

Partway up the lane, Zeb stopped, lightly grasping Katie's shoulders and turning her to face him. His hands moved upward, stroking her hair, then softly caressing her face. Invisible metronomes ticked a furious allegro in her heart and sent its tempo racing through every inch of her body.

Sturdy arms embraced her and warm lips pressed against hers. Lost in the moment, she let his lips carry her away, and the world existed for them alone.

Pulling back, he took her hands in his. "You mean a lot to me. An awful lot. If I ever lost you, I don't know what I'd do."

She struggled to prevent her voice from revealing the elation that flooded her body. "I'm not going anywhere. This is my home."

He planted a kiss on top of her head. "Thank you."

They reached Marcus and Ella's yard in what seemed like only moments. Giving her hair a little tug, Zeb turned to go. "I'll see you in the morning. Count on it." And he disappeared into the night.

The Banks' house was dark except for the glow of a single lamp in a front window. Aunt Nellie must be waiting up for her. She eased the door open and found the dear woman reclining on the daybed, her breaths coming in the slow, steady rhythm of sleep.

Katie blew out the light, crept to her room, and climbed into bed.

Chapter 28

"Mornin', Katie."

"Katie."

She forced her eyes open. A reptilian face materialized in her still-fuzzy vision. "Boys, I thought I told you to not bring that terrapin in here. Now take him outside where he belongs."

Luke backed up, staring sympathetically at the animal.

Duke plopped down on the foot of the bed. "Mr. Harlow's been here."

Katie, now fully awake, scooted to a sitting position. "Where is he?"

Duke shrugged. "Gone. But he said come to the store. Can we go with you?"

Katie weighed the situation. "No, better not. I don't know how long I'll be gone, or what they'll need me to do. Maybe your dad'll bring you by later."

The twins eyed each other, exchanging a silent communication. "Okay. C'mon, Luke. Let's go give Mr.

Olsen's terrapin back to him."

Duke bounced out of the room, and Luke followed, bearing the offending creature. The door slammed behind them.

Katie swung her legs off the side of the bed. Draped over a chair were overalls—beautiful, freshly laundered overalls. Bless Aunt Nellie's heart.

Dressed in her outfit of choice, Katie dashed into the kitchen and grabbed Aunt Nellie in a warm embrace. The woman's eyes shone. "So glad you're back. You head on out now. I hear there's a gentleman that wants to see you."

Snatching a biscuit, she started for the door, then glanced back for a split second. Her aunt flashed a broad smile and flicked her hand. "Get on outta here. Shoo."

Katie found Zeb on the front porch of Hollisters' store, nonchalantly lounging in a chair propped on two legs against the wall. He waved a welcome. "Good morning, sleepyhead. Do you realize it's almost seven o'clock?"

She cleared the steps in one leap, landing beside him. She gave him a playful punch. "Heard any news?"

He glanced down the highway. "Nope, but I'm expecting to hear something before the day's over."

The morning wore on with no activity, save the occasional caw of a crow or the lowing of a distant cow. Hunger pangs gnawed at Katie's stomach, reminding her that it had been several hours since she'd eaten anything.

"Stop!" Marcus's voice rang out as Duke and Luke

skidded to a halt at the end of Banks' lane. The three crossed the highway together and Marcus thrust a paper bag into Zeb's hands. "Ella said to tell you it's time for lunch, so she sent biscuits and apple butter for you and your gal." He winked at Katie, making heat creep up her neck and onto her face.

Zeb balanced the bag on his lap. "Tell Miss Ella we said thanks."

Mike waved from across the lane, and Duke and Luke made a beeline for the Slocums' yard. Marcus squatted and leaned back against a post. "Any news?"

Tearing into the bag, Zeb cast another glance down the highway. "Not yet. But I expect somebody to show up any time."

Marcus stood and stretched his arms behind his head. "Guess I'll take a little stroll down toward the school. The old building might be lonesome for some company on a Saturday." He directed a knowing glance at Katie, then strolled off down the lane.

After a brief blessing, Zeb handed Katie a serving of the delicious treat and took one for himself.

Katie had just swallowed her last bite and washed it down with a Coke, when Deputy Fox's patrol car slid to a stop beside the gas pump. The passenger door swung open and Brother Deren emerged, lifting a squirming Davey to the ground. When the child saw Katie, his eyes brightened and he made a run for her. "Tay-deee!"

Fighting tears, she scooped him into her arms and hugged him to her. Then, lowering herself onto the top step, she cradled him on her lap.

Spying Zeb, Davey broke free, sidled up to the man, and tugged at his pant leg. "Pway?"

As the melody of "Amazing Grace" filled the air, Katie's eyes pooled, and a single tear escaped and trickled down her cheek. A hand reached from behind her and wiped it away. "Hey, everything's okay now. Wasn't I right?"

She leaned back against her Uncle Rance and patted his hand. "One hundred percent right."

When the song ended, Mike and the twins raced across the lane. "Davey!" Mike knelt on the gravel, arms open wide, and the little boy rushed into them. Moments later, the four spun around and trotted back toward Zeb's yard.

Brother Deren and Deputy Fox made themselves comfortable on the edge of the porch along with Rance. Rebel eased between Zeb's feet for an ear scratch or a belly rub—or both. Zeb obliged. "Well, men, what can you tell us?"

The deputy clasped his hands around one knee. "To begin with, there's a prison cell calling out Lillian's name. I'm thinking they'll throw the book at her. Kidnapping, crossing a state line in the process, and terrorizing a woman into having a nervous breakdown."

Zeb breathed out an audible sigh. "What about Charlie Eugene?"

The deputy's mouth curled up in a mirthless smile. "Once he recovers enough, he's facing some jail time in Canada himself. And he and Lyle Piper also have a few little issues to settle with the law in this country when

Canada gets done with them. In other words, I don't think we'll need to worry about those two for a long, long time."

A thought gnawed at Katie's brain until she could hold it in no longer. "What about Hazel?"

Jesse Fox turned toward her, his eyes filled with compassion. "They're saying Hazel won't be charged, that her nervous breakdown was caused by Lillian, and Hazel wasn't responsible for her own behavior. They've got her in the mental hospital for evaluation, and are hoping that, with the proper counseling and therapy, she'll eventually be well enough to return to her normal lifestyle."

Not trusting her voice, Katie took a deep breath before speaking. "How's Fred?"

The deputy shook his head. "Fred's fine, but he won't leave his wife. He's rented a room in Farmington and plans to live there until things are squared away for Hazel."

Giggles sounded from across the lane, making Katie smile, and at the same time, breaking her heart. "Who..." Her voice broke, causing her to hesitate. "Who'll take care of Davey?"

Deputy Fox swiveled toward Brother Deren, extending an open palm. The beloved pastor rose and came to sit next to Katie. He laid a hand over hers, his face radiating kindness. "Don't worry, Katie. I've agreed to keep him till we can make other arrangements. I'll take good care of him, and you know he'll be loved."

Katie wanted to throw her arms around the man.

Bless his heart. She lowered her gaze, hoping he wouldn't notice the tears welling up in her eyes. "Thank you, Brother Deren. Thank you so much."

He patted her on the hand and rose to his feet. "That's what I'm here for."

She watched him make his way across the lane and into the yard where his little charge frolicked without a care in the world.

Rance stood, brushing the dust off his pant legs. "I'm gonna head on home. Who knows, Everett might have a good old bowl of biscuits and gravy waitin' for me. See y'all later. Glad everything worked out."

Deputy Fox clicked to Rebel and attached a leash to the little dog's collar. "Guess I'll be gettin' on back to town now. We'll be checkin' in every so often."

Zeb stood and shook the deputy's hand. "Thanks for everything. You guys are top notch."

Fox grinned. "Just doin' my job."

Katie pushed to her feet and watched him lead the little beagle to the squad car.

Deputy Fox. Jesse Fox. Dad. A heaviness filled her heart over missed opportunities.

The deputy had only moved a few steps when he spun around and motioned Katie to him. Surprised, she hastened to his side. He faced her, his eyes staring into her soul, serious, yet possessing a certain sparkle. Leaning down, he spoke in a low tone. "By the way, you've got a beautiful mother. I'd like to get to know her a whole lot better."

Katie's mouth dropped open. She felt as though she could leap fifty feet into the air and shout *hallelujah* all at the same time.

Fox tilted his head and winked at her. "Thought you might like to know." He ushered Rebel into the squad car and was gone.

Zeb leaned against a post, arms folded, eyeing her suspiciously. "What was that all about?"

She skipped over and punched him on the arm. "He was just letting me know that God answers prayers."

~

Zeb stared across the field, raising his eyes toward the sky.

You see, son, I told you I could handle it.

God's presence filled the valley, and Zeb wanted to shout.

He dropped his gaze and focused on the gal beside him. "That He does. Yes, He definitely does." He reached out and gave her hair a not-too-rough yank. "Ya know, you and I have a little unfinished business to attend to. How's about a walk?"

Her soft hand in his felt so right as he led her along the familiar path and up to the ridge—*their ridge.* Had it only been a short time since they'd sat here and planned a way to spy out the valley and catch Davey's kidnapper, then Zeb had gotten knocked cold in a squirrel hunt gone wrong--and he'd been afraid to tell Katie how he really felt about her? And look at them now. He smiled to himself and squeezed her hand, taking a deep breath that ended in an audible sigh.

She peered up at him, eyes questioning. "A penny

for your thoughts?"

He ran a finger over the smooth enamel of the bluebird pinned to the collar of her shirt. "It's not about the bluebirds, is it?"

Understanding flashed across her face. "No, it's not about the bluebirds. It's about the One Who created the bluebirds—and us—and everything."

"Ya know what?"

"Uh-uh. What?"

Heart thudding, he placed his hands around her waist and leaned forward until their foreheads touched. It was now or never. "I love you."

She pulled away, a huge grin on her face. "Love ya right back."

He lifted a hand and stroked her golden hair. His girl. "Then, Katie girl, do you think it might be nice if we got married?"

Eyes shining, she made a fist and punched him on the arm. "Best idea I've heard all day." Wrapping her arms around him, she buried her face against his chest.

He returned the embrace, reveling in the moment, and turned his eyes toward heaven. Then, placing a finger underneath her chin, he tilted her head and pressed his lips to hers.

She leaned into the kiss, and their heartbeats merged as one.

The End